PIONEER POST

Vietnam GZ Thriller Series
Book Twenty-Eight

Eric Helm

PIONEER POST

Published by Sapere Books.

24 Trafalgar Road, Ilkley, LS29 8HH

saperebooks.com

ISBN: 978-0-85495-287-8

PROLOGUE

THE VIETNAM-CAMBODIA BORDER

The Long-Range Reconnaissance Patrol's mission was to gather intelligence deep in enemy territory but not engage in a fire fight. Tracing their history back to units such as Richard Rogers' Rangers, Force 136 and into the modern era to any number of specialized military units created around the world, the United States Army's 101st Airborne Division in Vietnam organized the first LRRP unit in 1965. From there the concept spread to other major commands in Southeast Asia until General William Westmoreland authorized the formation of LRRP teams in every brigade and Division in Vietnam.

None of this history meant much to Sergeant First Class Sam Anderson as he lay hidden in the dense foliage near the Vietnam-Cambodia border in what was known as Three Corps. He and his team had been there for three days and were scheduled for extraction in twenty-four hours. He wondered just how he had gotten himself in this mess in the first place.

Anderson's mother had told him to take typing in high school because that was a valuable skill that could be converted into a good job. But he had been too smart for that, opting instead for a more fun elective. He had built the obligatory bird house, the iron chisel that didn't hold the edge because he had not used enough heat to harden it, and had written a series of meaningless essays.

After high school he had joined the Army to avoid the draft and because he had no prospects for higher education. The Army offered the chance to learn a trade, but basic training had no real analog in the civilian world. And, since he showed no aptitude for any specific Army job, he was sent from basic training at Fort Polk to Tiger Land, the advanced infantry training center at Polk. He was now in the long pipeline to be a grunt in Southeast Asia.

With his training complete, he was on orders for Vietnam, along with nearly everyone else he had trained with at Polk. Although he graduated from basic as an E-2, which was a reward for the top soldiers, that didn't mean very much in the way of prestige. The only real difference between him and the E-1s was that he made a little more money each month, but there was no rank insignia to mark his new-found status.

He had ended his Vietnam tour as a Sergeant E-5 with a Bronze Star Medal, a Purple Heart for a minor shrapnel wound, and a Combat Infantry Badge. He was also close to discharge. While in Vietnam he had dreamed about getting out of the Army, but once in the Land of the All-Night Generator, he had discovered that he didn't really want to leave the Army. At least not yet. Rather than taking the discharge, he had re-enlisted, understanding that he might draw a second tour in Vietnam.

So, now Anderson was crouched in the deep jungle with a satisfactory view of an infiltration trail used by the enemy. He had watched as the Viet Cong and the North Vietnamese Army had moved their supplies into South Vietnam. He had been astonished at how much materiel they managed to move on bicycles from the terminus of the Ho Chi Minh Trail. One man, pushing an overloaded and unbalanced bike, could transport enough ammunition and food to supply an eight-man squad for several days. Anderson had counted fifty such bicycles in the time he had been concealed, watching the trail.

His orders were not to engage, just to count and to mark the trails on his map. It would be the responsibility of someone else to stop the flood of materiel. His job had been to identify the route, or routes, and he had done that. The other three members of the team had been making their own observations while each member kept one of the others under surveillance so that they wouldn't be surprised by an ambush.

Slowly, Anderson reached down for his canteen. The water tasted of plastic and chemicals, but it would keep him hydrated. He took a sip and wished that it was anything else. As he put the canteen back, he noticed a Vietnamese boy moving across a rice paddy and into the jungle about a hundred meters away.

He was coming directly at Anderson as if he had spotted him. There was no way to wave him off that Anderson could think of, and in training he had been told anyone coming directly at him was a threat. But this was a kid — no more than fifteen at most — without any weapon that he could see.

Before he could react, a shot rang out. The boy turned his head, as if looking for the source. Then, suddenly, he spun, running back the way he come. He didn't shout. He just ran.

Anderson hissed, "Who fired?"

"We've got to get out of here," came a whispered response.

Anderson had figured that out. Their position was now compromised. It might have been an accident, or it might have been a probe looking for any American soldiers in the area. It didn't matter now because it was time to go. He slid to the rear, moving slowly until he found a place where he could stand without being seen easily.

He kept his eyes on the rice paddies and the tree line. There was a single house, but there was no movement near it. In fact, there had been no movement near the hootch the whole time they had been observing the area. He figured it was abandoned, but now he wondered if someone hadn't been using it as a concealed observation post. Vietnamese could infiltrate without causing much in the way of curiosity, which was an advantage that the Americans didn't have.

He pulled the team together and knelt on one knee. He got on the radio and spoke a single word. "Three."

A moment later there was a double click as the radio operator at the other end acknowledged receipt of the message.

Without a word, he pointed at David Sanders, who nodded, understanding that he was the point man. Sanders turned, took a compass reading and then stepped off. Specialist Steven Rogers fell into position behind Sanders, leaving a space of about ten yards between them. Anderson pointed at Carlos Martinez. He would be the tail-end Charlie. Anderson then followed Rogers.

They moved quickly and quietly, staying away from the game trails and human paths for two reasons. First, if there was an ambush, it would be set along the trails. And second, often those trails were mined. Anderson and his team knew this.

They were headed toward pick-up zone three, which had been designated before the team left their home base. They had pre-selected a number of zones and would use the one most convenient. It also meant a clearing where the trees and other foliage was low enough and the space big enough that two helicopters could get in and out with relative ease. The pick-up zones were not large enough to accommodate a flight of Hueys, which meant that the enemy might not be watching these smaller areas with the same enthusiasm they monitored the larger ones.

Martinez caught Anderson up and whispered, "I think we've got company."

"How many?" Anderson asked.

"A dozen. Maybe fifteen. They're moving faster than us and don't seem to care about the noise."

Anderson considered stopping, but he knew that would be fatal. Instead he needed to slow down their pursuers. A mechanical ambush would do it, but he was reluctant to create it. There was always the chance the VC would avoid it and that later some innocent Vietnamese civilian would trip it. But they were not on a path and he doubted that a civilian would be this deep in the jungle. It was more likely that an animal would trip it if the enemy didn't.

He pulled one of the grenades from his pack and then crouched down. Loosening the pin, he set the grenade aside and found a ball of dark-colored twine. He braced the grenade against a tree so that it wouldn't move, looped the twine through the pin and strung it about six inches above the jungle floor, tying it off on another tree. If the enemy followed their path through the jungle, someone would trip the ambush. That should slow them down, if for no other reason than they would now be looking for another booby trap.

Anderson got to his feet and with Martinez, hurried forward to catch the rest of the team. They had just caught them up when the grenade detonated and there was a wild burst of automatic weapons fire.

Martinez said, "They found it."

"Yeah. They're closer than I thought," Anderson replied.

Without a word, the point picked up the pace. It was clear that the enemy knew they were there so the noise discipline was no longer important. Now it was all about speed. They needed to reach the pick-up zone before the enemy closed on them and could engage them.

Suddenly, up ahead, the jungle brightened. Sanders held up a balled fist and dropped to one knee. Anderson moved forward and crouched in the waist-high grass at the edge of the small clearing. He knew that the pilots wouldn't like it, but he also knew they'd come and get him because they always did.

He raised the radio to his lips and said, "Talley Ho."

Two short clicks came as his answer. The message had been heard and understood.

Anderson scanned the clearing and found it vacant. He pointed to Martinez, and signaled for him to remain in place and watch their trail for any sign of the enemy.

Anderson waited five minutes, as called for in the mission plan, and then tossed out a yellow smoke grenade into the pick-up zone. For a moment, it was lost in the tall grass, but then the smoke began to billow upward and, in the distance, he heard the distinctive *whap-whap* of the Huey rotor blades.

Over the radio he said, "Lukewarm." That meant there were enemy in the area but, at the moment, not near the pick-up zone.

An instant later a Charlie Model Gunship flashed overhead and then broke to the right. There was no enemy fire.

A Delta Model Huey appeared over the trees, flared out, and sank toward the ground. The rotor wash pushed the grass down and the yellow smoke was caught up in it and blown away.

Above the engine roar, Anderson shouted, "Let's go!"

The team broke from hiding and forced their way through the grass. Anderson reached up and grabbed the skid, pulling himself up as the helicopter settled closer to the ground.

To the left, one of the gunships rolled in and began a run on the jungle. There was no real target. It was suppressive five.

As the rest of the team scrambled into the cargo compart of the helicopter, firing broke out. Anderson could hear four or five AK-47s, but the rounds were not coming close to them. Suddenly the nose dropped and the aircraft raced toward the far end of the clearing. Just as Anderson thought they were going to fly into the trees, the nose came up and they climbed out rapidly.

As they cleared the pick-up zone, the gunships rolled in. Anderson watched as the rockets fired by the gunships exploded in orange fireballs among the trees at the end of the zone, but he didn't see any enemy soldiers.

The crew chief looked around, into the cargo compart where Anderson and the team were sprawled. "We're clear!" he yelled above the noise of the turbine.

For the first time in days, Anderson relaxed.

CHAPTER 1

The conference room, buried in the interior of a larger building at the Bien Hoa military complex, could have been located in the Pentagon or any one of the congressional buildings in Washington, D.C. It was large, paneled in teak, with a screen at one end set up for both front and rear projection of 16mm movies and 35mm slides. The conference table was mahogany with four high-backed chairs on either side and one at each end. Other chairs were set away from the table for the various aides and supporting staff necessary for the briefings. Although there was a silver beverage service set in the center of the table, there was nothing in it.

Standing at the lectern in the corner of the room was Colonel Jesse Martin, the senior intelligence officer with the 25th Infantry Division. He had prepared the briefing after reviewing the intelligence gathered by his Long-Range Reconnaissance Patrol teams, reports from the aviation section of the division — known as the Little Bears — and other data collected from both the Hornets and the Crusaders of the 269th Combat Aviation Battalion that often supported the division's ground operations and were based in Cu Chi and Tay Ninh.

Seated at the table were the operations and intelligence officers from the 1st Cavalry Division (Airmobile) and the 9th Infantry Division, sometimes referred as the "Flower Power Division" because of the design of the unit patch. Of course, Colonel Martin would not comment on that. The 25th ID patch was referred to as the "Electric Strawberry," which was an outgrowth of the psychedelic world of San Francisco and the hippy movement.

Martin shuffled through the papers before him, all stamped in bold red letters "Top Secret." He was waiting for General Westmoreland, the theater commander. The others in the room sat quietly, knowing that Westmoreland would be there shortly and not wanting to be caught doing anything the general might find annoying.

The door was opened by an armed guard, positioned in the hallway to prevent anyone without proper clearance from entering the room. The officer who entered was tall, thin and wearing the stars of a major general. He was dressed in a khaki uniform with only the Combat Infantryman Badge pinned above the left breast pocket. He did not wear a nametag and the only other emblem were the two stars signifying his rank.

He did not introduce himself, though Martin recognized him as Major General Douglas Whitney, the theater intelligence officer. He took the chair at the end of the table that was designated for General Westmoreland. As he sat down, he said, "General Westmoreland is involved in a conference call with the Pentagon and the White House. Rather than asking you gentlemen to wait on that, he asked me to sit in for him."

Martin nodded and said simply, "Lights."

A moment later the lights were dimmed and the first slide — with the words Top Secret — was projected onto the screen. Martin's voice pierced the gloom. "This briefing is classified as top secret and is not to be discussed with anyone outside this room except those designated with a need to know. I stress here that no one, other than those on the approved list will be advised of the contents of this briefing, and that includes our Army of the Republican of Vietnam counterparts."

He waited and then said, "Next slide please."

The "Top Secret" warning slide disappeared and a map of the western portion of Three Corps and the Cambodian border was displayed. A series of red lines appeared in the north, west of the border, that then spread out and turned into South Vietnam.

"This shows the route of the Ho Chi Minh Trail from North Vietnam with the various penetrations into the South. As you can see, they seem to cluster west of Tay Ninh, then cross rice fields and using some of the easier paths to move munitions and supplies into the south, heading toward the Iron Triangle of War Zone C. This is the Hobo Woods area and it is being used by enemy forces as a staging area for mounting attacks on Cu Chi and Saigon." Using his pointer, Martin continued, "There is something of a choke point here. The terrain doesn't seem to dictate it, but it does seem that those infiltration routes narrow to a point just to the southwest of Tay Ninh. I suspect it is to avoid our major base at Tay Ninh, the cluster of villages here, and a Special Forces camp farther to the south."

Without asking, the next slide appeared. It was a close up of the choke point with both the geological features, the rivers, and the jungle areas shaded in. "There is a gap here, among our various installations that makes infiltration through that area prime. The enemy has identified it and I believe it has been used for many months, if not years."

"How accurate is your information, Colonel?" asked Whitney.

"I had a LRRP team in there monitoring the traffic. They supplied solid information, that is 'eyes on' information, to me."

"Who authorized that?"

"I suggested it to the division commander and he approved. It was a sneak-and-peek mission with orders to avoid contact."

"Was it successful?"

Martin set the pointer on the lectern and leaned forward. "It was cut short by inadvertent compromise, General."

"What does that mean?"

"It means they were discovered by a local boy and were extracted a day early. The enemy, while learning that we had been in the area, does not know the composition of the team, or its mission, only that they were pulled out before they could be engaged."

Whitney waved a hand, indicating for Martin to continue.

"I can supply a list of what they observed on a nightly basis. The one surprising feature was that trucks were being used to move some of the supplies, but mostly it was men and women pushing heavily loaded bicycles through the area, or who were carrying large backpacks. They moved through the area after midnight and by dawn the traffic had ceased. In that time, one hundred and seventy-two enemy soldiers were counted, each armed with at least an AK."

Whitney looked at his watch and then asked, "What is the purpose here?"

"You can see we have identified an important route for the enemy into Three Corps. The solution is to set a base in the middle of the area, making transport through it difficult if not impossible."

"They'll just alter their routes."

Martin held up a folder. "I have here a plan, devised by the Special Forces, written by an officer who, last year, reactivated a base in that general area. That caused a disruption in the flow of supplies."

"You're referring to the camp that, what's his name, Gerber set up without proper authorization?"

"Yes, General. There were two flaws in what he did. First, he had to gather support from other camps in the area, weakening them slightly. Second, his was a permanent base. It lacked mobility. In his after-action report, he suggested that mobility was the key to maintaining control of the area, which, of course, is the mission of the cavalry. Or as it has been said, 'Get there firstest with the mostest'."

One of the other colonels spoke up then. "It sounds like what this Gerber was suggesting was that he needed a base he could move around as needed."

Martin couldn't help smiling. "Exactly."

The view from the sixth floor of the hotel was spectacular and certainly better than that from the Visiting Officers Quarters. Major MacKenzie K. Gerber, US Army Special Forces, known as Mack to his friends, had seen the quarters and decided he wouldn't be staying there. It did not have a view of a beach, did not have easy access to a restaurant, and it was on post. It was the last thing he wanted now that he was in Hawaii rather than South Vietnam.

He turned from the window and looked at the double bed, which was softer than the single bed in the VOQ and probably cleaner. He had spent enough time in a tent in the jungle and a bunker on a Special Forces camp to appreciate a comfortable bed.

Now, it was just a question of what do first. There was a sparkling bathroom with a big shower, there was that bed that seemed to be calling to him, and there was room service. Not to mention the air conditioning that seemed to be set on artic. Gerber was used to heat and humidity with cooling provided by a large fan that circulated the air but did little else.

He had just about decided to call room service when there was a knock at the door. He walked over and unlocked it.

Sergeant Major Anthony B. Fetterman stood there, dressed in a loud Hawaiian shirt. Without waiting to be invited inside, he pushed passed Gerber and walked to the window. "Your view is better than mine."

"Privileges of rank. We field grade officers are authorized various luxuries that you lowly enlisted men are not. We appreciate them."

"Sure, Major." Fetterman sat down in one of the two chairs near a small table. "Mind if I sit?"

Gerber grinned. "What's on your mind, Tony?"

"Wondered what our next move is going to be."

"You know as much about it as I do. There was nothing in my orders that weren't in yours. Our presence is required for a briefing or a conference or something."

"You have any beer?"

"I just got here and haven't had time to stock up yet. Besides, there is no way to chill it."

Fetterman shook his head. "When has that ever stopped you?"

"What's on your mind, Tony?" Gerber asked again.

"I'm concerned that we have been brought here with little in the way of explanation other than we'll be here for about a week. The length of an R and R for which neither of us is eligible."

"What do you mean not eligible?"

"First and foremost, we haven't been in-country long enough. They just don't send you on R and R on the whim of someone at a higher headquarters. You know as well as I do that you have to put in for it. That means the R and R is cover for something else."

"And?"

"Hawaii is reserved for those who are married. The spouse is brought from the World to meet her husband here. We can choose from any of the other R and R sites, but we wouldn't be approved for Hawaii."

Gerber moved toward the bed, where he had set his suitcase. He opened it and brought out a bottle of Beam's Choice. He held it up so that Fetterman could see it. Fetterman nodded and held his hand up, the index finger a half inch from the thumb, asking for that much of the bourbon.

Gerber went to the low table that held a pitcher, an ice bucket and four glasses on a fake silver tray. He poured the liquor into one of the glasses and handed it to Fetterman, before pouring a stiffer drink into another. He took a sip and remarked, "That's smooth." Ice simply wasn't necessary for Beam's Choice.

"Major, there is something going on here that I don't like and I think it has to do with the camp you established on the last tour."

Now Gerber chuckled. "If there had been any repercussions from that, they'd have fallen on us by now. I wouldn't have been promoted and neither would you. We'd have found ourselves in our terminal assignments in Bumfuck, Egypt."

"I just wondered if you had heard anything that I didn't. You being a field grade officer and all."

"I would expect you to have heard something before I did with all the contacts you have around the world. You senior NCOs have a better communication network than AT&T."

Fetterman finally lifted his glass and drank about half the alcohol. He hesitated for a moment and then said, "The only thing I've heard is that someone at a higher pay grade than either yours or mine was impressed with that little operation."

Gerber sat down where he could see out the window and wished they were on the ground floor. There were many people on the beach and he wanted to get a better look at some of them. To Fetterman, he said, "I had the distinct impression that the only reason there hadn't been repercussions then was that the mission was considered successful. We did inhibit the flow of men, munitions and supplies in that region."

"And nearly got our asses shot off in the process," said Fetterman. He held up the glass in a semi-salute.

Gerber shook his head and said, "I haven't heard anything about that since we rotated into the World."

"My sources, well, my source, said that someone liked the idea of putting camps in those sorts of areas. It was one of the things the Special Forces was created to do. We had to steal manpower from the surrounding camps, we had to manipulate the system for the supplies we needed and we were walking on the very edge of our authority."

"I know all that, Tony," said Gerber. "It seemed to me that nearly everyone in the chain of command hated the idea, fearing that it put too many soldiers in harm's way without sufficient planning, but couldn't say anything because the plan had worked up until the time they jerked us out of the field."

Fetterman finished the drink and carefully set the glass on the table. He stared at it for a moment and then said, "I'm just telling you what I've heard. It might mean nothing at all. It just seems strange that we're here, early for R and R and in a place reserved for the married personnel."

"Anybody ever mention not looking a gift horse in the mouth?"

"Well, I could say that we need to beware of Greeks bearing gifts, but then we are in Hawaii, so there is that."

Sergeant First Class Sam Anderson was sitting in the NCO Club at the 25th Infantry Division headquarters in Cu Chi, Republic of Vietnam, enjoying a relatively cold beer. It was his second, but then, even if it was only just after 1600 hours, he was off duty and was not the only non-commissioned officer in the club. True, most of them never left the sprawling base at Cu Chi unless it was to head into Saigon or go to the in-country R and R center at Vung Tau. Anderson didn't have much to do with those NCOs. They wouldn't understand him and he didn't like them. That might be because they never went into the field and he did. They had easy air-conditioned office jobs while he was humping through the boonies with enemy forces shooting at him.

A Spec Five, the company clerk named Clark, came over to him, saw the beer and shook his head. "CO wants to see you."

Anderson looked up at him. He was just a kid. Maybe twenty or twenty-one and had the job he did because he knew how to type. That reminded him, again, of what his mother had said. Then he wondered how he would feel if he was stuck at the base camp all the time while his fellow soldiers were out in the bush.

"Now?" said Anderson.

"That's what he said."

Anderson drained his beer, pushed back his chair, and said, "Let's go."

They walked out into the heat and humidity of the late afternoon. Anderson looked up toward the sun without looking directly at it. There was nothing to see but building clouds that hinted at some rain that evening.

He followed the clerk to the orderly room and waved toward the battalion commander's office. He knocked on the door and heard, "Come."

Following military protocol, even here, in a combat zone, he stopped three feet from the commander's desk, stood at attention and saluted. "Anderson, Samuel T., reporting as ordered."

The commanding officer, Lieutenant Colonel Robert Cornett, looked up, seemed startled and asked, "What in the hell is this, Anderson?"

He held the salute and said, "I was summoned, sir."

Cornett grinned and returned the salute. "Sit down, Sam. Where have you been?"

"At the club, sir." He sat in one of the two chairs situated in front of the somewhat beat-up desk that looked as if it had been rescued from the city dump.

"I got a strange message, today. Seems there is some sort of meeting or debriefing in Hawaii and they have asked that you attend. Or more specifically, ordered that you attend."

"They asked for me? Specifically?"

Cornett wiped his lips and said, "Not exactly. They were interested in talking with a LRRP who had been in the field recently close to the border here in Three Corps. I figured you'd be the man to send since you were the man there. Those other kids are, well, just kids on their first tour. Good at what they do, but I don't think they have the observational skills that you bring to the table."

"I don't know, Colonel."

"Why the hesitation? Here's a chance to go to Hawaii, all expenses paid, well, except for the booze. It gets you out of here and it's not chargeable as R and R or a leave. Means you can get an R and R later. This is a bonus."

Anderson repeated himself. "I don't know, sir."

"I was asked to supply an NCO, preferably a senior NCO, who knew the score and could answer some specific questions and provide some specific guidance to them about operations near the Cambodian border. I figure it's some sort of staff study on the viability of the LRRP program. Westmoreland thought LRRPs were a good idea. This might be a staff study that would expand the program throughout the Army rather than just here, in Vietnam."

"I'm not very good at that sort of thing. I don't have the proper uniforms. I think I have one set of khakis that would get me home. It's all that I needed."

"Jungle fatigues are probably the order of the day. There is a war on, you know."

"When would I leave?"

"Chopper to Hotel Three tomorrow. There will be someone to meet you there and get you on an airplane to Hawaii with all the other lucky guys going on R and R."

Anderson grinned. "I really don't have a thing to wear."

"I'll want a full report when you get back," said Cornett. "This'll be a nice break for you."

Anderson understood that he was being dismissed. He stood up and saluted again. "Thanks, Colonel."

"See the First Sergeant. He should have the rest of the travel details and any specifics of what you might need. You'll have to turn your weapon into the armorer for the time being and I'll ignore that pistol that you don't hide very well in violation of Army regulations."

Anderson turned and left the commander's office. He didn't like this at all, but had he been in trouble for some reason, the conversation would have been significantly different. Besides, a week or two in the World would be a nice break to the routine in-country.

CHAPTER 2

Warrant Officer, W1, known by everyone in aviation as a "wobbly one," Steven Douglas, was the youngest pilot in the company and one of the most senior. That was a result of the Army policies in affect during the Vietnam War. The aviation company had deployed from the United States as a single, full-strength unit when orders had been issued. Tours in Vietnam, for the Army, were one year. At the end of that year, everyone would have been eligible for rotation back into the World.

To correct that problem, once in Vietnam, soldiers were moved from one company, battalion, or brigade to another so that the DEROS would not strip a unit of everyone with combat experience at the same time. This meant, of course, that a pilot right out of flight school, assigned to one of the companies would, after six or seven months, be one of the senior and most combat experienced pilots in that company. There was an influx and outgo of soldiers throughout the year, but no unit was stripped of all the experienced men on the same day.

Douglas had been appointed a warrant officer by the Secretary of the Army and awarded the wings of an Army Aviator, as were all his classmates on graduation. He was then handed orders for the Republic of Vietnam just weeks after his nineteenth birthday. He then had three weeks of leave before he was required in San Francisco for transportation into Saigon. He spent those three weeks at home, visiting with friends who were freshmen and sophomores in college, with friends from high school and trying to ignore, as much as possible, what he thought of as his impending doom.

The only prior military experience Douglas had was in the movies and he figured that it wasn't a good indication of what he would find when he arrived in the combat zone in Vietnam. That was verified almost the moment they landed at Tan Son Nhut in Saigon and climbed onto the bus with open windows that were covered by screens that had a mesh that was nearly an inch square. Someone, new in-country, said, "These screens won't keep the insects out."

"They're to keep the hand grenades out," said a voice in the back. "Now they tie fish hooks to the grenades so they can hang them there."

It took Douglas a moment to figure out what that meant and he was suddenly aware of all the Vietnamese around the bus on their motor scooters and Lambrettas, staring up at him. None of the Vietnamese looked particularly friendly.

At home he had stayed away from the network evening news, not wanting to hear about how the war was progressing. He had vivid memories of long lines in flight school as the warrant officer candidates had decided to drop out of the program after learning about the slaughter of helicopters in the A Shau Valley during a week of heavy combat.

Douglas hadn't actually thought about dropping out then because he knew that it was better to ride than walk and better to fly rather than ride. He thought his chances of survival were better in the air and besides, at that time he was only eighteen and what eighteen year old thought about failing to survive the war. The failure to survive was what happened to someone else. He thought of flight school as a delay of the inevitable.

Douglas was just over six feet tall, thin, with light colored hair and an angular face. He was something of a smartass, given that he was now nineteen and some things just didn't strike him as important because he was still a teenager. But he was a good pilot, having graduated to aircraft commander early once he had arrived in Vietnam. Some of it was the need for aircraft commanders, but more of it was his ability to fly. There had been talk of moving him to the gun platoon, and he had even flown with them a couple of times. Neither his platoon leader nor the company commander thought that all the good pilots should end up with the weapons platoon, so he stayed a slick driver. He didn't particularly care about that as long as he got to fly.

For the day's missions, his platoon had been assigned the trail end of the flight while the other platoon had the lead. Douglas, because he was one of the senior pilots, had the last place in the flight. His job was to watch the flight, advise lead when everyone was off, or down, when they were loaded, and to make sure the flight stuck together. Douglas liked that position because no one was watching him except for C&C and if he wasn't way off base, no one said a word to him about his position in the flight. The downside was that if there were follow-on missions that required a single ship, which was often, then, while the rest of the flight was shut down and resting, he would be flying off on some other task.

He walked down the steps, into the operations bunker and looked at the assignment board, which posted the names of the co-pilots, often called the "Peter Pilots." He was flying with one of the FNGs who had just been cleared for the flight after his in-county check rides. Douglas wasn't even sure he had met the guy, though he had been introduced in the officers' club to the other FNGs when they had arrived at the company.

Douglas signed out an SOI that held the various call signs and other aviation codes. Because of that, it was a classified document. The SOI was attached to a piece of white cord and was hung around the neck. Douglas had seen some of the more senior of the Peter Pilots sign one out. That wasn't against any rule, but it was a sort of status symbol. Those who had the SOIs were identified as the aircraft commanders and some of the FNGs didn't know all the ACs. Douglas thought of it as an annoyance because if it was lost, there would be hell to pay. The more SOIs out there, the more likely someone would lose one.

Another AC, holding his SOI in one hand and his helmet in the other, was studying the tactical map marked with the locations of suspected enemy positions. Looking at it, it seemed that they were surrounded by the VC and NVA units, but they almost never fired at the flights coming and going into the base camp and never really caused much trouble. While they had Cu Chi surrounded, they had little power and did little to inhibit the normal aviation operations.

The AC looked over at Douglas and asked, "Hey, Douglas, you got a note from your mother to be here?"

Douglas looked at him and smiled. "Nope. Can I go home?"

"Afraid not," said the aviation company commander, Major Nathan Fox, who was standing in an alcove so that he was nearly invisible. He was a somewhat small man, with his hair cut to about a quarter of an inch.

Douglas hung the SOI around his neck and put it in the pocket on the ceramic chest protector. It would stop almost anything fired at the flight except for a .51 calibre heavy machine gun round. An armor-piecing round from an AK, if fired within a hundred yards, might penetrate. If it didn't, it would leave one hell of a bruise.

Without another word, Douglas climbed the narrow steps up, out of the air-conditioned operations bunker and into the uncomfortable world of high temperature and the higher humidity of the morning. It was going to be a nasty day, weather wise.

Sitting on the troop seat of the Bell UH-1D Huey helicopter, Douglas saw First Lieutenant David Hampton who was always David and never Dave and certainly not Davy. He was twenty-four, short and stocky with dark hair that needed a trim and tailored jungle fatigues that were frowned on by some of the brass hats. He was reading a paperback novel and waiting for the day to begin. He was supposed to have completed the pre-flight inspection.

Although Douglas never really thought about it, this was one of those strange situations that often cropped up in Army Aviation. Here, on the ground, with the aircraft shut down, Hampton outranked Douglas. But Douglas was the aircraft commander, and once the engine was cranked and the airlift missions began, Douglas was in charge, rank be damned. Hampton was obligated to respond to the order Douglas gave.

Douglas opened the cockpit door, climbed up onto the skid and hung his helmet on the hook over the left seat. He looked back at Hampton and said, "You finished the pre-flight?"

Hampton glanced up and nearly said, "Yes, sir," but caught himself in time and merely said, "Yes."

"Any issues?"

"None that I could see."

"You make commo check?"

"We're good to go. No problem."

Douglas climbed into the left seat. Bell Helicopter had designed the Huey with the aircraft commander's seat on the right side, unlike airplanes. But here, in Vietnam, the aircraft commanders sat in the left seat, the co-pilot's seat, because the visibility outside the aircraft was better. It was something done throughout the battalion. Douglas didn't know if it applied to other aviation units in Vietnam, but it was the way they did it here.

"We've got about five minutes to crank. You want to get settled in up here?"

Without a word, Hampton put the book into one of the pockets of his jungle fatigues and then climbed into his seat. Once he was buckled in, he looked over at Douglas. They quickly ran through the start procedure. Douglas was staring at the sweep of the second hand on his watch rather than the cockpit clock and when it touched the twelve, he said, "Crank it up."

While Hampton started the engine, Douglas reached over and turned on the Automatic Direction Finder. The radio picked up the signals from navigation aids, which were not readily available in Vietnam. However, it also covered the commercial broadcast bands, which meant that they could pick up Armed Forces Radio in Saigon. All crew members could listen to the popular music from the United States. It was not uncommon for someone in the flight to say, "ADF," meaning there was a good tune on the radio. It was as if they were driving around in a convertible listening to a top forty station.

There was a high-pitched whine as the turbine began to spin. When it had reached 6000 rpm, Douglas keyed his mike and said, "Trail is up."

"Roger, Trail."

After all the aircraft had reported they were ready, Lead said, "Let's form on the Assault Strip in Chalk Order."

Douglas said, "I've got it."

Hampton replied, "You've got it," and released the controls.

With his hands on the cyclic and the collective, Douglas lifted to a three-foot hover. Over the intercom both the crew chief and the door gunner said, "You're clear."

He hesitated, watching the other helicopters as they maneuvered to the Assault Strip. He moved forward, clearing the walls of the revetment, turned, and joined the flight at the very end. As soon as his skids hit the asphalt, he radioed, "Lead, you have ten on the Assault Strip."

Lead lifted off, dumped the nose, and began his climb out. Over the intercom he said, "Come up a staggered right."

One by one, the others did the same, with Douglas, in the last aircraft, following. Once off the ground, he said, "Lead, you're off with ten."

To Hampton, Douglas said, "Lead will climb to fifteen hundred feet and level off. He'll hold sixty knots so that the rest of the flight can catch up and join. In trail, we sometimes have to fly at ninety or a hundred knots to catch the flight."

Once they caught up and had slipped into position, Douglas radioed, "Lead, you're joined with ten."

"Roger. Rolling over."

Douglas looked at the instruments. Everything was in the green. His position in the formation was where it should be, about three rotor disks separating him from the aircraft to his left.

To Hampton, he said, "If you look at the skids and see the way everything is aligned here, that puts you in the correct position. We can get a little sloppy in Trail because there is no one behind us. Major Fox, if he's in C and C, will probably tell you to close it up."

Now that they were off the ground, away from Cu Chi, and heading to the PZ, Douglas relaxed slightly. Turning to Hampton, he said, "There's little chance that we'll be engaged flying at 1500 feet over rather open rice patties. Things might get tense as we start to land at PZ but I doubted it."

He didn't say that they'd be picking up the grunts near an American fire support base, which meant a well defended PZ close to a battalion of American soldiers. The ARVN were sometimes less than prepared.

They started the descent toward the PZ. A cloud of yellow smoke was billowing from the grenade tossed to mark the forward position of the soldiers and provide the wind direction. As they touched down, the waiting grunts swarmed onto the helicopter. When all were loaded and Dougals saw no soldiers standing around, he said over the radio, "Lead, you're down with ten and loaded."

The air mission commander, orbiting near the LZ, cut in. "Lead, hold your position."

"Roger that."

Hampton asked, "What's going on?"

"Don't know," Douglas replied. "Maybe they're having trouble finding a suitable LZ. Maybe they're waiting on an arty prep. Maybe they have to coordinate with another unit or with Cu Chi arty."

Ten minutes later, C and C said, "Lead. Let's go."

"Lead's on the go."

As the skids broke free, Douglas radioed, "Lead, you're off with ten."

In the distance, Douglas watched as the arty prep hit the ground. Instead of the explosions he had seen in the movies, fountains of gray, brown and black shot up into the air and then slowly fell back to earth. The idea was to clear the LZ of any landmines or booby traps. The arty prep shifted toward the trees, to keep the enemy guessing — if there was an enemy around — and to kill as many as possible.

Over the radio came, "Lead, make an orbit."

"Lead, roger."

They began a circle to the right. It was just a way of delaying the flight from arriving before the arty prep was finished. Then, over the radio, "Last rounds on the way. Tubes clear."

Hampton asked, "There VC in the area?"

"Not necessarily," said Douglas. "Okay. Which way is it to Cu Chu from here?"

Hampton looked confused. He glanced at the compass and then pointed.

"Close. Head in that direction. Eventually you'll see a cloud of thick smoke. That's always there and marks one end of the base camp. I think they're continuously burning garbage."

"Okay."

"What's the closes medical facility?"

Hampton shrugged.

"That'd be the Twelfth Evac Hospital at Cu Chu. They monitor sixty-two decimal five. When you get close, you need to contact the tower and the hospital."

"Why are you telling me all this?"

"Because it's information you need to know if something happens to me. I expect you to get me to the closest hospital. They had medical facilities at Dau Tieng and Tay Ninh. All monitor the same freqs. Cu Chi is the closest to us today."

From C and C came, "Flight, you have full suppression."

One of the gunships came toward the flight and then made a hundred-and eighty-degree turn. Lead followed him as the flight continued descending. As they approached the LZ, the gunships rolled in, raking the tree lines on either side of the flight with machine gun and rocket fire.

"Chalk Three is taking fire on the right."

The door gunners opened fire; the muzzle flashes nearly lost in the bright sunlight.

Douglas glanced to the right, but couldn't see any muzzle flashes. That suggested that there weren't many enemy down there.

"Chalk Seven is taking fire on the right."

Douglas could hear the door guns of the flight and the sporadic burst of the enemy AK-47s. He couldn't see any tracers, but that wasn't all that unusual. Bright sunlight hid them, or the enemy might not have loaded tracers into their weapons. The firing was getting heavy.

A green smoke grenade tumbled from the gunship. "Lead, land fifty meters short of the smoke."

"Lead, roger."

A moment later, the flight touched down. The grunts leaped from the aircraft, dropping to the ground. They opened fire, raking the tree lines with their M-16s and M-79 40mm grenades. There were explosions at the tree line and rockets hitting a few meters in.

"Five's down. We've lost the engine."

"Five, understood. Trail?"

"Lead, you're down with ten and unloaded. I've got Five."

"Lead's on the go."

Douglas pulled pitch, dumped the nose, and hovered forward. As he neared the stricken helicopter, he jerked back on the cyclic, stopped his forward motion and settled to the ground. The landing zone was alive with fire, door guns hammering at the base of the tree line. The gunships started their attack, their rockets firing and exploding in bright orange flashes while the grunts continued to pour fire into the trees all around the LZ. Douglas heard rounds striking the aircraft and felt the impact through the pedals.

Hampton sat straight up, wanting to grab the controls. He wanted to get out of there. The flight crew of Chalk Five scrambled from their aircraft toward them. They carried their personal weapons and equipment, but not the M-60 machine guns.

The AC, the last in the line, ran across the grass and leaped into the cargo compartment shouting, "Go! Go!"

Douglas turned in his seat and saw four men in the cargo compartment. The flight crew was all there. Again, he pulled pitch, dumped the nose, but this time he was speeding across the ground, gaining altitude along the way.

From the C and C, he heard, "Trail, give me a status."

For the moment Douglas ignored the request. He had his eyes on the instrument panel, but everything was in the green. There was no indication that anything vital had been hit. He wasn't losing power and there was no indication he was losing fuel.

Over the intercom, he said, "How is everyone?"

"No one is hit. We're good back here."

"Six, we're out with the flight crew," said Douglas on the radio. "We have no wounded."

After dropping off Chalk Five's crew at Cu Chi, Douglas caught up with the flight when it had shut down at a small base known as Duc Hoa. It had a long landing area next to a pond that was inside the wire and could accommodate the whole flight. They didn't have any immediate follow-on missions. It was almost as if someone had arranged for a long coffee break at mid-morning.

With the aircraft shut down, Douglas climbed into the cargo compartment and sat on the troop seat. He pulled a paperback from one of his pockets and started to read. For him it was the best way to pass the time as they waited for the next mission.

Hampton had been walking around the aircraft as if he wanted to burn off excess energy. Douglas understood. The adrenalin of a hot LZ still excited the NFGs, making it difficult for them to sit still. For the first couple of months, Douglas had been the same way, but he had learned to calm down quickly. After sitting in a couple of dozen hot LZs, he recognized that there was nothing he could do. He let training take over, did his job, and then put it all behind him as quickly as possible.

Hampton finally sat down in the cargo compartment, leaning back against the pilot's seat. He hesitated and then said, "Is it always like this?"

Douglas almost answered with "What do you mean? That was quiet," but he knew that Hampton deserved a real answer. Instead, he said, "No. Sometimes it's worse, but most of the time the LZ is cold and all the shooting is from us. Sometimes someone with an SKS might take a shot at the flight, but often we don't know it and they don't hit anything anyway."

He was about to say more when he heard a distant pop. He recognized the sound immediately. "Incoming!"

Hampton moved to the cargo compartment door but hesitated there. Douglas wanted to get out of the aircraft and pushed him gently. Hampton tried to jump, but instead he stumbled and fell, nearly landing in the water as another round detonated in the wire. It hadn't landed very close.

Douglas leaped from the aircraft and sprinted toward Lead. As he neared, he shouted, "The tube is to the southwest, maybe a hundred fifty yards away."

He skidded to a stop and saw the Lead AC, WO Johnson, on the PRC-25, talking to the company executive officer, serving as the air mission commander, in orbit somewhere to the west of them. Douglas heard Johnson say, "The tube is southwest of us, in a clump of trees."

There was another explosion, this one at the edge of the wire. At the same time, the .50 calibre mounted in the southwest corner opened fire, followed by an M-60 machine gun. Douglas saw the tracers flying toward a finger of the jungle. He didn't know how affective the fire might be, but thought it might suppress the mortar.

The Lead AC looked at him. "What you got?"

Standing there, almost oblivious to the mortar, Douglas said, "Wanted to get the information to C and C." He turned, shaded his eyes and thought he saw the gunships beginning their suppression run.

A moment later there was a series of explosions in the tree line. As the gunship broke away, the second rolled in using the mini guns. A red stream of tracers, looking more like a death ray than machine-gun fire, probed the tree line.

The gun team made another run, but there was no return fire from the enemy. If they were still there, they had either taken cover or were dead. The tube was silent.

At the gate, on the southwest, a platoon had assembled, carrying only their weapons, ammunition and canteens. They spread out and headed toward the trees while the gunships continued to provide cover.

The Lead AC put down the mike and said, "That should take care of it."

"We got any idea of the next lift?" asked Douglas.

"Haven't a clue."

Douglas shrugged. "Well, I guess I'll go apologize to Hampton. I pushed him out of the way and he fell in the mud."

"You mean Lieutenant Hampton?"

Now Douglas smiled. "No, I mean my Peter Pilot Hampton."

Sitting in the cockpit of the helicopter, now parked in the revetment, Douglas was filling out the book at the end of the day. It was a green, loose-leaf binder that held only a few sheets. Later, someone from operations would collect the information about the hours flown, and the number of passengers carried.

Hampton was sitting quietly, looking drained. Finally, he said, "That was quite exciting."

"Yes," said Douglas, realizing that after he had returned to Cu Chi, it meant additional flying hours for him and Hampton. Trail always logged additional time, sometimes as much as double the rest of the flight.

"I wondered if today was typical?"

Douglas put the pencil in his pocket, closed the book and put it back in the slot at the end of the center radio panel. "Typical? No. We haven't been mortared like that for a while. Usually, we'll get mortars at the PZ as we extract the grunts. Some fire, poorly aimed, is about all we see."

Hampton nodded and looked as if he had another question. Before he could speak, however, one of the operations' specialists showed up. He said, "Mister Douglas, the CO wants to see you in his office."

"I'm surprised he wants to see me."

"I don't think he likes to be kept waiting."

Douglas laughed, "Who does?" He looked over his shoulder at the crew chief. "Make sure the guns are cleaned properly this time and don't let Hernandez fill the can all the way to the top."

Last time Hernandez had filled the ammo can, used to clean the machine guns, to the top with JP-4. He had then spilled it under the aircraft. It had not been an ideal situation.

"Yes, sir."

To Hampton, he said, "That's it for the day."

Douglas climbed out of the cockpit, then walked across the road and entered the Orderly Room. The first sergeant said, "He's waiting."

"Thank you, First Sergeant."

The CO's office was set in one corner of the building. Outside the door, Douglas set his flight helmet on the floor and knocked. He heard, "Come in," and entered. The room had paneled walls, an air conditioner built into the wall, and a woven mat covering the floor. A desk was set at an angle in one corner, facing into the room. There was an old, green settee along the wall opposite the desk and a table surrounded by six chairs at the other end. Over the door was a captured RPG launcher with an engraved plaque.

Standing at attention in front of the desk was First Lieutenant John Williams. He didn't move as Douglas stopped beside him and saluted.

"Warrant Officer Steven Douglas reporting as ordered."

The company commander, Major Nathan Fox, returned the salute. "At ease."

Douglas relaxed slightly and noticed that Fox's fresh uniform was heavily starched, with knife-edge creases and not a sign of sweat. The sleeves were rolled to a point halfway between his elbow and shoulder as the current regulations prescribed. He had no facial hair and, had you passed him on the street, you probably wouldn't have noticed him.

Fox set his pen down on his desk and looked up at the two officers. "I called you here because we have been tasked with a special assignment in Hawaii, which means both of you will be traveling in the next day or so."

Douglas wanted to ask a question but knew better than to interrupt Fox. The major didn't take kindly to interruptions. He continued, "This was something of a difficult decision. I was asked for experienced pilots and my first thought was for aircraft commanders, especially those who were married. But they've all been on R and R and Douglas, I believe you are the most experienced of the aircraft commanders available to me. However, I don't want to strip the company of all my experienced ACs."

Douglas, believing that Fox was waiting for a response, said, "Yes, sir."

"Why don't you two sit down."

As they dropped onto the settee, Fox stood up and walked around his desk so that he could sit back on it. He reached around and picked up a sheet of paper. "According to this, I'm to select two pilots for a special assignment —"

Williams interrupted. "Aren't we supposed to volunteer for special assignments?"

"There is nothing in this document that suggests a search for volunteers. It orders two pilots, that's you two, for a special assignment. It says nothing about any danger involved. Only that you will travel to Hawaii to arrive in the next forty-eight to seventy-two hours based on the availability of the air transport. That good enough for you, Lieutenant?"

"Yes, sir. Fine, sir."

"I know nothing about the assignment, but they are looking for pilots with combat experience and at least six months in-country."

Fox looked at Williams and said, "Before you interrupt again, I will point out that you are the senior Peter Pilot in the company and while you don't have the six months, you have a wide range of experience in our operations. You'll be transitioning to AC sometime in the next few days or weeks, so I take that as close enough for government work."

Williams had learned his lesson and said, "Yes, sir."

Fox looked at Douglas. "What's that dangling from your holster?"

Douglas wasn't intimidated. He had strung the leather neck strap holding a peace symbol through the loops on the holster that were meant to hold six rounds of .38 caliber ammunition. The rounds tended to fall out so he had used it to create a leather thong that had part of the leather pulled up over the hammer.

"Peace symbol I bought in San Francisco. The battalion commander has one painted on the doors of his aircraft."

Fox rubbed his chin with his thumb and then grinned. "I guess he does."

"And there is one slick in second platoon that has a big one painted on the bottom of the helicopter."

Williams chimed in, "There is one that says 'Here we come,' painted on the bottom."

"I don't need to be reminded what is painted on the bottom of our aircraft, Lieutenant."

Douglas realized that the aircraft commanders were allowed a little leeway in their interactions with Fox.

"Before we get too far off course," said Fox, "is there any reason that either of you can think of that would disqualify you from this mission."

"We don't really know anything about it," said Douglas.

"That's the rub," said Fox. "I don't know any more than I have told you. You'll be on TDY to Hawaii for an unspecified period."

Douglas closed his eyes for a moment. According to his count, he had one hundred and four days left in-country. Like nearly everyone else, he knew exactly how many days were left on his tour. About the only ones who didn't know were the FNGs who had only been in Vietnam for a couple weeks. No one started counting carefully until they reached about two hundred days left.

"Does that time count for DEROS?"

"That I don't know, but I would suspect it will be treated in the same fashion as an R and R. You're gone for a week or ten days; it doesn't add time to your tour. This assignment is part of your job here."

Douglas thought for a moment and then said, "I'm not really sure this is something that I should be doing."

Fox sighed and said, "What's your problem Mister Douglas?"

"Sir, I'm only nineteen. There might be some question about my competence here."

"You have accumulated nearly a thousand hours of combat flight time in a variety of missions including single ship medical evacuations. You have flown with the gun team, and into LZs under heavy fire. You have been shot down twice. You have as much experience or more than the other ACs and have been nominated for the Distinguished Flying Cross. You are as qualified as any of the pilots in the company."

"A commissioned officer might be considered more qualified."

"That's why I'm sending Williams. He's a commissioned officer." Fox now looked at Williams and said, "But you have to understand that Douglas here, is the real expert."

Williams had the good sense to say nothing.

Fox stood up. "If there are no other questions."

"Itinerary?" asked Douglas.

"We'll fly you to Tan Son Nhut in the morning. Operations will coordinate with them in Saigon so that you're met at Hotel Three and taken over to the terminal for the flight to Hawaii. Nothing for you to do other than follow their lead and get on the aircraft."

Douglas was about to stand up and then had another thought. "I don't have much in the way of civilian clothes and only have one set of khakis. Other than that just jungle fatigues."

"That shouldn't be a problem. They have good laundry facilities in Hawaii. Oh, you'll have to turn your weapons in to supply while you're on this mission."

Douglas stood then, saluted and said, "Thank you, sir."

Williams followed him out of the office.

CHAPTER 3

Gerber was wearing a freshly laundered khaki uniform with branch insignia, combat infantryman's badge and his jump wings. Fetterman, similarly attired, sat in the back seat of the taxi with him. Neither man knew, precisely, what the meeting they had been asked to attend was about, though they suspected it had something to do with their last tour in Vietnam.

Neither said much on the taxi ride from the hotel to the military installation. When they neared the gate, they saw a small group of men and women carrying signs and placards. There were away from the road and the MPs at the gate were keeping them under surveillance.

Fetterman was about to say something when Gerber burst out laughing and pointed at one of the signs. It read, "I thought there would be cake."

As the taxi approached, the protesters moved toward the road as if to block it. The taxi driver knew what he was doing. He didn't slow as the crowd surged and was past them before they could block the road. He stopped at the gate and one of the MPs looked into the rear seat. He saw Gerber and said, "Can I see your ID, Major?"

Gerber pulled his ID out of his pocket and flashed it at the MP.

"Thanks." The MP looked at Fetterman. "Sergeant Major?"

Gerber said, "He's with me."

"Yes, sir, but I need to see ID anyway."

"Tony?"

As Fetterman dug for his ID, Gerber asked, "Is this usual?" He pointed to the demonstrators.

"They're here every day but don't really do much. Just stand around and wave their signs at the traffic. They aren't doing anything illegal. They're on public property. We just ignore them unless they get too aggressive or stop traffic."

"Noticed the guy with the cake sign."

Fetterman held up his ID and the MP nodded. "Thank you, Sergeant Major." To Gerber, he said, "He's new. I don't think they've figured out he's mocking them. Where you headed?"

"Building two three four."

To the driver the MP said, "Down the main road and turn at the post theater. It's up on the slight rise." He waved them on.

They made their way along the road, turned at the theater and drove up to the front of the building. It was white with a red roof and surrounded by tropical plantings. It looked as if it belonged to a different era, like something from before the Second World War.

Having paid the driver and added a substantial tip, Gerber opened the door and got out. A cool breeze was blowing and there wasn't the overwhelming humidity that he had come to expect in the tropical heat.

When the taxi pulled away, Gerber asked, "You ready to beard the lion?"

Fetterman just shrugged as they walked up the steps to the door. He opened it and bowed Gerber through. Inside was a large room with a red carpet that looked as if it had been laid the day before. An NCO was sitting behind a desk. Behind him was a door that looked solid.

"Can I help you, Major?"

"Major Gerber with Sergeant Major Fetterman. We're scheduled for a meeting here about now."

The NCO asked for ID, examined it, and then said, "Through the door. Second door on the right."

There was a buzz and Gerber realized that the sergeant had pressed a button to unlock the door. As he moved toward it, he saw that the man was armed with a pistol. There was also a shotgun concealed by the desk.

Gerber opened the door and stepped through into an air-conditioned corridor, with more of the red carpet on the floor and walls painted a stark white. There were the typical military paintings on the wall showing scenes from past battles, mainly from the Civil War.

At the second door on the right was another armed guard. Gerber whispered to Fetterman, "I don't know who they expect to attack here."

"Maybe those kids out front protesting the war."

"Looking for that cake?"

The guard checked their ID and then opened the door for them. They entered a conference room that looked as if it belonged to a general whose taste ran to the 1890s or maybe to a high-class bordello. In the middle stood a highly polished table surrounded by eight high-back chairs. Each place was set with a notepad, pen and pencil, and nameplates. There were no windows in the room, but there was a movie screen at one end.

Fetterman pointed at the nameplates. "Looks like we were expected."

The door opened again and a colonel entered. He was dressed in khakis with his ribbons on display, suggesting service in both Korea and Vietnam. He didn't have jump wings or a combat infantry badge, but he did wear an expert infantryman's badge, which was strange given his rank. His collar insignia indicated that he was assigned to JAG. His nametag read "Larson."

"Major Gerber?" the colonel asked, holding out a hand. Gerber noticed that it was small, but then Larson wasn't a big man. He had a bookish look, which probably explained the lack of valor awards.

"With Sergeant Major Fetterman," said Gerber.

It was a study in contrasts. The two men were physically similar, both being fairly short, but it was clear there was a difference. Fetterman stood a shade over five foot six and couldn't have weighed more than one hundred and fifty pounds sopping wet. But his small stature belied what he actually was: probably the most dangerous man in Southeast Asia. He was a hardened and much decorated veteran of three wars and in his long military career had earned well over a hundred confirmed combat kills. Gerber had seen Fetterman in several firefights. He was as tough as they came.

"Of course. Sergeant Major." Larson held out his hand to be shaken. He didn't bother to introduce himself but instead gestured at the chairs. "Have a seat. The general will be with us in a few moments. I will say that the other participants in our little project are still enroute. They should be arriving in the next day or two, but we can get the preliminaries out of the way."

Gerber pulled out the chair in front of his nameplate. He said, "Why does that make me suspicious?"

"Nothing to worry about, Major. There are some things we can do before the others arrive."

The door opened and the guard shouted, "Atten-hut!"

Gerber got to his feet. With a full colonel in the room already, it could only mean that the man about to enter was a brigadier general or higher. He was surprised when the first man through the door was a captain in a Class A uniform that displayed all his awards and decorations, the crossed rifles of the infantry but no combat infantryman badge and no combat awards. Somehow, he had avoided service in Vietnam even at the height of the war.

Right behind him was a brigadier general in a khaki uniform who wasn't wearing a name tag and whom Gerber didn't know.

As the general took his place at the head of the table, facing the screen, he said, "As you were. Be seated."

Once everyone was comfortable, the general began. "For those of you who don't know me, I'm General Thomas Jones. I have been given the task of getting this operation off the ground."

The projection screen lit up in white with bold red letters that read, "Top Secret."

Jones grinned. "That says it all. I know that you all know the rules, but I'll remind you that anything discussed in this room is classified as top secret and the information is not to be mentioned to anyone who does not hold the proper clearance for it. The penalty is twenty years in jail and twenty thousand dollars in fines, not to mention the cost of a defense and other ancillary expenses that go along with defending yourselves at court martial if you violate these rules and regulations. Is that understood?"

When all had acknowledged the warning, Jones said, "Colonel Larson, would you care to take over?"

Larson stood up and said, "Next slide."

Both Gerber and Fetterman recognized the scene immediately. They were looking at the smoking remains of the camp they had established fourteen months earlier after they had beaten back an effort by a reinforced NVA battalion to take it. The bodies of the strikers killed were still laying where they had fallen, and at one point the wire surrounding the camp was visible. The bodies of the enemy were still there as well. Two of the American soldiers were off to the right, one holding an M-16 and the other with only a holstered pistol on his hip.

"This is the scene about noon on —"

Gerber interrupted. "We know what it is, Colonel. We were there."

"Of course," said Larson. "The briefing was prepared for those who were unfamiliar with the attack."

Gerber turned his attention to Jones. "General, if I may be so bold, but just what is going on here?"

"We are about to expand on your theory, Major. While I'm thinking about it, just what in hell possessed you to establish that camp anyway? That was not in the briefing material that I was provided."

"I told General Crinshaw exactly what was going on."

"Then tell me."

Gerber rocked back in his chair, closed his eyes for a moment and then leaned forward, looking at Jones. "A smartass reporter in Saigon was pontificating on his perspective of the war. He was telling all who would listen, in a voice that was unnecessarily loud, that the war couldn't be won and what was worse, he was saying that we didn't know how to win it."

"So, you thought you would show him."

"Not at first, General. At first, I thought I would enlighten him by suggesting that the limitations put on us by the politicians in Washington, far removed from combat, were part of the problem. They were blocking what seemed to be good military tactics because they didn't understand asymmetrical warfare."

"You weren't worried about providing the press with some useable quotes to stir public opinion against us?"

"No, sir. I just didn't want him to think that we didn't know how to win. I wanted him to know that the reporting — that was often less than accurate — might be suggesting to the public that things were worse than they were. And, I wanted him to know that some of that reporting was giving aid and comfort to the enemy."

"You didn't think about the concept of free speech, not to mention freedom of the press?"

"General, my concern was for the soldiers in the field engaged in combat operations. That certain limitations on free speech and free press were necessary to protect the lives of the soldiers."

"Not your call, Major."

"I wasn't telling him what to report or not to report. I only suggested that it would be beneficial if the reporting was a little more accurate and a little less filled with a reporter's opinion."

"Such as?"

"General, I'm not sure where this is going."

"Humor me. Such as?"

"I knew that the reporting that the TET offensive was a great surprise for the Army was simply not true. It seemed that everyone knew that something was going to happen during TET. General Wheeler even mentioned, in November of 1967, that we expected some sort of attack around TET because the Vietnamese had done that when fighting the Chinese centuries earlier. Plans were set in motion in Vietnam to counter the enemy attack."

Now Jones smiled. "You're particularly well informed about this."

"Yes, sir. I pay attention and I read after action reports when I can get them, and I read newspapers so that I know where the errors are made."

"So, you took it upon yourself to provide a practical demonstration."

"Well, yes, sir. It wasn't completely outside my authority, given the orders I had been issued."

"Since we're off on that tangent, why don't you fill me in?"

Gerber looked at Fetterman, who knew the whole truth. It hadn't been the repelling of the assault on the camp that had proved the point. It had been another operation. But Gerber could think of no good reason to mention it. He said, "They threw a reinforced battalion, maybe a regiment at us not long after we had occupied the area."

Gerber recalled the incident like it was yesterday. He remembered sitting on a sandbag wall hoping that there might be a cool breeze blowing off the South China Sea, but knew it would never happen because it was so far away. Instead, he had heard a distant pop and knew immediately that someone had fired a mortar.

Gerber had experienced dozens of mortar attacks. Rather than sprinting for a bunker, he had slipped from the wall and crouched, listening for the impact. He heard the mortar fire, but the round landed far away from him.

Mortars didn't particularly scare him, especially when the rounds seemed to be walking away from him, but then he had heard a rocket being fired. They didn't have guidance and the VC normally tried to aim for the center of the camp, hoping to hit something. Rockets were more dangerous and could seriously damage or destroy a bunker.

Additional mortars were fired, but Gerber couldn't spot the flashes. If the fire control tower had been up, he might have been able to direct counter-mortar. Instead, he ran toward the bunker line closest to the enemy positions. Keeping his head down, he ducked into the command bunker and found Fetterman already there.

He asked if Fetterman could see anything, but the master sergeant had replied, "No movement yet."

Gerber had grabbed the field phone, spun the crank and when it was answered, said, "Bocker. Get me a status report."

Just as he hung up, the jungle around them seemed to explode in a mushroom of fire and flame. A dozen or so mortars began to fire and more rockets came off the rails as shrapnel buried itself in the sandbags of the bunker. Gerber ducked and then stood straight again. He remembered saying, unnecessarily, "Here they come."

Fetterman had moved away from the firing point and set the starlight scope to the side. "They're dropping a lot of stuff on us."

Gerber had wanted to say, "Yeah, I noticed," but the timing wasn't right. They had to deal with the mounting attack. He could hear the slow chugging of one of the .50 cals, and he heard the M-60s open fire.

When the field phone buzzed he had picked it up.

It was Bocker. "We have the perimeter manned. Captain Parker had his men fill the gaps and Tyme reports he's ready with the counter-mortar."

"Who's spotting for him?"

"One of the listening posts."

Gerber had been surprised that the listening posts hadn't already been overrun. He knew from experience that they usually fell first. Gerber couldn't remember exactly what he had said, only that he had told Tyme to open fire.

He remembered wondering about the fate of the other listening posts, but didn't attempt to contact them. If they had anything to report, they'd have called in and if they didn't, it might mean they were surrounded but hadn't been detected.

Fetterman said, "I have movement in the trees."

Firing erupted as the strikers began to shoot at the movement. Gerber hadn't worried about them wasting their ammo. They had plenty of that.

A mortar round fell close to the bunker. Both Gerber and Fetterman had instinctively ducked as dirt, shaken from the sandbags, drifted down.

The noise and scale of the attack was increasing. The continuous detonation of mortar shells was like thunder. The M-60s hammered into the trees and the hot brass from the weapons bouncing around only added to the noise. The air inside the bunker was becoming oppressive.

Fetterman said, "I don't know what I hate most. The incoming or when it stops."

They both knew that when the shelling stopped, the ground attack would begin.

And then suddenly the mortars fell silent. The calm before the storm. Fetterman used the starlight scope. There were now shapes in the tree line, human shapes. He said, "They're massing in front of us."

Gerber had picked up the field phone to tell Tyme to concentrate his mortars on the eastern side of the camp where the enemy was massing for the assault.

From the jungle came the sound of a bugle that Gerber knew signaled the beginning of the ground attack. There were now more whistles and bugles and the enemy swarmed from their cover. They were screaming and shooting, their green tracers in stark contrast to the ruby-coloured tracers of the strikers.

Standing in the command bunker, Gerber had a good view of the open fields leading into the trees. He saw the enemy racing toward the wire, some of them firing wildly.

Fetterman, who had been watching the attack, said, "Getting close, Captain."

Gerber had picked up the firing controls for the claymore mines. They were loaded with hundreds of ball bearings that would explode outward at high speed. A perfectly placed claymore was a devastating weapon.

As the first of the enemy hit the wire, Gerber had pushed the button. There was a flash of orange fire, followed by another and another as he detonated the mines in sequence.

That had momentarily stopped the assault. Gerber had been surprised that the enemy hadn't broken and run. Instead, they forced their way through the wire, firing at the bunkers. An NVA solder stood to throw a satchel charge but was hit as he let go. The explosive detonated behind him in a fountain of sparks and shrapnel that killed all those around him.

Then, as quickly as it had started, the attack broke. Those enemy soldiers still alive turned to run back the way they had come. Gerber grabbed the field phone and ordered, "I want the mortars to hit the tree line."

"Will you spot?"

At the same time, the mortars fired, hitting the ground near the trees.

Fetterman said, "Add fifty."

Gerber relayed the message and then said, "Fire for effect."

In seconds there was no one moving between the camp and the trees. They had disappeared into the night.

"Major?"

Gerber looked around the office, almost as if he had forgotten where he was. The photograph on the screen of the smoking remains of the camp, much of it damaged by the mortars and rockets, had brought the memories back. He could feel sweat bead on his forehead though the room was air conditioned.

Jones said again, "Major?"

Gerber swiped the sweat with the palm of his hand. "What did you want to know, General?"

"Tell me something about your overall plan."

"The mission was simple. This had been a VC stronghold and I wanted to take it away from them. I wanted to show our own press that we could push the enemy out of the area and turn it into a government stronghold. It wasn't just about defeating the enemy but also about gaining the support of the local population. But to start, we had to show them we were stronger than the VC."

"It wasn't just about throwing a base up in a specific location?" asked Jones.

"We knew that we'd need the support of the population, so we did what we could to help them. The VC stole their rice; we'd try to replace it. They denied the people medical attention and we'd provided medical assistance. We worked with the local leaders."

The slide changed, showing the camp a few days later. Jones said, "You made some rapid repairs."

"We had a good strike force and we had some help from the local population."

Jones leaned back in his chair and said, "I was under the impression that when you repelled the attack, that made all the difference."

Gerber sat quietly for a moment before he spoke. "We ambushed an enemy force that had just crossed into South Vietnam sometime later. They were a klick or so on our side of the border. I think that had a great deal to do with it."

But that wasn't the whole truth. They *had* ambushed an enemy force and nearly destroyed it. But what Gerber didn't say was that they had carried out an earlier attack on the wrong side of the border. That might have been the deciding factor. The imaginary line on the ground would not offer the enemy the protection it once had.

Jones flipped through a folder of papers bound by a cover sheet stamped "Top Secret." "General Crinshaw made no mention of anything like that."

Gerber shrugged. "The general was in Saigon and didn't make a trip out to our location. He was working off material that was incomplete because he didn't bother to talk with us."

Jones didn't respond. The criticism wasn't very pointed, more of a statement of fact. He closed the folder and said, "I think that's it for today. Take some time off and we'll meet again when the other participants arrive."

Gerber remained seated. "Can we get some clarification on what is going on here?"

Larson, who had remained silent, said, "We're gathering information for a possible mission later on. What we —"

Jones interrupted. "This is just some preliminary work. We'll get more information to you later. Make sure that my aide has contact information for you and check in each morning at zero eight hundred and each evening at sixteen hundred."

Gerber stood and Fetterman followed. Gerber said, "Thank you, General."

Once outside the building, Gerber turned to Fetterman. "Do you know what they're doing?"

"I suspect that they're thinking of running the experiment again in an attempt to strengthen the strategic hamlet concept."

"I'm just glad you didn't mention that little excursion into Cambodia. I don't think that even Crinshaw knew we had done that."

"It's the reason we succeeded," said Fetterman.

"But they don't have to know that. Yet."

CHAPTER 4

Neither Colonel James Larson nor Brigadier General Thomas Jones moved as Gerber and Fetterman left the conference room. Jones waited until the door had closed and the NCO who had been running the slide projector had packed up his gear and left. When they were alone, he asked, "What were they not telling us?"

Larson looked at the folder in front of him. He opened it but didn't look at any of the documents inside. "There was that ambush at the river, just on the Vietnamese side of the border as Gerber said, about the time a VC compound in Cambodia was attacked. Seems to be too much of a coincidence."

"Or the result of some incredibly good intelligence. If Gerber and his team had managed to convince the locals that they could end the VC terror tactics, someone might have told them about the river crossing."

Larson wanted to stand up and walk around. He could think better when he moved around. He had realized this in high school during a history test. He had been staring at the blank test paper as if it had been in ancient Greek. He'd asked for a hall pass to use the restroom and as he had walked down the hall, he had suddenly known the answers. The walking around had gotten his blood flowing, had stimulated his brain to shift through all the data he had collected while studying.

Naturally, the teacher had thought he had stashed the answers in the restroom and had gone to consult them. Larson had told him the truth: that the moving around allowed him to sort through the problem.

The teacher suggested he take a make-up test, which would cover the same general material, but have a different series of questions. Larson had sat there, with the test in front of him for several minutes and then asked, "Mind if I move around?"

Now, he was in the conference room with a general who had asked him a very specific question. Larson knew the answer was buried somewhere in the documents that he had read over carefully in preparation for the meeting. Without a word, he stood up, and walked around the table as if looking for something. He returned to his seat moments later. "There was something in one of the intel reports that I read that suggested an attack on a VC camp in Cambodia around that same time."

Jones nodded. "You think that's the connection?"

"Gerber had built his camp close to the border to disrupt the flow of men and equipment into Vietnam. Maybe he got a little ambitious."

"That would end up in a court martial and an international incident, if you could prove it."

"Currently, I have no evidence that he had done anything like that," said Larson. "It just feels right."

Jones rubbed his lips and stared up at the ceiling. "This really isn't our purpose here."

"No, sir. But don't we have an obligation to report this sort of thing if we learn about it?"

"We haven't learned anything yet," said Jones. "You've linked a couple of separate events and come up with this theory that Gerber attacked an enemy base in a neutral country."

"Allegedly neutral," said Larson, grinning.

"I have the report written by General Crinshaw but there is nothing in it to suggest that Gerber engaged in a cross-border incident. He criticizes Gerber for setting up the camp without specific, written orders to do so, but it seems that Gerber wasn't operating in a complete vacuum. There were orders that allowed for some flexibility."

Larson reached into his briefcase and took out a three-ring binder. As he flipped through it, he said, "I pulled some of the documentation about all this. Granted, there isn't much here, in Hawaii, just classified copies of some of that documentation while the rest of it is buried at the Pentagon."

"Let's cut through the bull and get to the point," said Jones, making it a point to look at his watch.

Larson ran a finger down the page until he found what he was looking for. "Gerber had a couple of strike companies at this camp of his. If he arranged for them to cross into Cambodia to attack..."

Jones held up a hand and said, "You say that there were strike companies there. Under Vietnamese leadership?"

"Status of forces agreements, not to mention the SOP for Special Forces, allows for the training of the local, indigenous populations but they are under the command of the Vietnamese officers."

"Okay," said Jones. "Then if the Vietnamese officers arranged for the cross-border operation, and there were no American or Special Forces personnel involved, what is the problem?"

"It has been my experience, General, that the Vietnamese do not have the initiative to plan such an operation without the American advisors providing a great deal of assistance."

"But if they only advised, and maybe advised against such an operation, then they would have no responsibility for that operation. Gerber and Fetterman would be in the clear."

"They should have contacted the next higher level of command to suggest that such an operation was in the planning stages so that the Vietnamese chain of command could stop it."

Jones rubbed his eyes as if he was tired. "If, for some reason, charges were brought, wouldn't Gerber just have to say that he advised against the operation?"

"I believe it goes deeper than that, General. I think it was Gerber's idea from the very beginning. He understood that the base, inside Cambodia, was a threat to him. Their heavy artillery could lend fire support to an attack on Gerber's base and that was a threat he had to eliminate."

"I still don't see what you're after here, Larson."

"I want to know if there was someone at a higher headquarters that was participating in all this. Someone who wanted to prove a point. It just doesn't seem to me that a captain would come up with such a strategic thought and implement it on his own. There had to be someone else, in Saigon or Nha Trang, that had a hand in this."

"Aren't those Green Berets supposed to think in the long term? Isn't it their mission to engage in asymmetrical warfare?"

"General, I believe that some sort of, well, I don't want to say war crime, but some sort of violation of our restrictions in Vietnam have been violated. I believe that we should look into it."

"That is certainly in your wheel house, Colonel. You don't need my permission to pursue this. But be careful that you are not smearing a decorated and respected officer because you think he might have overstepped his authority."

"I will need your permission if I have to travel overseas, General. I will if I need to penetrate some of the classified operations that have been run in Vietnam. Just to get at some of the documentation is going to be a problem because of need to know."

Jones shook his head as if he was about to end the discussion and issue an order that the investigation, or the request for an investigation, end at this point. It wouldn't be good for the Army and it wouldn't be good for his career — unless there was something to it.

Both men got to their feet. Jones turned to Larson and said, "Proceed with caution. Extreme caution. If you hit a snag, contact me, but don't make any waves."

"Yes, General. Thank you."

Gerber said little on the trip back to the hotel, given they were riding in a taxi. He was concerned about the inquiry into his establishing the camp at Xa Cat. That could lead to some trouble, depending on the interest in what happened there and how deeply they probed into it.

The driver pulled to the curb. As Fetterman got out, Gerber paid the driver and then they walked through the hotel lobby. They rode the elevator up to Gerber's room. Once inside, Fetterman said, "Well, that went nicely. You have anything to drink? I mean, left over from last night?"

Gerber waved at the dresser where the bottles were set. "Help yourself."

Fetterman poured himself two fingers of bourbon in a water glass and then sat down at the table. He raised the glass in a semi-salute then took a deep drink.

Gerber stood at the window, looking down at the beach that was curiously deserted. He turned back to look at Fetterman. "I've said it before and I'll say it again. I don't like this. It smacks of an ambush and I wonder if Crinshaw isn't pulling the strings from somewhere."

"Major," said Fetterman, "both of us were promoted after we DEROSed. That seems to indicate that all is good. That seems to suggest that the matter is closed."

Gerber pulled out the other chair and dropped into it. "But that doesn't mean that someone hasn't been working to catch us in a lie. We were both in Cambodia, even if we did try to disguise it as an ARVN operation."

"There is nothing that can lead back to us. None of the team would say anything about it."

"I don't know, Tony. We are skating on awfully thin ice here. I have a bad feeling about Colonel Larson. It's almost as if he is a copy of Crinshaw."

"What do you propose?"

"The team is scattered all over the world. We need to talk with some of them to see if anyone has been asking questions about Xa Cat."

Fetterman shrugged and pointed at the telephone. "You can talk to them any time you want."

"You know where they are?"

"Come on, Major. You know how to find them as well as I do. A call to Mackall will provide the information."

"I thought about that, but I think a call there looking for several of our pals might tip them off that we're onto what they're doing, or provide them with names that they might not have."

Fetterman finished his bourbon and set his glass down. "So, what's Plan B?"

Gerber shook his head. "I might be paranoid. This might not have anything to do with that cross-border op, but I don't like it coming up now. We've got a general asking questions and I don't think Larson was thrilled with our answers."

"I've never seen you so ambivalent, Major."

"That's because we're in uncharted territory. We don't have Alan Bates running interference for us, and we don't have the CIA looking out for us. We're on our own in this."

"You know what Georgie Patton used to say. The real one, from World War Two. He'd say, 'Don't take counsel of your fears.'"

Fetterman leaned back in his chair and added, "We have the rest of the day off. We don't have enough intelligence to make any real guesses and if we start asking questions, we might find ourselves having to explain what interests us. Nothing is going to happen today, so we might as well relax."

Gerber took a deep breath and nodded. "We could tour the *Arizona*. Might provide us with a different perspective."

"Are you suggesting something about a surprise attack?"

"No. I'm just suggesting that since we're here, we might as well do something that is educational."

Colonel James Larson sat at his desk, which looked to be nearly new. That was an oddity in the military because it seemed that everything had a worn and well-used look to it. In fact, nearly everything in the office was new with the exception of a settee pushed up against one wall. While it wasn't new, it didn't show much wear either.

Larson was sitting in front of a stack of documents that related to Gerber's experiment during his last tour. He had scanned them once but had seen nothing extraordinary in them. Nothing had leaped out at him.

He sat back, picked up the bottle of Pepsi and took a drink. It was still nearly ice cold, which was another benefit of being one of the highest-ranking officers around.

But he knew that was about to change. He was at the extreme end of his career if he wasn't selected for promotion soon. Colonels had only so long to move up the chain, and the positions available for colonels to become brigadier generals were limited. He was within a year of mandatory retirement if he didn't find a way to move up.

The problem was, his had not been a distinguished career. He had checked all the necessary boxes, attended all the proper schools including command and staff. He had not graduated at the top of any of the classes, but was well down in the middle of the pack. Which rarely mattered.

He had served in Korea. Not as a combat commander but as a staff officer at the Corps Headquarters. He had not fired his weapon while there, had not earned any awards for valor, but he had done his job as an assistant operations officer. He was rewarded with an Army Commendation Medal which the enlisted troops called the Big Green Weenie. The fact that he had only received the Army Commendation Medal told all who looked at his records that his service had been adequate but not spectacular. Had it been spectacular, or even above average, he might have earned a higher award.

Like many of his colleagues, he had a single tour in Vietnam. He had held a higher rank but had been assigned to MACV Headquarters in Saigon. Had he been there during the TET offensive, then he might have had the opportunity to distinguish himself, but he arrived after the fighting was over — with the exception of the siege at Khe Sanh and the final push into Hue. He had participated in none of those battles but had reported on them to the other colonels and generals stationed in Saigon.

Sitting in front of him, in the stack of files and reports, might be the salvation for his career. True, he had reached the upper echelons of the military structure and would retire as a full bull colonel, but he had hoped for more. He had hoped for the star that would propel him into the stratosphere of the military organization. Answering the telephone as a general was better than answering as a colonel because even a lieutenant colonel could do that.

The potential for that promotion was there, in those folders, if he could navigate it properly. He just didn't know which way to jump. The Special Forces, that is the Green Berets, had become the darlings in the Pentagon since the Kennedy administration. That Special Forces tab, as did the Ranger tab, provided some push for promotion, but he had neither. It was one of the things that the promotion boards looked for beyond just the normal schools and training assignments.

As a young second lieutenant, he had not gone to jump school to earn his parachutist's wings. Nearly every officer in the Army went to jump school, with a few notable exceptions. Army Aviators, who had been recruited to fly helicopters didn't go to jump school, but then, they did fly helicopters into hot LZs and rescued downed flight crews, and evacuated the wounded. They performed difficult and dangerous missions and nearly every officer who had served in Vietnam could tell of a helicopter rescue, critical supply run, or close air support that the Air Force couldn't or wouldn't perform. The Army Aviator's Badge was nearly as important as jump wings.

Larson took another swig of his Pepsi and then opened the top folder to begin the task of reading the reports carefully and attempting to learn which side of the fence he should jump to.

He was almost sure that both Gerber and Fetterman had crossed the imaginary line into Cambodia at some point. But Gerber was too smart to give anything away and there was no way that Fetterman would spill the beans. Fetterman had been around too long, been in too many units and assignments not to understand how the system worked. Fetterman would have contacts all over the Army that would protect him. Larson needed to find someone else, and try to pry the truth out of them. The question was how to do it.

Before he could do that, however, he needed to understand what had gone on in Vietnam and in Cambodia during that period in the war. He was sure that Cambodia was the key to understanding the situation.

He shifted through the stack of documents and finally found a roster that provided the names of the Americans involved at the camp and those who had supported Gerber at other camps. The majority of the soldiers had been Vietnamese and they probably would be of no help, but there were a couple of dozen American officers and NCOs who had participated. He needed to find two or three of them.

He pulled the roster out of the folder and shouted, "Wilcox?"

A moment later Wilcox appeared at the door. The administrative assistant was a stocky man who looked as if he should be leading a patrol into the jungle rather than sitting behind a typewriter keeping track of Larson's paperwork. He was wearing a khaki uniform that held only his branch insignia on one collar, a "US" insignia on the other and a nametag as required by installation regulations.

"Yes, sir."

"Come in. I have a list of names here, all Special Forces, and I need to find out where they are. We can assume that some of them will be in Vietnam, but others could be practically anywhere in the world. I want you to find them for me without raising suspicion."

"Yes, sir," he said, not quite sure what he should do.

"Try to learn where they are through the Special Warfare Center at Bragg. They usually have a good idea of who is where, but you must be a little cautious about it. I don't want them to know why we need to know or that we're even looking for them."

Again, Wilcox said, "Yes, sir."

"If someone pushes for a reason, tell them that we are in the preliminary stages of putting together a special team for a classified mission. There is nothing scheduled yet and we are assembling information for a general on this."

Wilcox grinned. "Yes, sir. I get it. But if you want to hide what you're doing, you might want to add names that have nothing to do with, well, whatever you are doing."

It was Larson's turn to grin. "That's a very nice touch. Get ready to make the calls, but don't do anything yet. Let me get the names of some other Green Berets to add to the list."

"Yes, sir. Will that be all?"

Larson rocked back in his chair, pleased with himself. "Yes, that's it."

As Wilcox turned to go, Larson shouted, "If you can find it, get a list of the Green Berets assigned to Vietnam and those deployed to Africa. Anywhere in Africa because that doesn't matter."

"Yes, sir."

Master Sergeant Galvin Bocker, who had served in Vietnam with the Special Forces as a communications specialist and who had cross-trained as a small weapons expert, was happy with his current situation. He was sitting in a hotel room on the ninth floor with a window overlooking Denver, Colorado, and had a partial view of the Rocky Mountains. He was on leave, thirty days, accumulated after DEROS, about ten days earlier. He was on orders to report to the Special Warfare Center by the end of the month, but he wasn't thinking about that. He was thinking about women and a new car and where he would live when he got to North Carolina. At the moment, life was good.

Bocker had been a staff sergeant when he first deployed to Vietnam, trained to work the radios, though the job was more than that. He had to be able to repair them, to build a working transmitter from the parts of other radios, to understand the dynamics of communications in the short wave and long wave arenas. He had to be familiar with the Fox Mike, meaning, of course, FM, the Uniform which was UHF and about everything else used in communications in Vietnam.

But right now, what he would rather do was find an interesting movie in downtown Denver and spend the evening immersed in someone else's fictional problems. He wondered if James Bond was the solution, or maybe one of those westerns by that Italian director. It was nice to have that sort of weighty decision to make, without worrying about Charlie dropping a mortar on him while he was watching the film.

Bocker had actually joined the Army, rather than being drafted, because that gave him the chance to decide, within reason, what he wanted to do. He had thought about helicopter flight training, but being color blind had disqualified him. Offered the opportunity to take the communications course, he opted for it, because he was just nineteen and thought that it would be communicating to others, through radio and television or even a training film or two, what they needed to know. He was surprised when he learned it had to do with repairing the radios, ensuring the equipment was in top shape and communicating with others in the field.

When he learned that upon completion of the school, he would probably be deployed to an infantry unit in Vietnam, he decided that he needed parachute training. That should have happened after basic training, but Bocker had lucked out. He could get qualified as a parachutist and more importantly, it would delay orders to Vietnam.

The downside, besides jumping out of a perfectly good airplane, was that the school was only three weeks long. That wouldn't delay his deployment by all that much, and the news suggested that the war wouldn't be over by the time he pinned on his silver wings.

But the fates intervened again. It turned out that the Special Forces was looking for those who were jump qualified and who had an MOS for communications. There were other qualifications, such as a tour in Vietnam, but that could be waived for someone who was both a paratrooper and a communications specialist. Training would delay his deployment even more, and completion of the training would almost certainly result in a promotion to Sergeant E-5, as opposed to Spec Five.

His training in communications and later in the Special Forces hadn't delayed his deployment long enough, and Bocker found himself in South Vietnam, assigned to a team at Camp A-555. He worked with Captain — now Major — MacKenzie Gerber and Master Sergeant — now Sergeant Major — Anthony Fetterman, when they established a camp in a province that had seen little in the way of South Vietnamese government interest. He'd seen, for the first time, how asymmetrical warfare worked when properly conducted and well thought out. He had also witnessed the value of close air support when in a defensive posture.

Now he was a master sergeant with combat experience who was home from his last tour in Vietnam. Instead of working with an A-Team, he had been assigned to a headquarters where he coordinated the communications of teams scattered around

Three Corps and War Zone C. An interesting tour where the most danger he saw was from the random mortar attacks as he rode along on some of the resupply convoys.

Bocker watched the sun sink toward the mountains, waiting for his room service dinner and thinking that this was much better than suffering in the heat and humidity of South Vietnam. Lights were coming on in buildings across the city and he could see the traffic crawl along on Colfax.

The ringing of the telephone startled him. It was a holdover from his time in a combat environment. He thought he was over the sudden surge of adrenaline that came with sudden loud noises. And he realized that it could not be good news. Although he was on leave, he had been required to provide contact information to the receiving headquarters, which meant those awaiting his return to Fort Bragg knew how to reach him. They would have to go through his parents to do it, but his parents would relay the message.

His first thought was to ignore the phone because his parents wouldn't be calling at this hour. It was too early for them. But then he pushed himself out of the chair and walked to the telephone. He picked it up and said, "Hello?"

"Galvin, honey?"

"Yes, Mom."

"Are you okay?"

"Yes, Mom. Just waiting on my dinner and looking at the mountains."

"We got a call from a Major Forrester. At Fort Bragg. He said that he needed to talk with you."

Bocker looked at his watch. It was half past six, which meant is was eight thirty at Bragg, which was late for a peace side, state side, assignment. It meant that whatever he wanted, it couldn't be good.

"He say anything else?"

"He gave me a number and said that you could reach him there at any time." She hesitated and then repeated, "He said that he needed to talk with you."

Bocker reached for the pen that the hotel had left by the telephone for his convenience. "Give it to me."

She read off the number and then asked, "Is there trouble?"

"No, Mom. Probably something routine."

"Then why call so late and want you to call him back right away?"

Bocker laughed. "That's because it's the Army. Hurry up and wait. Probably something he forgot to do during normal duty hours. I'll give him a call."

"And you'll be coming home soon?"

"Couple of days. There's a guy I want to see while I'm here."

Now it was his mother's turn to laugh. "What's her name?"

"There is really a guy here. I'll probably be home in a couple of days."

"You be careful."

"Bye, Mom."

"Goodbye."

Bocker didn't like the sound of her voice when she had said "Goodbye." It had the same tone in it when he had called home just before his last tour in Vietnam. A sadness, as if they might never speak again.

CHAPTER 5

Gerber sat in the hotel room chair, his feet up on the bed and the telephone pressed to his ear. He was listening intently to the person at the other end of the line when there was a knock at the door. He had flipped the security device over so that the door wouldn't shut completely because he knew that Fetterman was due at any moment.

He called, "Come on in." He saw Fetterman and waved him toward the other seat and then said into the telephone, "I'll meet you at the airport in the morning."

When he hung up, Fetterman asked, "That Morrow?"

"She's in San Francisco and will catch a flight out later. Be here in the morning."

"That a good idea?"

Gerber dropped his feet to the floor and turned his chair so that it was facing the table. The remains of his dinner were there and he drained the last of the Pepsi. "What's the problem, Tony? You know that Robin would not do anything to harm us."

"But we're here, in Hawaii, and there are indications that the reason is the little project we set up in Vietnam. Or rather some of the ancillary operations needed to make the point."

Gerber grinned. "And she already knows about that and hasn't printed a word."

"Only because the brass in Saigon couldn't really find anything wrong with what we did. Might have overstepped our authority, but not by much and we were successful."

Changing the topic, Gerber asked, "You want to go for a run?"

"I've got a date," said Fetterman.

Gerber raised his eyebrow and asked, "A date?"

"Not what you think. I ran into an NCO I know and he has a poker game planned for tonight. Invited me to play."

"I didn't know you are a poker player."

"Haven't had much chance. Didn't want to get into a game with the other members of the team. It's just not good form to take money from your subordinates, and neither you nor Bromhead seemed interested."

"Bromhead was a babe in the woods when he joined us. You might have been able to pick him clean," said Gerber.

"Not a good idea to take money from the team's exec, either. Who knows what sort of retribution he could inflict."

"Jonathan wouldn't do anything like that," said Gerber.

"Not then, but now he's a captain and a little more worldly. He might remember if I picked him clean in a poker game and find some way to get even."

Gerber looked out the window onto the beach and said, "I don't know what time we might be summoned in the morning."

"I think if they had anything planned very early, they would have let us know by now."

Fetterman stood up. "I will assume that if you're going for a run that you'll have no need for the car tonight."

"If I need to go anywhere, I'll grab a cab. Keys are over there." Gerber pointed to the low table that held the ice bucket and four glasses.

"See you in the morning." Fetterman grabbed the keys and left.

As he entered the room, Fetterman saw a large round table in the center covered with a green, felt cloth. The host for the evening, George Forman, was at the side bar pouring himself a drink. On seeing Fetterman, he announced, "Gentlemen, some of you might remember Sergeant Major Tony Fetterman. I've known him for twelve years and I don't hold it against him that he is a Green Beret or that he jumps out of perfectly good airplanes."

One of the men seated at the table said, "I don't believe we've met, Sergeant Major. I'm Master Sergeant David Culhane, Infantry. I've jumped out of some perfectly good airplanes myself. There are times that it's a good idea to do that."

Fetterman reached across the table, shook his hand and asked, "David or Dave?"

"Dave is fine."

The man seated next to Dave introduced himself. "Virgil Johnson. I go by Bill because I have never liked the name Virgil and in poker, I'm the Bill you pay."

Fetterman shook his hand and then looked at the next man. "Don't I know you?"

"I just finished the Q Course. You spoke to us about some of the things that you had observed in Vietnam. Gave us a rundown on what to expect once we were in-country."

Fetterman grinned. "You asked the incredibly stupid question."

"That was me. I wanted to know why the North Vietnamese and the VC seemed to be better soldiers than the ARVN."

"And I told you that part of it was because they believed in the cause, weren't filled with corrupt officers who bought their rank and position, and that there were some very good soldiers in the South Vietnamese Army. I have worked with several them."

The man nodded. "So, I did a little research to see if you were full of shit."

"First, you really shouldn't say something like that to me because I'm a Sergeant Major." Fetterman smiled to show he was only having a little fun with him. "Second, I'll bet you found that I was right."

"Certainly did, Sergeant Major."

"I'm Tony here, at the table."

The man held out a hand and said, "Jesus Gonzales."

The last man at the table said, "Now that you Green Beanies have gotten old home week out of the way, can we get started?"

"You are?"

"Sergeant Thomas Zimmerman. I'm assigned to the 25th rear detachment."

"Glad to meet you, Sergeant."

Forman looked around the group of faces and said, "Now that we have everyone introduced, we can get started. The game is five card stud, table stakes during a hand, but you can dip into your cash reserves between hands. No automobiles will be used for collateral and no IOUs for over twenty bucks. Any questions?"

As those at the table shook their heads, Fetterman pulled out a chair and sat down. "What's the buy in?"

"Whatever you feel comfortable. Ante is a buck. Raise whatever you want but let's keep the game friendly." Forman sat down, set a glass of bourbon on the table, and then said, "Unless there is an objection, I'll deal the first hand and then we'll rotate clockwise."

Fetterman noticed that everyone else had a glass of liquor or a beer close at hand. He wasn't going to drink, at least, not much. He'd wait until someone asked what he wanted to drink.

He'd watch the other players, to learn how each of them played. The first hour was for observations and quick folds unless the cards fell in his favor.

Poker was a game of strategy. You had your forces, which might be weak or strong, facing off against the opponents, who were in the same boat. Fetterman didn't engage in the general banter around the game, saying just enough so that the others didn't take offense. He watched the cards, watched the men, and kept track of who was bold, who was cautious, and who knew how to bluff. He looked for tells, that is, body language, nervousness, blinking; anything that might hint at the strength of the hand being held by the other players. A spotted tell was a big advantage for those paying attention.

There was a great deal of information on the table for the careful observer. Although he couldn't see his opponents' hole card, he could see all those dealt face up. The trick was to remember which cards had been dealt face up for hands that were then folded. Knowing which cards were out of the game helped Fetterman gauge the hands of those who remained in the game and the odds for who held a winning hand.

They were a dozen hands in when Fetterman realized that he couldn't be beat. His hole card was the ace of diamonds. His four face-up cards were all diamonds but there wasn't a sequence that might have masked a straight flush. Looking at the other players, there was no one who could be holding a full house. That would require two pair showing with the hole card matching one of the pairs. There were simply no other combinations that would beat him. The best was the hand with two queens showing. If the hole card was a queen, the guy was sitting on three of a kind.

The pair of queens bet and Fetterman took a chance, raising him. It was a large increase. The queens reraised, telling

Fetterman that the guy had the queens and since there were three diamonds in one of the other hands, and a fourth had been folded, the queens thought they had a lock.

Fetterman called and the man flipped over the third queen. And Fetterman flipped over the ace of diamonds. After that, he knew that the others would watch him a little more closely, but more importantly, it allowed him to set up a bluff or two. They would see him as a tight player, who was cautious and would bet heavily with a good hand.

Forman, it turned out, was something of a bully at the table. He bluffed frequently with big bets to buy the hand. He didn't seem to watch the other players and bet on instinct that turned out to be reliable, but Fetterman knew that he could use that information against him.

Johnson was a careful player, folding the moment that someone on the table picked up a pair. Johnson seemed to fear the ambush, that is a player with a hole card that made three of a kind.

In one case, Fetterman had seen that others had folded the two cards necessary for three of a kind. The best Culhane could do was two pair and Fetterman had that beat. Culhane was a cautious bettor, who tried a small raise, which Fetterman called, but didn't reraise. When the last card was dealt, Fetterman knew that he held the winning hand. Culhane bet again and Fetterman raised. Culhane folded.

Fetterman watched as those who were drinking the bourbon became more aggressive as the night progressed. They would push their cards, trying to buy the pot, but it rarely worked. Fetterman knew who was getting wild and depending on his hole card, he would fold after two or three cards had been dealt.

He also began to slip money into his pocket, so that he didn't have a big stack of bills in front of him. Ten or twenty dollars at a time until he had more money in his pocket than he had brought to the table. He would leave a winner without the others realizing it.

Finally, as it was getting late, and because the others were drunk, Fetterman said, "Last hand for me."

Forman looked across at him. "The night is young."

"It might be," said Fetterman, "but I'm not. And, I might have an early morning meeting. I need to get my beauty sleep."

"You can say that again," said Gonzales. "In fact, I think you might need a coma to catch up."

Fetterman ignored him. After looking at his hole card again, and then the jack on the table, he said, "I'll bet a buck."

Forman shook his head. "That's not a bet. Ten bucks is a bet."

Zimmerman, who'd had more to drink than he should have, said, "I call."

Gonzales called and Culhane folded.

Johnson hesitated and finally folded.

Since he had a pair of jacks, Fetterman shrugged and said, "I call."

No one paired on the board with the next round, but Forman now had an ace showing. He said, "Ace bets. Ten bucks."

"Your ace doesn't scare me. Up ten," said Zimmerman.

Gonzales looked at the cards, then checked his hole card. "I fold."

"Chicken?" asked Forman.

"Nope. Wise."

Fetterman, still sitting with only a pair of jacks but knowing that Forman would bully the table, said, "I call."

When the last card was dealt, Fetterman had a pair showing to go with his two jacks. "Ten bucks," he said.

Forman grinned, as if he had Fetterman trapped. "Raise to twenty."

Fetterman studied the board and knew that the best Forman could have was a pair of aces. Since he had two pair, but only one showing, he had the winning hand. He hesitated, as if signaling a weak hand, which, if Forman knew what he was doing, would have alerted him to the trap.

"Fifty," Fetterman said.

"I thought this was a friendly game," said Culhane.

"That was a friendly fifty," replied Fetterman.

Forman grinned. "Your little pair won't beat my aces. I call."

Fetterman flipped over his hole card. "I knew that. But two pair will."

"I should have known that a sergeant major would not be caught by ambush." He didn't show his hole card.

Fetterman collected the pot and asked, "Is there gratuity for the host?"

"Whatever you think appropriate," said Forman.

Fetterman peeled off a twenty from the roll of bills and said, "Thanks, George."

"You're welcome back at any time, Tony. Just bring your money."

Major Joshua Corley sat in the semi-darkness of the operations bunker, one of the few air-conditioned structures on the base camp, and studied the fire support base plan. It was not something he wanted to do. He'd have been happier as a captain commanding an infantry company during combat assaults, but he had been promised a more rapid rise if he changed jobs. There were hundreds of captains who could command infantry companies, but few with the training to be assistant division engineers.

Like his contemporaries, Corley was a young man, twenty-six and in good physical condition. He had graduated from West Point and had been assigned as a second lieutenant to one of those infantry companies as a platoon leader. Corley knew, from the many conversations held late into the evening about a career in the military, that most senior NCOs would be capable of running a company or a battalion and it was the smart second john who listened to them. Corley believed that he should stay out of their way and let the platoon sergeant run the platoon while he watched and learned how it was in the real Army as opposed to the Army as taught at the Point.

Like those who graduated with him, he was promoted on time to first lieutenant because he could hear thunder and see lightning and had not gotten caught up in any sort of scandal, such as impregnating a willing female to whom he was not married, bouncing a check — even if it was an arithmetic error that caused it, or been caught drunk driving, for which there was no excuse. And just before deployment to Vietnam, he had been serving as the executive officer of one of those infantry companies that he believed he could command.

In Vietnam he learned that a company was not comprised of two hundred or more soldiers, but only eighty or ninety. This was because that was the number of soldiers that could be carried into combat on a flight of ten, and later nine, UH-1D or UH-1H Huey helicopters. That kept the company together and if more men were required for the mission, another company would be inserted, or as many additional companies as needed.

Like all the FNGs sent to Vietnam, he was assigned to a battalion and then on to a company in that battalion, to learn the ropes before being turned loose with a command of his own. The unwritten rule was that he would spend the first six months of his tour deploying into the field, sometimes for a day, or a week, and one such deployment for two weeks. For the last six months, if he survived the combat role, he would find himself assigned to another job. The statistics showed that the turnover for young lieutenants was high because of their inexperience in the combat arena.

He was surprised when the battalion commander called on him and asked if he was interested in filling in as the assistant division engineer. When he started to interrupt, the BC held up a hand to stop him.

"Before you speak, hear me out. We have a need for someone with your training in engineering and I have all the bright-eyed lieutenants I need for the positions with the companies. They'll be living out in the field, humping the bush, and you can stay at the base camp working. Air conditioning, steak dinners and movies every night if you have time to go to them."

Corley sat on the edge of his cot, his sweat-soaked jungle jacket hung on a nail nearby. The ceiling fan turned slowly overhead but did little to cool the room. After a day in the field, they had been extracted about sixteen hundred and returned to the base.

"This is a chance to move up the ladder a little faster than your peers. Position calls for a major and since this is a combat theater, some of the regulations can be suspended for the good of the service. That major leaf won't be far away."

Corley shrugged. "But isn't combat experience at a premium for officers?"

"Of course, but what makes you think this isn't a combat assignment? We're here, in the heart of Three Corps and

Charlie is dropping mortars on us on a regular basis. We are, in essence, on the front lines. It's a good job and it broadens your skill set. You become a good utility player who could be plugged into any assignment."

Although he would never mention it, he was worried about being left out of combat where officers earned valor awards and those enhanced careers better than a choice assignment. There was no way to mention the concern without seeming to be a glory hunter. A reputation as a glory hunter could end a career faster than almost anything else.

The BC leaned closer and lowered his voice. "I know what you're thinking. You're afraid that taking the assignment will look as if you are trying to dodge combat. But I can tell you that if you do a good job as the assistance engineer, you'll get an OER that will cover that, not to mention a Bronze Star Medal as you DEROS."

He had been in Vietnam for only a couple of months, but he understood the philosophy of comfort level. Patrolling in the field and living at a fire support base was not high on the list of plum assignments. Living at a base camp with the division or brigade headquarters was higher on the list. The good things could be had daily, while those at the fire support bases were rewarded with a few days at a base camp when they could be spared from their duties.

"Corley, you don't have to decide on this right now, but I don't understand the hesitation. All the benefits are here and not just the living conditions. You'll be working with senior staff, which never hurts a young officer's career. You'll be in a position to learn things that some officers never learn."

"What would I be doing, exactly?"

"Engineering stuff… Oh, you wouldn't be trying to clear mine fields or anything like that. This is more of a planning assignment. There'd be some design work involved, supervisor in the field for a few days here and there, but no long-term deployments into the field."

Corley shrugged. "I had wanted to command a company. A combat command can go a long way in the Army."

"True enough. However, planning the operations from an engineering point of view is more valuable. While you haven't had, strictly, a combat command, you have served as an executive officer. That's nearly as good because everyone will understand that there were times that you were in command. It all shakes out in the end."

"With all due respect, Major, why are you pushing this?"

"I… We, recognize potential when we see it and we thought this opportunity would be a valuable asset on you record, not to mention the accelerated promotion."

Corley looked across the room, at the M-16 standing in the corner with mud on the butt and a magazine inserted. There wasn't a round chambered, but the weapon was ready. It was a symbol of the situation. A loaded weapon just in case the VC hit the perimeter in the night.

"When would I start?"

"Just as soon as I can get a replacement for you. Ford is a good commander, a senior commander, so he's used to having to train an exec."

Now Corley smiled. "I can hear the excitement. He'll be delighted to get a new guy to train."

"Then it's settled?"

"Yes, sir."

Now he was looking at the plans for a new type of fire support base, but they didn't require an engineer because the plans were standardized. He had looked at the terrain earlier, seen that there was an area of slightly raised ground that was perfect for the base. If attacked, the enemy would have an uphill charge, not that it was much of a climb. He could see no reason that the base shouldn't be located on that elevated terrain. It dominated the surrounding ground and had good open fields around it. Still, he sometimes wished he had been given a company instead.

Gerber was watching the morning news when there was a knock at the door. He stood up and opened it. "Good morning, Sergeant Major."

"Good morning, sir."

Gerber grinned and said, "What in the hell is that you're wearing."

Fetterman spun slowly to give him a full view. "It's all the rage here in Hawaii."

"That is the loudest shirt I have ever seen."

"I think of it as camouflage. I look like a tourist and can blend in with the crowd."

"I take it you're going to wear that out in public."

"Yes, sir. I've still got the keys, so I'll drive?"

Gerber nodded and said, "You've got a deal."

As they walked through the hotel lobby, Gerber noticed that Fetterman was not alone in his untucked, short sleeve shirt. Only the colors varied, though they were all bright and, in some cases, looked as if someone had thrown paint on a clean, white shirt.

The scene didn't change much at the airport, though it was early morning. Gerber looked at the schedule. "Robin is due in about thirty minutes. You eat breakfast?"

"Of course," said Fetterman. "It's the most important meal of the day."

"So I've been told."

"Major, I am a little worried about this. She is a reporter."

"We've been through this before, Tony. We can trust her."

Fetterman nodded. "What are we going to do?"

"Walk out to the gate and wait. No time to do anything else."

Fetterman did a double take and then pointed to a man wearing a blue sport coat and khaki trousers, which was the unofficial uniform of a soldier off duty but who had a new purpose. "Do you know that man?"

Gerber searched the crowd and then said, "Can that be Bocker?"

"If it's not, then it's his twin."

"Let's ambush him," said Gerber.

Although trained in situational awareness, Bocker was intently studying a map of the local area. Gerber put a hand on his shoulder and said, "You're going to have to come with us."

Startled, Bocker spun round, then he grinned. "Mack, I mean, Major. What are you doing here? And Tony too. It's old home week."

"I could ask you the same thing," said Gerber. "What *are* you doing here?"

"Got orders," said Bocker. "Needed to get me here quickly for some sort of debriefing."

"Any hint about what?" Fetterman asked.

"I think it has to do with the base we established. I'm not sure what the rush is, but with you two here, that makes some sense to me."

"We've got a car," said Gerber. "We're waiting for Morrow, who should be here in a few minutes. We can get you to the hotel. We can think about dinner later today."

"I've got orders to report in as soon as I arrive. There's supposed to be transportation for me here. I don't know what the schedule is."

"You have any documentation with you?" asked Gerber.

"Nothing except my orders. I wasn't asked to bring anything with me, not that I had much to bring. I'm delighted to be here on the one hand. Free trip to Hawaii where no one will be shooting at me. If I stay in the visiting NCO quarters and eat in the mess hall, then it doesn't cost me a thing, other than my entertainment."

"I'm not going to ask about that entertainment. I will say, however, that staying on post is not as relaxing as it is in the hotel."

"I've got two beds in my room," Fetterman said. "You're welcome to one of them."

"Let me report in and see what the schedule is. I can always call you this afternoon when I know more."

Gerber looked at the arrivals board. "Robin's flight has landed."

Fetterman handed Bocker the telephone number of the hotel. "Call me when you know."

As they reached the gate, they saw an aircraft parked there and a stream of passengers getting off. Unnecessarily, Fetterman said, "Guess they were a little early."

Robin Morrow appeared then, surrounded by the other passengers. She was dressed in a short skirt, light blouse and black shoes. She was tall, had hair bleached light brown from the sun in Vietnam, and bright green eyes. When she spotted Gerber, she smiled and waved and headed toward him.

She stopped short, looked at Fetterman and asked, "What in the hell are you wearing, Master Sergeant?"

"That's Sergeant Major, and he is caught up on the local color," Gerber said.

"My apologies, Sergeant Major. I forgot you had been promoted."

Fetterman nodded but he looked serious. "I will only accept the apology if it is accompanied by a drink."

"Here? Now?"

"Later. In nicer surroundings."

"Deal," said Morrow. "So, what are you guys doing here?"

"Let's grab your luggage and we'll talk in the car."

She tapped her carry-on. "This is it. Everything I need is in here."

"No typewriter?" asked Fetterman.

"I'm off the clock, Tony."

Fetterman shrugged but it didn't look as if he believed her. She was a reporter and, as far as he knew, they were never off the clock.

Once they had recovered the car, Fetterman got behind the wheel. Gerber and Morrow climbed into the back seat.

"What's going on? You guys weren't in Vietnam long enough for an R and R," Morrow asked.

"We have orders to be here to participate in some sort of meeting or planning session. We don't really know the exact reason for those orders," said Gerber, choosing his words carefully.

"You're not in any sort of trouble, are you?"

Fetterman, watching the road, said, "We don't think so. If we were in trouble, the orders would have read differently and we wouldn't be running around loose. They'd be keeping us holed up somewhere."

"Tony and I are staying in a hotel."

Morrow grinned. "Not in the same room, I hope."

CHAPTER 6

The set up in the conference room was the same as before. The only change that Gerber could see was that there were more men in the room. Bocker, of course, he recognized. The other newcomers had the look of a recent visit to Vietnam. They were tanned, though one of them looked sunburned, as if he hadn't been out in the sun much until recently. Given the uniforms, Gerber could see that two of the men were aviators and one wore no qualifications badges other than jump wings. He was wearing the crossed rifles of the infantry that told Gerber nothing about him.

Fetterman, as was his habit when required to wait, closed his eyes and relaxed. Since neither he nor Gerber would be leading the meeting, he was at the mercy of those who were. Meetings, Fetterman knew, were mostly worthless, but there were times when questions were answered and something important was accomplished.

The door opened and General Jones entered. He was followed by Larson, who went over to the lectern set in the corner of the room, near the screen. He set a notebook on the lectern, flipped it open, and then stood waiting.

Jones took the chair at the head of the table. "Be seated. I know most of you here. We've all met once or twice, but let's get acquainted so that everyone knows all the players."

Then, without pausing, the Colonel pointed at Gerber, telling the others who he was. He then pointed at Fetterman and Bocker. Sitting next to Bocker was the engineer, Joshua Corley. On the other side of the table were the two Army Aviators who looked as if they hadn't slept in a couple of days. Their khaki uniforms were wrinkled and the only items were their branch insignia, rank and wings. Jones made it clear that they had come from the airport directly to the meeting.

To them, he said, "I'm sorry that you were rushed here. Let's see if I have this right." He consulted a paper. "Warrant Officer Steven Douglas and First Lieutenant John Williams. I understand that Mister Douglas is senior based on his time in-country though Williams holds the superior rank."

Douglas wasn't sure if he should stand when addressing the general, but then they were in a meeting so it seemed he should remain seated. "I have about seven months in-country, General. I'm an aircraft commander and Lieutenant Williams is what we think of as a Peter Pilot, meaning that he hasn't accumulated sufficient flight time to be considered for aircraft commander."

Jones grinned. "*About* seven months? I thought every soldier in Vietnam knew exactly how long he had been there, down to the hour, and when he would be going home."

"Yes, sir. We know exactly how long we have left."

"And that is?"

"One hundred and fifty-seven days and a wake up, sir."

"You, Lieutenant?"

"Around two hundred and eighty days. Too much time to keep an accurate count, especially with all the short timers around, sir."

Jones laughed and then turned to Larson. "We can begin now, Colonel."

Larson glanced down at his notes before warning them about sharing information with anyone other than those in the room because of the high classification. "The President, along with Secretary of Defense and the Joint Chiefs of Staff have suggested that they are interested in advancing the

Vietnamization program in the war, which is to say, it has become something of a priority for them. One of the things that has caught their attention, as we have mentioned in other meetings, was the mission completed by Major Gerber. In short, he moved into an area and convinced the locals that it was in their best interest to cooperate with his Special Forces soldiers and, of course, the South Vietnamese government and the ARVN."

Jones interrupted. "Let's drive on. We all know this."

"Yes, sir. We have been building fire support bases throughout South Vietnam as the war progresses. These are artillery bases that are protected by the infantry and used to provide artillery support to units engaged in combat operations in their area. They are, for our purposes, somewhat fixed bases, not easily established and moved. They become targets for enemy attack, both with ground forces and artillery."

Larson moved through the slides, briefly showing pictures of the typical fire support base. He had never been to one himself, but he was familiar with the concept. He didn't realize that everyone in the room had been to fire support bases with the possible exception of Jones.

"Major Gerber, when he reestablished the Special Forces camp near the Cambodian border, changed the game to an extent. He moved in and got the camp running in a matter of hours, and was able to finish most of the work in forty-eight to seventy-two hours. The enemy was ill prepared to engage him, at first, providing the opportunity to establish the camp. We thought it an interesting concept that might be modified to a more mobile exploitation."

"Colonel, there is no point in repeating this," said Jones.

"Yes, sir. Major Corley has come up with a modification of the concept that we have found interesting." Larson looked directly at Corley and said, "Major Corley, you now have the floor."

Corley stood and walked to the lectern that Larson had just vacated. He adjusted the microphone, looked at the screen and then at the others in the room. "I don't want to take all the credit here because the idea was inspired by Major Gerber and I was handed a modified plan that I, well, modified a little more. If I might have the first slide, please."

The photograph changed to a diagram. It was of a circular base that showed bunker locations and a fire control tower in the center but no emplacements for heavy artillery and no indications that one bunker was different from the one next to it.

"The concept," said Corley, unnecessarily loud, "was to create a base that could be established in a single day. There would be an open field in the morning and by nightfall, there would be a completed compound ready to repel any enemy force."

Corley grinned. "I almost said, 'To repel boarders.'"

No one else smiled.

He looked down at his notes before continuing. "The construction materials will be flown in by helicopter on pallets, each pallet holding the materials for a single bunker —"

Douglas interrupted. "How much would these pallets weigh?"

"I haven't worked out those figures yet. I don't know what a sandbag weighs, for example."

"Thirty-five to forty pounds depending on the material used to fill it," said Jones.

"That much?"

Douglas spoke up again. "Then ten sandbags could weigh as much as four hundred pounds and one hundred would weigh four thousand pounds."

"I believe that a Huey can lift a sling load of that weight."

"You need a Chinook," said Douglas. "The Huey doesn't have the capability to carry much in a sling load and most Huey pilots have limited experience in carrying sling loads."

"You just said it could carry four thousand pounds," countered Corley.

"No, I said the hook strength is rated to four thousand pounds. The problem you face is that the airlift capability is reduced for the actual weight when you factor in the armament on the Huey, the ammunition that is carried, the weight of the fuel and the atmospheric conditions. In Vietnam you're operating with a high-density altitude, meaning heat and humidity that reduces the lift capabilities of the aircraft."

"Didn't you take any of this into consideration, Corley?" Jones asked.

"Mine was a preliminary study on the best type of base to construct as quickly as possible. I hadn't had the opportunity to take the logistics of the situation into consideration other than suggesting that we palletize the loads with specific equipment and materiel to be flown in."

Gerber spoke for the first time. "We found that a star-shaped camp was a better design for defense. It allowed for interlocking fields of fire from machine guns and other small arms."

Corley looked at Gerber as if he had just broken an unspoken bond between majors. "The circular construction allows for quick assembly and there is no single point that can't be supported by those on either side of it."

"You said something about Chinooks, Douglas," said Jones.

"Yes, General. They have a much greater lift capacity than a Huey — something like twenty thousand pounds — and they're designed to carry sling loads. I always thought that sling loads on the Huey was an afterthought."

"Are there Chinooks in your aviation company?"

"The battalion has a company of Chinooks, General. But I'm not qualified in them and neither is Lieutenant Williams."

Now Jones looked at Larson. "All this seems to be a little premature now, Larson."

"I was told to look at this idea of Corley's and bring in the experts for a consultation. Gerber was the one who started it." He held up a hand to stop Gerber's protest. "I don't mean that he called the meeting or knew about Corley's idea, only that his setting up that camp seemed to be the springboard for the idea that Corley and others grabbed."

"I didn't know about Major Gerber and what he had done," said Corley. "I was looking for a way to interdict the enemy lines of communication without putting our soldiers at greater risk than necessary."

Jones closed the folder in front of him, suggesting that the meeting was over. "Major Corley, I'd like to see your plans as they are today. You and I can meet after lunch."

"Yes, sir. I think the briefing here would have accomplished that."

"After lunch, Major." Jones turned to Gerber. "Major Gerber, what have you brought with you?"

"Nothing related to this, General. We were summoned to the meeting without being advised of its nature. Just that our presence was required. Everything about our establishing the camp is in the after-action reports and the investigation conducted by General Crinshaw. I'm sure that you can get those. I think Crinshaw's findings were only classified secret, though I'm not sure exactly why they were classified at all."

"Douglas, you and Williams can supply me with figures on the aircraft capabilities Both Hueys and Chinooks."

"Everything you need to know would be in the dash-tens, sir. They should have the manuals here, in the post library," said Douglas.

"You're the expert on this. Why don't you search that out, and we'll talk about it later. You can provide the proper figures and capabilities. I'm sure that as pilots with experience in Vietnam, you'll have a better idea of what is needed and how it all works."

"Yes, sir."

Finally, Jones turned his attention on Galvin Bocker. "Master Sergeant, I don't know why you were summoned."

Larson immediately said, "I thought that the insight of one of the subordinate NCOs would be of benefit to us in understanding how this worked. I'd like to talk to him once we're done here."

"Unless someone has something to suggest that we haven't thought of let's meet here at, say, fifteen hundred."

As Jones stood up, so did the others. He walked to the door and once he was out of sight, Gerber turned to Fetterman. "I thought that went well."

Larson led Bocker down the hall to his office. He told the NCO at the outer desk, "I don't want to be disturbed unless it's the General and then not if it isn't important."

"Yes, sir."

As the entered the inner office, Larson said, "Take a seat. You want coffee or a soft drink?"

Bocker was taken aback by the sudden courtesy. Officers were only polite when they wanted something. He shook his head. "No, thank you, sir."

Larson sat down behind his desk and Bocker wondered about that. Larson had tried to establish rapport with him by offering the coffee and then ruined it by setting up a barrier between them. Anyone skilled in interrogation would have known better. It suggested something about Larson and what was going on, but Bocker wasn't sure what it could be. It worried him.

"How was your trip?"

"A little hectic, sir. I was in Denver relaxing and next thing I know, I'm catching a flight to Hawaii."

"Well, it was lucky you were at Lowry Air Force Base so that you could catch a military ride without having to spend money on an airline ticket. Got you here faster than commercial."

Bocker had to laugh. "I guess you haven't made one of those flights. The back of a C-130 isn't all that comfortable, especially on a long-haul flight."

"Well, that couldn't be helped."

"Just what am I doing here, sir? You have Major Gerber and Sergeant Major Fetterman here. They were running the operation. They planned the whole thing. The operations NCO might have some insight into the plan. I was just doing the communications."

"But there were a limited number of Americans in that camp."

Bocker was suddenly wary. He knew that there were officers involved and some of what they did was not strictly by the book. He didn't like the direction this was going.

Larson opened a file on his desk. "That ambush at the river, just inside of Vietnam was a stroke of luck. How do you think that happened?"

"Good intelligence?"

"Well, yes, certainly." Larson leaned back in his chair and clasped his hands behind his head. "According to the information I have here, there was an attack on a VC or NVA camp on the other side of the Cambodian border that same night about the same time. Just a few klicks into Cambodia."

"I wouldn't know about that, sir."

"But you were there at the time, we're you, Sergeant?"

Bocker shrugged. "I was just the communications sergeant and sometimes helped with the small arms and the like. I would think that Sergeant Tyme would have more information about that."

"Sergeant, I'm not trying to bust your chops here. I'm just wondering about some of the things that might not have made it into the after-action reports. I'm trying to get a feel for how Major Gerber was able to pull off this ... this change in the attitudes of the local population."

"I had nothing to do with the after-action reports, sir. Besides, the camp was pretty shot up after the VC attacks. We had to do something."

"There," said Larson, sharply. "You had to do something. Do you think that Major Gerber thought a cross-border attack was needed?"

Bocker knew that he had screwed up. They had been taught to not get caught up in a discussion during an interrogation and he had relaxed. He had to be careful at this point. If he tried too hard to correct the mistake, then Larson would know that he knew more than he was willing to tell. He didn't know what Larson was after, but the red flags were waving.

"The Major — he was a captain back then — knew that cross-border operations were against regulations."

"That doesn't really answer my question."

"But it does. Major Gerber would not violate regulations." Bocker knew that was a flat out lie. He knew that sometimes the rules established by the chairborne commandos in Saigon or Washington were in conflict with a winning attitude.

"Sergeant, I must remind you that lying to a superior officer is a court-martial offence."

Bocker felt the sweat break out even though the office was well air conditioned. "How did we get to that point, sir?"

"I have testimony here that there were American soldiers involved in a cross-border operation that was not authorized by MACV or the Special Forces chain of command in Vietnam. I just want to clear that up so that there can be no further interest in this."

"I wouldn't know about that," said Bocker, trying to relax.

Larson wasn't fooled by that. "Sergeant, it is clear that you know something about this. I need to know what you know. Simple as that."

Bocker said, "This line of interrogation…"

Now Larson smiled. "This is not an interrogation, Sergeant. If it was, I would have to remind you of your rights under Article 32 of the UCMJ. I haven't done that, have I?"

"No, sir. But I thought I was summoned here quickly, and we talked about setting up some sort of new camp…"

"You are moving close to revealing classified information."

"Yes, sir. But you know what is going on because you were in the room with us. We talked about establishing that camp and realized that there were logistical aspects that we didn't know about. Things that I don't know about."

Larson sighed and closed the file in front of him. "I think we might have gotten off on the wrong foot here. I was just trying to understand the sequence of events that lead to the ambush that was clearly on the Vietnam side of the border. A military operation that was well within the rules of land warfare."

"Major Gerber can tell you all about that," said Bocker. "He was the officer overseeing the operation, which, if I'm not mistaken, has been investigated and found not to have violated any regulations or international law."

"Well, yes, I just said that. But I wanted to understand this from the NCO point of view. NCOs often know quite a bit about the daily operations at the company level because they are directly involved in them. I just wanted some further insight before we progressed in developing our operation here. I have talked to others about this."

"Yes, sir."

"Let me see if I can get us back on the right track. I noticed the coincidence between the ambush and the attack on the enemy camp in Cambodia. You weren't involved in that ambush?"

Bocker didn't blink. Body language could give away more than the spoken word. He said, "Well, sir, on that night, the night of the ambush, I was in the camp to maintain communications between the strike force and the camp in case they needed reinforcements. I wasn't brought into the details of the operation."

Larson realized that he had lost the advantage, and anything he said now might reveal what he really wanted. Bocker, as the commo sergeant, might not have been told the full story of the operation. Rather than tip his hand, Larson stood up and came out from behind his desk. In a friendly voice he said, "Well, I guess that's all for now. I have another meeting in a few minutes. We'll chat again."

Bocker came to his feet and saluted. "Yes, sir."

When his salute was returned, he walked to the door and into the outer office. He wasn't sure exactly where he was in the building, but he knew that he had to talk to Gerber soon. He had the feeling that this exercise was a cover for some sort of investigation about the raid into Cambodia. Larson might know something more and he wanted to let Gerber know about it. He didn't think that either Gerber or Fetterman would fall for that sort of a trick, but he thought he should talk to them about it.

Once Bocker left his office, Larson turned and walked to the window. He had a great view of a parking lot and beyond that, palm trees. There was a hint of the ocean, but it was too far off to see and he often wondered if it really was the ocean or his imagination. He slammed his hand on the desk and knew, just knew, that Gerber had violated international law. It was his job to see that Gerber was prosecuted for that violation.

He took a deep breath, scrubbed a hand through his hair to calm himself, and then called out, "Wilcox."

Wilcox appeared in the door. "Yes, sir."

"You have your list of Special Forces soldiers that were with Gerber?"

Wilcox retreated to his desk, grabbed the paper, and returned. "Yes, sir, right here."

"There a sergeant named Tyme on it?"

Wilcox ran a finger down the list. "Yes, sir, there is a Sergeant Tyme, first name Justin. He's stationed in North Carolina. You want I should put in a call to him?"

Larson looked at his watch. "It's nearly eighteen hundred there. You'll just get the duty officer or the charge of quarters."

"Those Special Forces guys are pretty hardcore. They work late. I might have some luck."

"See who you can get on the horn and then put the call through to me."

"Yes, sir."

Larson returned to his desk and opened the file again. It contained nearly a hundred pages. There were unit rosters, a TO&E, after-action reports, assessments of the jobs done by those involved in the firefights. A list of potential awards and decorations with a Silver Star recommendation for Gerber and one for Fetterman. The other Special Forces soldiers were all recommended for the Bronze Star Medal for Valor, with a single exception. Larson found that odd and wondered if that man who was not nominated for an award might harbor some ill will. It might be productive to find him and, at the very least, speak with him.

Wilcox knocked on the door and said, "Got a charge of quarters. He said that Tyme was unavailable. He was engaged in an overnight training exercise. He'd be in sometime tomorrow but would be released from duty for the day."

Larson held up his hand. "Let me see that list of names you have."

Wilcox had left it on his desk when he went to call Tyme. He grabbed it again. Handing it to Larson, he asked, "Is there something you want me to do?"

"No, I just want to review it one more time." As Wilcox left, Larson scanned the list. He found the name he wanted and saw that the man was assigned to the west coast. It would be easy to bring him to Hawaii, if Larson wanted him as a witness. He rocked back in the chair and wondered aloud, "Have I found a chink in your armor, Major?"

Bocker found Gerber and Fetterman sitting in the hotel restaurant looking at menus. Robin Morrow was with them and Bocker marveled at the way she seemed to show up at the right place at the right time. He liked Morrow. She actually understood the Special Forces and their role in the war. She wasn't the type of journalist to sit around Saigon, drinking cold beer. She got into the field, talked to the men, and learned exactly what was happening. Besides that, she was easy on the eyes.

"Mind if I join you?"

Fetterman waved at the vacant chair. "No need to ask, Galvin. We invited you."

Bocker sat down and then grabbed one of the water glasses. He drank deeply and said, "That Colonel Larson is something else."

"Meaning?" asked Gerber.

Bocker glanced at Morrow.

"She's with us," said Gerber. "She's not in her reporter mode."

Still, Bocker hesitated and then asked, "What do you know about Larson?"

"Not much. Talked to him a bit. He's interested in the base we set up which seems to go with the job. Asked a lot of questions about the operations including the ambush. Didn't seem overly interested in the logistics, or how we had gathered our force."

"I was with him for about an hour and he talked to me about the raid into Cambodia that has him worried."

Fetterman sat up straighter and asked, "Just what was he wanting to know?"

"It all centered around the ambush we conducted on the Vietnamese side of the border. He seemed to think that it was a remarkable coincidence that we were waiting there for the bad guys." He glanced at Morrow again, but she didn't seem overly interested in what was being discussed.

Gerber knew that Morrow knew about the raid and had never said a word about it to anyone. But then, she didn't have all the details and he wondered if Bocker might feel more comfortable talking about the raid if she wasn't sitting at the table listening to all that was being said.

"Give us a minute or two, Robin. I'll fill you in later."

She smiled sweetly at Bocker and said, "I'll just stroll around the lobby for a while. Maybe look for a nice soldier to talk to." She pushed back her chair and walked to the door.

"He knows you guys were in Cambodia. I played dumb for him, suggesting that I was just the commo guy, but then screwed up, saying that Tyme was the intelligence NCO."

Fetterman grinned. "No, you set him up. If he tried to find Justin, that tips his hand because Justin will tell us that someone is snooping around about the raid."

"He said he had witnesses."

"Who?" asked Gerber. "The only witnesses are our team, a few of the other SF guys and the Vietnamese, most of whom can't speak English and who wouldn't know where we were even if they wanted to talk. They have no concept of international borders."

Fetterman interrupted. "Did he say that he had witnesses or something else?"

Bocker thought for a moment. "He didn't use those words, but I sort of got the idea that he was saying he had witnesses."

"That's not quite the same thing," said Fetterman.

"Then you're not worried?"

Gerber shrugged. "Let's just say that I'm concerned. The press is always looking for stories about our violation of neutral countries and mistreating the enemy combatants. It could cause trouble, but there are some important officers, way above Larson's pay grade that would rather the lid stay on this. There is no physical evidence that we were in Cambodia and I think the worst he could prove is that a company of our strikers attacked that enemy camp — but they were under Vietnamese control and that's a whole different problem."

Fetterman added, "And their excuse is that it was so close to the border, they didn't know they had crossed into Cambodia. It's not like there is a line on the ground or a border guard station."

"So, what do we do?"

Gerber laughed. "Well, you continue to play dumb because you're very good at that. Tony and I will keep our eyes and ears open, but I don't see how any of that it going to bounce back on us. For some reason, Larson is fishing for more information."

The waitress appeared then and asked, "Are you gentlemen ready to order?"

Fetterman stood up. "I'll go fetch Robin. I just want a hamburger, lettuce and tomato but no onion, fries and coffee."

As the waitress turned her attention on Gerber, a hotel employee approached the table and asked, "Is one of you Major Gerber?"

"I'm Gerber."

"I have a message from a Colonel Larson. The afternoon meeting is cancelled and you are expected tomorrow at eight in the morning."

"Thank you."

Brigadier General Thomas Jones was not sitting at the main conference table, but had taken a seat in one of the chairs near the door. While he was interested in the discussion, he didn't want to take part and he certainly didn't want to direct it. Larson could do that. Jones would be able to leave, nearly unobserved, if he decided that he had better things to do.

Sitting at the table were Colonel Larson, Major Joshua Corley, the engineer and First Lieutenant John Williams and Warrant Officer Steve Douglas, the pilots. Absent were Major MacKenzie Gerber, Sergeant Major Anthony B. Fetterman and Master Sergeant Galvin Bocker.

When everyone was settled, Larson asked, "Did you review the weight limits for the Huey?"

"I was accurate in what I said," Douglas answered. "If you are going to move a large sling load with a Huey, you are going to run into trouble, especially operating in Vietnam. I don't know how many sandbags you need to erect a bunker, but I suspect it might be more than the capability of a Huey. And that doesn't count the structural elements necessary."

Corley spoke for the first time. "We can reduce the number of sandbags by digging a little deeper in the ground. We will still need PSP or plywood to form the roof and more sandbags for that."

"Why don't you just ship in the empty bags and fill them on site?" asked Douglas.

"Because," said Corley, "the whole purpose here is to pre-form the bunker, palletize it, so that the only thing that needs to be done is assemble it on site. And, where would we get the sand to fill the bags?"

Douglas couldn't resist stating the obvious. "Well, if you're going to build part of the bunker underground, then you have to put the dirt somewhere. Put it in the sandbags."

In the background, Jones chuckled and said, "A very good point."

Corley jumped in. "It strikes me that if we have some of the sandbags filled and on the pallet, that would allow us to build part of the bunker. We could fill others while part of the structure is being erected. Won't have the soldiers standing around and waiting. It reduces the load for the helicopters."

"Or," said Douglas, "we could just use Chinooks to carry the load. Hueys to move the soldiers and Chinooks with the equipment and the pallets."

"I believe we need to run an experiment here," Jones said. "We need to palletize a load and see how well that works. If we can move everything by helicopter, and learn how long it will take to create a bunker, we will have some of the logistics figured out without having to guess about them. How long to put the pieces together for such a practice mission?"

Corley nodded. "I was thinking along those same lines. I think we need one hundred sandbags, which shouldn't be hard to find. The structural components would be the same as those used to erect a bunker. We'll need an explosives expert to use the shape charges to excavate the bunker and then the soldiers to work the problem."

Larson, who had been writing this down, said, "Let me pass this along to operations and see what they say. We might be able to do it tomorrow with the right priority."

"I'll call Pete Johnson over in operations and provide the priority. I think that's got it for today." Jones stood up, signaling the end of the meeting.

CHAPTER 7

It had taken nearly forty-eight hours to set up the exercise. Even with the push by Brigadier General Jones, it had been impossible to fill the sandbags, cut the supporting four by four wooden posts to hold up the overhead, and arrange for the Huey and Chinook aircraft for use in the exercise. There was also trouble in finding enough soldiers to participate, brief them, and have them ready. Normally, an exercise is scheduled weeks in advance, not mere hours.

Colonel Larson had Specialist Wilcox contact what he now thought of as the staff for the project and alert them to the new schedule. He was standing on the tarmac outside the Flight Operations building. In keeping with the nature of the exercise he was dressed in jungle fatigues, wearing a steel pot and a pistol belt complete with a holstered Colt 1911A pistol.

Next to him, dressed in khakis, were Major Gerber and Sergeant Major Fetterman. They hadn't arrived in Hawaii with fatigues. Given their orders, they had brought only Class A uniforms and khakis, but then they weren't about to engage in manual labor. They weren't going to be riding in the helicopters, directing the soldiers, or digging the bunkers. They were there as observers only and planned to stay that way.

Major Corley, however, was dressed in stateside fatigues. He held a set of plans in his hand which he consulted regularly. He saw the pallet holding what he thought of as the pre-fab bunker. It contained the sandbags, the four by fours cut to various lengths and numbered. There was PSP on top of the sandbags and the posts and there were pioneer tools strapped to the very top, which meant there were shovels, axes, sledgehammers and smaller tools as well. Everything that they thought would be needed to create the bunker in one compact package.

Brigadier General Jones arrived in a staff car flying the general officer red flag with the single white star in the center. The car stopped and the driver leaped out to open the rear door. Jones climbed out, spotted Larson, and then diverted to Corley. The driver remained with the car.

"Major?"

Corley saluted. "Yes, sir?"

"Fill me in."

"I calculated the number of sandbags needed and then increased that by ten percent. The structure of the bunker is based on what we've been using in Vietnam. We palletized the load and have a Chinook helicopter ready to pick it up. In the next ten minutes, I hope that the infantry company arrives so that we can brief them and move into the field. This is a modified company meaning it had about ninety members, including the officers. It is set up according to the TO&E in Vietnam."

Corley pointed at a deuce and a half sitting on the edge of the tarmac. "There is an engineer squad there, including their demolitions personnel. We had a jeep carry the explosives and another one with the det cord and detonators. As per regulations, we kept all the elements separated for safety purposes."

"And then?"

"Once everyone is here, we'll move to the demolitions range and work as if this was the real thing. The grunts will be in place as the helicopter brings in the pallet. I'll designate an area, and the demolition team with excavate the bunker using shape charges. The grunts will begin the assembly. The only thing we won't be doing is landing the grunts by helicopter. We already know how that works."

Jones nodded. "It seems that you have this well in hand."

"Yes, sir. Thank you."

Jones walked over to Gerber and Fetterman. As they all saluted Jones asked, "What is your role here today."

"Well, General, we're observers. We're looking for ways to speed up the process and for anything that might be improved. We're looking for flaws that might occur to someone who hasn't tried all this before."

"So, you're basically just standing around doing nothing."

Gerber grinned. "That about covers it."

Jones rubbed his chin. "Either of you know the real reason you were pulled out of the field?"

"I was under the impression, General, that our expertise in setting up a quick camp in enemy territory would be of benefit to Major Corley in his planning of the operation."

Two pilots left the operations building. Both were dressed in the Nomex flight suits that were issued to the pilots. Jungle fatigues burned too quickly in the event of a fire. The Nomex was fire retardant and could reduce injury. That was the theory.

Both were warrant officers, though one of them was a CW-3, meaning he was a senior warrant officer and had been around a while.

They approached Jones and saluted. The senior pilot said, "Warrant Officers Leonard and Peters, reporting as ordered. We're ready whenever you are, sir."

Jones grinned at them and pointed at Corley. "He's the man in charge here. I'm just an observer. You'll have to talk to him."

"Yes, sir. Thank you, sir."

They approached Corley, saluted and Leonard said, "We're ready whenever you are, sir."

Corley returned the salute and responded, "You're not the pilots I briefed yesterday."

"No, sir. They briefed all of us when they returned and this morning the commander selected us for this specific mission. It's fairly routine for us. We just carry the sling load to wherever you want it, and drop it where the soldiers want it. We do it all the time."

"I'm not sure that I like this," said Corley. "Your commander didn't say that he'd be switching the pilots."

"It's really no big deal, sir. It's a routine mission, one that we trained for. Huey drivers practice once or twice and that's about it for them. We do this on a daily basis."

Corley stared at them for a moment. "You know where you're going? Where to drop the load?"

"We have the location of the LZ on the map. We were given the impression that there would be grunts there to throw smoke and that someone would direct us to a specific spot to drop our load."

As the pilots talked to Corley, Larson walked over to Jones. "I have some work to do back at the office and I'm not needed here now. Corley knows what to do. It's really his show and I won't be there in Vietnam."

"I thought you'd want to watch this, Jim."

"Corley can brief me later. Besides, he's the one who will have to make the corrections."

"This is his show and if you're not needed here, then head on in."

"I'll see you this afternoon, General, once there is something to report."

Jones merely nodded. He watched at the pilots approached their aircraft and as the trucks carrying the infantry company arrived. Corley dispatched them to the test site and then joined Jones.

"The infantry company will be in place in about twenty minutes."

At that point the first of the engines on the Chinook began to whine.

"Here we go," said Corley.

Colonel Larson returned to his office and found Wilcox relaxing with a book rather than working on something else. When Larson entered, Wilcox dropped his feet to the floor and came to attention. "Good morning, Colonel. I didn't expect you this morning, sir."

Without preamble, Larson said, "Did you learn anything on the telephone?"

"We should be able to talk with Sergeant Tyme later today, and I found Sergeant Jeffords at Fort Leonard Wood. That's in Missouri."

"I know where Leonard Wood is. Why is he there?"

"Looks like he's changing his MOS to military police. They train there."

"I thought he was in Special Forces."

"No, sir. He was attached to them in some fashion when Major Gerber began drawing on personnel for his base. That's all I know."

"Can you get him on the phone?"

Wilcox looked at the clock. "Probably, if the phone system is up and running for a change."

"Then do it, and put the book away."

"Yes, sir."

A few minutes later, Wilcox shouted from the outer office, "I have Sergeant Jeffords on line two, Colonel."

Larson picked up the telephone and said, "Sergeant Jeffords, I'm Colonel Larson. I'm doing a follow up after-action report about the engagement that you were in last year."

"Yes, sir," said Jeffords cautiously.

"I want you to know that I have spoken to both Major Gerber and Sergeant Major Fetterman about this, and I thought I would get the reactions of some of the enlisted men who were involved. I'm just looking at the after-action reports and want to fill in some details. You're not to worry about it. This is just a routine follow up report."

"Yes, sir."

"Specifically, there was an ambush of VC or NVA just on the Vietnamese side of the border..."

"I wouldn't know much about that, sir. I was at the base when all that took place. Captain Gerber can fill you in."

"Gerber has been promoted, as have most of the men who were working with him."

There was silence on the other end of the line. Jeffords hadn't been completely truthful because he had been there at the river ambush with a M-79 grenade launcher. He had liked that weapon because it was a 40mm shotgun if loaded with a canister round. It was single shot and didn't have much range compared to the M-16s, but it was difficult to miss an enemy soldier running at you.

He hadn't been in the forward area, where the main part of the ambush had been deployed, but to the right flank with the job of ensuring that the enemy didn't attempt to break the ambush by flanking them. He had been crouched by a fallen tree, one knee in the damp and rotting vegetation around it.

The tree offered some protection and Jeffords believed any protection was better than no protection at all.

He had been nervous because he wasn't used to deploying for a night ambush. His experience had been daylight search and destroy missions. They rarely stayed in the field at night. They went back to the fire support base which provided better protection. Where they could rest and get a hot meal.

Now he was staring into the darkened jungle, looking for the enemy.

There was a crashing in front of him, as if someone was running through the jungle. Gerber had been clear in the briefing. None of his soldiers, American or Vietnamese, would be in front of him. That was an enemy soldier running through the trees, though Jeffords couldn't see him. Then a shadow loomed out of the darkness and Jeffords aimed his weapon. He was surprised by the recoil and the muzzle flash that seemed to illuminate the jungle around him.

To his left a machine gun opened fire, the red tracers stabbing out and bouncing around. The strobelike flashes gave the jungle the look of an old black and white movie. As he struggled to reload, he saw two men fall and heard someone scream. When the machine gun fell silent, he could hear nothing more in the jungle near him. The fighting had shifted to the main ambush and the firefight that was developing there. Jeffords didn't realize that even though he had only fired one round at the enemy, there were thousands of soldiers in Vietnam who hadn't even done that much.

"Sergeant," said Larson into the receiver. "Are you there?"

Jeffords shook himself, almost as if he was trying to shake off the memories. "Yes, sir."

"It seems that nearly every one of the Special Forces soldiers was decorated in some fashion, but I didn't notice your name on any of the special orders."

"I was not, technically, in Captain Gerber's chain of command."

Larson thought he detected a hint of anger in Jeffords' voice. The Green Beret officer taking care of the other Green Berets but ignoring the straight leg infantryman. That was a problem he could exploit.

"I was released to my unit a couple of days later," Jeffords continued. "I was there as an engineer to help set up the land mines and site the crew-served weapons."

"Didn't they have a man trained in that?"

"Yes, sir, but some of us were brought in to get the base up and running quickly. It was temporary duty. We were helping where we were needed."

"So, Gerber just overlooked your contribution to the defense of the camp?"

"No, sir."

Larson didn't like that answer and turned the conversation back to the ambush. He asked, "Was the ambush set up to cover the soldiers after the raid into Cambodia?"

Again, there was silence at the other end of the phone before Jeffords answered. "I don't know anything about a raid into Cambodia, sir. I was there to set up some of the defenses, as I said, and was not privy to the planning of any military operations. All I know is that I was assigned as part of the flank guard during the ambush. We were all in South Vietnam at the time. Both Captain Gerber and Master Sergeant Fetterman made sure that we were on the right side of the border."

Larson realized that he wasn't going to get much more from Jeffords with that line of questioning. He changed tack. "Everyone was decorated after these actions. It seems to me that Gerber should have put you in for a Bronze Star Medal, at the least. Doesn't it bother you that he didn't do that?"

"As I said, sir, I wasn't in his chain of command. He sent the recommendation for the Bronze Star to my chain of command and it was approved there."

Larson almost fell back in his chair. He hadn't thought about that. Gerber could have recommended the medal himself, and did, but by putting it through Jeffords' chain of command, there would be more recognition for Jeffords than if it had been approved by the Special Forces. This wasn't going to lead anywhere. He didn't have a disgruntled soldier, but an NCO who seemed to understand how the game was played. There was nothing to learn from him.

"Thank you, Sergeant. You've been a big help," Larson said. He hoped that Jeffords didn't hear the sarcasm in his voice and hoped he wouldn't think about contacting Gerber to ask questions.

He carefully cradled the telephone and then picked up a paperweight that looked like one of the old "pineapple" hand grenades. He wanted to throw it through the closest window. He wanted to scream because he knew the truth, the absolute truth. Gerber had been in Cambodia and no one seemed to care about the violation of Army regulations and international law.

Then he took a deep breath and set the paperweight down carefully, just as if it was a real grenade. There had to be some way to get the truth out, even if he was the only one who cared about it.

Major Joshua Corley stood off to one side, near the trucks that had brought in the infantry soldiers, holding a clipboard, and wearing a stopwatch on a lanyard around his neck. He was hot and sweaty and wanted to be somewhere else. Somewhere cooler, where he could find a cold beverage, even one that didn't contain alcohol.

He watched the soldiers dismount and form up in platoons, waiting to begin. Not far away were the engineers and beyond them was the truck with the explosives and the jeep with the detonators.

One of the engineers approached and saluted. Corley recognized Sergeant Collins. "We're ready when you are, sir."

"I have marked the limits of the bunker. I'd like to see it as square as you can make it, and I don't want it deeper than five feet."

Collins grinned. "You sure don't want much. We'll do what we can, but we need to move the men behind the trucks now just in case something goes wrong."

Corley was about to say something and then stopped. A mistake by the engineers could be catastrophic. He merely nodded and watched as Collins walked back to the others, picked up what looked like a small duffle bag and then headed to the marker area. From the earlier briefing, Collins knew the dimensions of the bunker and he knew that Corley's plan was for them to create a squared crater, which wasn't quite as difficult as it sounded.

With the other engineers, they walked, carefully, to the designated area and using shovels, began placing the shape charges. The concept was simple. The charges were designed to explode in a certain direction. In this case, it might be said that they explode down, and when placed in the proper position, would excavate the bunker. Shovels would be used to square it all off and remove the extra dirt. Ideally, they would have an excavator to do that, but Corley had doubted there would be one available in the field. He planned the work in the theory that it would have be to excavated by hand.

After twenty minutes, Collins approached. "We're about ready to go here."

"Once you have detonated the charges, I'll call in the helicopter."

Collins turned and watched as the engineers laid the wire from the charges back to where the engineers would trigger the explosive. He waved a hand and then ducked back, behind the truck.

Someone shouted, "Fire in the hole! Fire in the hole!"

A moment later there was a sequence of four explosions, one after the other. When the last one detonated, there was another shout: "All clear!"

Corley looked over at the RTO and said, "Call in the helicopters." He then walked over to the excavation. It wasn't as square as he hoped, but two of the engineers were already in the hole, working to straighten the sides. They were throwing the dirt out of it, creating piles around the excavation.

Corley made a note to have the pallets waiting before the excavations because they could be filling the extra sandbags with the dirt. That way, they didn't need to fly in as many filled sandbags as he had estimated they would need.

In the distance, he heard the sound of the approaching Chinooks. One of the grunts tossed a smoke grenade, indicating where the Chinook pilots should set down the pallet. Since it was close to the hole, the engineers in it climbed out and moved away from it.

Moments later the Chinook appeared. It approached slowly, descending toward the billowing smoke until it came to a hover above the ground. Once the pallet was on the ground, the chopper released the sling, dumped the nose of the aircraft, and moved away in a swirling cloud of dust and dissipating smoke.

The engineers began to remove the cargo net over the pallet so that they could get at the sandbags. Corley realized the mistake in the load. The support beams and the planks for the flooring were on the bottom of the pallet. They should have been at the top because they would be used first. Corley made another note.

Gerber, who had been watching, walked over to Corley. "You have a real problem. You have everyone working to build the bunker but you have no one for security."

"We don't need security," said Corley, annoyed by the interruption.

"Not here," said Gerber. "But when you move into the field, up to a third of your force will have to be used for security."

Corley was about to protest and then realized that Gerber was right. They couldn't count on the enemy being slow to react.

"I can get the information I need here and then as we write the Op Order for the mission, I can up the estimated number of men needed so that there will be a security force."

"You're going to need a water supply," said Gerber.

"The men have canteens."

"That water won't last long and you need to keep them hydrated. A water buffalo would do it for a platoon. The water will warm up rapidly in the sun, but it's better than losing men to heatstroke."

Corley made a note.

The engineers continued to remove the sandbags from the pallet. They didn't bother to stack them, just tossed them into a pile closer to the bunker. Others were still digging out the interior and Corley realized that empty sandbags at the top of the pallet would be useful. The men digging could be filling the sandbags, which meant they had a purpose for the dirt as had been suggested earlier.

With the sandbags out of the way, the engineers began to remove the planks and beams, carrying them to the bunker excavation site. They laid them out in the pattern they would be used. When one corner was prepared, they anchored the beam in place. Once all four beams were in place, they laid horizonal beams to hold up the planking for the floor which were set in place and then nailed.

It didn't take long to erect the sandbag walls, which were set on the ground in front of the bunker. The walls were only four feet high, but a soldier standing on the planking inside the excavated part of the bunker would be completely protected. There was a firing port in front and a doorway in the rear.

Other horizonal beams were attached to the top of the vertical beams and held in place with long nails. More planking was spread on the top and then sandbags were laid on those planks for overhead protection.

Corley kept a record. He knew how many sandbags had been used because he knew how many had been delivered. He noticed that the process might be speeded up by bringing in chainsaws.

After ninety minutes, they had a workable bunker. There were no weapons emplaced and the overhead protection needed strengthening, which could be accomplished later. The bunker was ready to withstand a frontal assault but it was still weak.

Corley looked at Gerber and asked, "Is this satisfactory?"

"For a preliminary bunker, sure. But how many can you erect between sunrise and sunset?"

"Depends on the number of assets assigned to the mission."

Gerber nodded. "What are your plans for dinner?"

Corley misunderstood the question and said, "We can bring in cases of C-rats. Food isn't the problem."

Gerber grinned and said, "No. I meant for tonight."

"Oh. I've made no plans."

"Then how about we sit down with Sergeant Major Fetterman and those helicopter pilots, and we work out some of the details based on what we learned here today. My hotel? About seven?"

Fetterman walked up as Corley went to talk to the engineers. He'd overheard the dinner arrangements. He said, "Robin is going to be annoyed."

"I'll think of something."

"Colonel, I have Sergeant Tyme for you on line one," called Wilcox from the outer office.

"Thanks." Larson picked up the phone and said, "Sergeant Tyme?"

"To whom am I speaking?"

"This is Colonel James Larson. I'm doing some follow-up on that mission you were on with Mack Gerber last tour."

There was silence on the other end of the line, so Larson said, "I just have a few questions about the cross-border operation."

Tyme spoke without hesitation. "I'm unfamiliar with any cross-border operation. We were close to the border but were careful not to cross it, even with the NVA running up and down the Ho Chi Minh Trail and taking pot shots at us every chance they got."

"That angered you?"

"Of course it angered me. We are observing international law by staying on our side of the border while the North Vietnamese routinely crossed the border without any condemnation from the world community. Then, having attacked us, they would run back across the border because they knew we wouldn't follow."

"Then you would have crossed the border if the situation demanded it?"

"Who did you say you were?"

Larson avoided the question and asked again, "You wouldn't have objected to a cross-border operation?"

"We obeyed the invisible line on the ground. We would patrol close to it because that was about the security of our base, but we would not cross it. We were careful to avoid crossing it."

"Sergeant, I'm just trying to clarify the situation that you found yourself in. I'm not looking to cause you any trouble."

"Yes, sir."

"But you wouldn't have minded if there had been a cross-border operation, if it enhanced the security of your base camp?"

Very quietly, Tyme hung up.

Major Gerber had arranged for a large table in a quiet corner of the restaurant. He knew that he was skating on thin ice because he was directing the conversation to what they had done during the day, and he didn't want to inadvertently compromise the classified information.

Sitting around the table were Fetterman, Bocker, Corley, Douglas and Williams. Colonel Larson was not present, but only because Gerber had failed to invite him. Larson would add nothing of value to the discussion and would inhibit the free exchange of ideas. There were some colonels who were so caught up in being colonels that nothing else mattered other than how they could become generals.

As they settled down, Gerber said, "I think this might be a shade more productive than if we were in a conference room with a general listening to our every word and Larson asking irrelevant questions."

"What, exactly, do you have in mind?" asked Corley.

"Let's have a drink and order dinner before we get too serious." Gerber studied the menu. He wanted a rare steak, baked potato with sour cream, a small salad, and a soft drink rather than something with a little more kick to it.

As he closed the menu, the waitress appeared. She smiled at Gerber and asked, "Are you ready to order?"

He looked at the others and said, "Gentlemen?"

Fetterman started with his order and when he finished, Bocker, who was sitting next to him, followed suit. It went that way around the table until Gerber gave his order and said to the waitress, "Give us about ten minutes before you bring the drinks and salads."

"Certainly," she said with another smile and retreated at that point.

Corley picked up his glass of water and took a sip. "It might have been nice to get our drinks first."

"I just wanted some time to set the ground rules," said Gerber. "We all are cleared for the mission but I want us to avoid specifics. Let's just talk in generalities, though I doubt anything we say here would be of value to the enemy."

Fetterman couldn't let that pass. "Major, there is always value in little bits of information."

"Tony, I doubt there are any spies here that we need to worry about."

"Yes, sir. That's what Custer thought at the Little Big Horn and that didn't work out all that well for him."

"Point taken, Sergeant Major. Gentlemen, let's be circumspect in what we say here. What I want is to hear about what we learned about erecting a bunker and how it needs to be palletized to speed that erection and yes, I used that term on purpose."

There was some polite laughter. Gerber continued, "For example we learned how long it takes to create the bunker and I think we learned the order, or can deduce the order that certain steps need to be taken so that we operate in the most efficient way."

"Such as?"

"We need to have the location of the bunkers marked so that pallets can be set down close to them. We can do all that with a minimum of people on the ground, though we'll need a security force with them which, of course, means more people rather than fewer."

Douglas spoke up. "The Huey is rated to carry eight fully equipped American soldiers or ten Vietnamese because they are generally smaller. Depending on the fuel load and how far we need to fly, we can carry ten Americans without too much stress and one or two more depending on the weather conditions."

"Ten helicopters with twelve soldiers, who wouldn't need a full pack, means a hundred and twenty on the first lift."

"Yes, sir."

"Well, this is a start," said Gerber.

Corley looked like he was getting angry. He didn't like a Special Forces major telling him how to set up what was a personnel and an engineer problem. He could figure it out himself. He just hadn't had any time to do that, but the exercise had provided him with valuable insight.

He pointed at Douglas and asked, "Just how old are you anyway?"

"Nineteen."

"Then you don't have any college. You have a high school diploma?"

"Yeah, I have a high school diploma. Is that relevant?"

Corley looked at Gerber and asked, "Why is he here?"

"Because we need someone who knows about air mobile operations. Someone who has flown them in combat conditions. Who has experience in dealing with the weather conditions in Vietnam and not some high-ranking guy who had gotten himself a free trip to Hawaii."

"And they couldn't find someone a bit older?"

"I don't need a college education to do my job," Douglas snapped back. "I just need the training, which I have, and the experience, which I have. I understand the dynamics of the various missions where helicopters are used and I know the limitations of the helicopters, not only from the Dash Ten, but also in the environment in Vietnam. Lieutenant Williams has been in Vietnam for only a couple of months and has the rank but not the experience."

Fetterman had been watching the exchange with a bemused look on his face. "Is this getting us anywhere?"

Corley had been around the Army long enough that he wasn't going to challenge a sergeant major who had asked a simple question. He merely nodded and said, "I just want to be sure that everyone knows what he's doing. That's all."

"We will assume that Mister Douglas is a competent, qualified and experienced combat pilot, especially as it relates to helicopter operations in Vietnam.If the challenge is to erect the base during daylight hours on a single day, then we're going to have to reduce the size of the base. I had thought about modeling it on a fire support base, but I don't think we could erect it in a single day. Besides, we're not going to put an artillery battery in there so that reduces the overall footprint.What we need," continued Fetterman, "is a comprehensive list of the requirements for the construction of the bunkers, and a plan for the base so that we can extrapolate the manpower requirements from there. Major Gerber and I can come up with the manpower requirements for the security force, which will have nothing to do with the construction crews."

"And young Mister Douglas can tell us about the lift capabilities of the Huey, including the operating parameters."

"All the information is available from non-classified sources, so we won't be violating any regulations here. We can be ready to tell the general just what will be needed to complete the mission."

"I think," said Corley, "we'll need a full test to make sure that we can do it all in a single day."

Gerber nodded. "The general will have to arrange that and we'll want to do it away from prying eyes."

He was going to say more, but the waitress had returned with a huge try that held the beginnings of their dinner.

CHAPTER 8

Major Nathan Fox sat behind his desk and looked across the office, at the closed door. On the wall above it was a captured RPG launcher, mounted on wood with an engraved plaque, looking for all the world like a trophy fish. The door opened and four officers, both commissioned and warrant, entered. They stopped two feet from his desk and saluted. The senior of them, a first lieutenant named Gates, announced, "Aircraft commanders from the First Airlift Platoon, reporting as ordered."

Fox returned the salute. "Gentlemen, please be seated."

Three of them sat down on the battered, green settee, while the fourth found a chair at the conference table and turned it around to face Fox. Not one of them knew why they had been summoned into the commander's office.

By way of preamble, Fox asked, "You guys enjoying your day down?"

One of the men chuckled and said, "I have a bad feeling about this."

Fox looked at him. He was a warrant officer, but was slightly older than most of the other warrant officers. He wore a pistoleer's mustache but his head was nearly shaved. There was just a shadow on his head showing that he was not balding.

"Well, Oliver, it's not all bad. Sometimes it's good news." He paused before continuing. "Unfortunately, this is not one of those times." He grabbed a sheet of paper from his desk and said, "I — and by I, I mean you — are going to be tasked with a special mission. The purpose is classified, which means you don't explain what you're doing to your crews, only that you have orders to carry out the mission, if they bother to ask."

"Yes, sir," said Oliver.

"Over the next two or three days, there will be several single ship missions to the area around Tay Ninh and near the Cambodian border. The idea is to find suitable locations for the establishment of a small camp with the purpose of interdicting the traffic from the Ho Chi Minh Trail."

"Are we supposed to cross the border?"

Fox looked horrified. "Hell no. We will be scouting the area on the Vietnamese side of the border and we need to be careful because of the anti-aircraft capabilities on the Cambodian side."

All the pilots were aware of the cautionary notes on the maps that suggested a Triple A capability to eleven thousand feet. That meant that the border was protected by, at the very least, .50-caliber machine guns, or more accurately, the 12.7mm machine guns and even larger caliber weapons including 20- and 30mm anti-aircraft weapons capable of shooting down a high-flying jet fighter.

"The orders suggest we stay five klicks from the border so that there will be no inadvertent penetration of Cambodian territory."

"What's this all about, sir?"

"I thought you would never ask. I don't have any idea what is being planned, other than we are required to scout the locations, looking for areas that can be easily defended. This suggests that we're going to put a base in there and don't want to have to find the location on the fly. Top brass want to know what the terrain looks like before they select the site."

"When do we begin this mission?"

"I thought that we could send out two of you this afternoon. Different routes, twenty miles apart, though you could probably fly formation to Go Dau Ha before you split up."

"And we're just supposed to fly around the countryside looking for a good place for a base camp?"

"It was suggested that someone take photographs. Photos as opposed to slides. There are photographers scheduled to arrive here later this morning who will be responsible for the photographic work."

"This seems fairly haphazard to me," said Oliver.

"I think this is just the preliminary. The likely spots, once we identify them, will be subjected to additional recon." Fox shrugged. "What can I say? We don't want to tip our hand, and a single ship flying around isn't going to be of much interest to Charlie."

The major looked down at the paper on his desk. "I hadn't planned to do this now, but since I have you all corralled for the moment, let's do it."

He moved to a map of Three Corps displayed in his office wall. It was a standard map and held no information that was classified. He gestured at the area southeast of Tay Ninh. "The infiltration routes meander through this general area, sometimes over the open territory. We're looking to place a camp in there to stop — or at least slow down — the flow of munitions and personnel."

"Wouldn't it be better to have the Air Force do this. They have the equipment to make those runs from high altitude. Then the photo interpretation guys can figure it out."

"I had thought of that, but pictures taken from high altitude don't provide a good look at the terrain. We're just cutting out the middle man here."

Fox turned away from the map. "It's just an extension of an ash and trash mission. It's just a couple of hours of flight time with little overt risk."

"It just seems stupid to me," said Oliver.

Fox ignored that because it was the same thought that he'd had when he had received the orders. Instead, he said, "Was that you volunteering, Oliver?"

"Of course, sir. Nothing I'd like better than flying around close to Cambodia on this bright and sunny day with my ass hanging out for any dummy with an AK or SKS."

"Who else?"

First Lieutenant "Curly" Behr, who was called curly because he was nearly bald, even at twenty-two, said, "I might as well try it."

Oliver spoke up again. "I do have one question. Does this have anything to do with the sudden R and R for Douglas?"

"Mister Douglas is not on R and R. He's on TDY on a special, classified mission for a few weeks. He'll return when that mission is completed."

"Who do we take as co-pilots?" Behr asked.

"Take whoever you want," replied Fox, "but take the most senior of the Peter Pilots just in case."

He didn't have to explain what 'just in case' meant.

Warrant Officer Richard Oliver, carrying his flight helmet in one hand and an AK-47 in the other, walked into the operations bunker to check the situation maps before the flight. These were classified maps that listed the known enemy positions and the enemy units operating in the area. On paper it looked like the entire base camp was surrounded by large enemy units. In reality, many of the VC or NVA units identified were little more than a headquarters or cadre with fifteen or twenty men assigned to them. If given orders for an attack, they would have to recall their men from all around the area and that could take days to accomplish.

Sitting in a chair was a soldier that Oliver didn't recognize. He walked over and saw a bag of what looked to be photographic equipment. "You must be the photographer."

The man stood up. He was a slight man in perfectly starched jungle fatigues that looked as if they had just come from the laundry. He had a Smith and Wesson thirty-eight in an Army issue holster that was on an Army issue pistol belt strapped around his waist. It didn't look as if the pistol had ever been used for anything other than decoration. Oliver wore an old-fashioned leather holster that looked as if it belonged in the wild west. It came complete with loops along the back that had been filled with spare ammunition.

The man nodded. "I'm Specialist Five Larry Underwood."

"You ready to go?"

"Yes, sir." He looked uncomfortable.

"Surely you've flown on helicopters before."

"Yes, sir. It's just that I haven't had to take pictures from them while hanging out of the door. Flying in a helicopter isn't my favorite thing to do."

"There's nothing to it. We'll be flying about five hundred feet, at about ninety or a hundred knots. You can be strapped onto the troop seat if that helps. Might make it difficult to get good quality pictures, but we can worry about that later. Do you have a helmet?"

Underwood held up a steel pot.

"I meant a flight helmet. It might be a good idea to have you plugged into the intercom system."

"No, sir."

Oliver thought for a moment and then said, "Well, you'll just have to tell the crew chief if you need anything and he can relay the message to me. If you're ready to go…?"

Underwood picked up his camera bag, put his steel pot on his head and followed Oliver, who signed out an SOI. They then walked back up the narrow steps to the surface. As he climbed the stairs, Oliver could feel the heat and humidity increase. The air conditioning in the bunker had been refreshing.

Together they walked across the dusty road to the revetment area. When he reached the aircraft assigned for the mission, the co-pilot, WO1 Frank Resor, the crew chief Spec Five Ruben Garcia and Spec Four Edward Anderson, the door gunner were already there, waiting.

"This is Spec Five Underwood and he'll be taking pictures. Help him out when you can."

Oliver then noticed Behr was at his aircraft, the blade already untied, indicating he was about to start the engine. Oliver said, "Let's get strapped in and prepare for takeoff."

Minutes later, with the engine started and the blades spinning, Oliver reached for the company fox mike. "I'm up and ready to go. You want to lead?"

Two clicks over the radio told him that Behr was taking the lead. They came up to a hover, held there for a moment and then began to slide forward toward the runway.

"We clear?" asked Oliver.

"Clear right."

"Clear left."

Oliver held at three feet by easing the cyclic forward and pulling pitch. He backed out of the revetment, used the pedals to turn to the left, and joined Behr close to the runway. Behr called the tower for clearance, and then began to climb out. At fifteen hundred feet and over Highway One, they turned to the west in a loose formation.

The one landmark that everyone recognized at Go Dau Ha was the bridge that was down in the river. Oliver had never seen the span intact, but it was a good landmark for them.

"Breaking to the left," said Behr. He didn't bother with a call sign because there were no other aircraft using the company fox mike.

Oliver continued to fly due east. He turned to Resor. "Keep track of the grid coordinates on the map. We'll want to mark the locations of the areas photographed."

They continued toward the Cambodian border before turning to the south and then back to the east. The landscape flashed under them — rice paddies, fingers of jungle, and a terrain that was more flat than hilly. There were hootches scattered around, many of them set in the shade of tall palm trees. Small farms with a single water buffalo to help with the field work. There were few roads and several paths that were too narrow for anything other than a man walking along it.

Underwood leaned over and shouted at the crew chief that he would like them to circle one spot. Oliver banked around and Underwood gasped, as if surprised by the maneuver, but as they flashed over he managed to take several photographs. Resor marked the location on the map.

For an hour, they searched the area for suitable locations for the camp. With the sun dropping toward the horizon Oliver turned back to the east, heading for home base. They were only at five hundred feet, flying above a stream that provided little in the way of ground cover. Then suddenly there was a burst of automatic small arms fire.

Oliver felt the rounds hitting the aircraft as he pulled back on the cyclic and up on the collective to gain altitude. He turned to the north, away from the stream and then turned to the south again. He couldn't see anything below him except the stream and the vegetation near it. Nothing was moving, that he could see.

Oliver was surprised that there had been no return fire by either the crew chief or the door gunner, but then, by the time the door guns could have been brought to bear, they were out of range. Without a good idea of where the enemy was, how many of them there were, or anything else, there was nothing more for Oliver to do. Instead he asked, "Everyone good back there?"

"We're all okay."

"Then let's head for the barn unless you saw something on the ground."

When there was no reply, he asked, "Did Underwood get what he needed?"

"Yes, sir," replied the crew chief. "I think this might be the first time he was shot at. He seems to be a little unnerved."

"Tell him you'll buy him a beer."

"Yes, sir."

When Oliver landed, the company first sergeant was waiting for him. As soon as the engine was shut down and the book entries completed, the first sergeant stepped up on the skid. "Major Fox wants to see you."

"Now?"

"He said as soon as you land. I don't think he'll wants to be kept waiting."

Oliver had heard that before, but he didn't say anything. Instead, he said, "I'll hit the latrine and be right there."

"Suit yourself."

Oliver outranked the first sergeant, but the first sergeant of any military organization had a great deal of power. He was a senior NCO who worked directly with the company commander. He ran the administration of the unit and if he was pissed off, there were many ways that he could make a soldier's life miserable, even for those who outranked him.

Wearing his weapon and carrying his flight helmet, Oliver knocked on the CO's door and waited until he heard Major Fox call, "Come in."

Oliver walked up to the desk and saluted. "Warrant Officer Richard Oliver reporting as ordered, sir."

Fox stared at him. "I thought it was made clear that you were supposed to come here before anything else."

"Yes, sir."

Fox took a deep breath and then asked, "How many hits did you take?"

"About half a dozen. I didn't have time to count. The crew chief will let me know."

"You didn't report to operations?"

"First sergeant said to report immediately. I have reported immediately."

"Okay, Oliver. Take a seat and tell me what happened."

"We were heading back, following a stream that was lined with vegetation. Maybe a couple of short trees and lots of bushes. I didn't see anything. All of a sudden, someone is shooting at us. I climbed up and hightailed it out of there."

"You return fire?"

"By the time the crew chief and door gunner got their weapons swung around, we were too far away to engage."

Fox nodded. "You didn't think about calling in the gun team or artillery?"

"I thought this was a sneak-and-peek mission and that if I engaged, it might suggest something important. No one was hurt, the engine wasn't damaged and the rotors were fine."

"How do you know the rotors weren't been hit?"

"We didn't pick up a sudden vibration. Had we taken a round through one of the blades, it would have set up a vibration."

"Okay. That makes sense. Probably best that you didn't return fire or call in artillery. Did the photographer get what he needed?"

Now Oliver laughed. "I think he got more than he needed." He held up a hand before Fox could say anything. "He wasn't exactly thrilled with the helicopter ride. Anyway, we scouted a half dozen sites. From the air, I thought two of them showed promise, at least, from my point of view."

"Meaning?"

"Out in the open. Good lines of fire in all directions and they seemed to be on short hills, maybe five, ten feet higher than the surrounding terrain. No real place for Charlie to hide."

"You have the grid coordinates for all of them?"

"Marked on the map. What happens to that?"

"Goes with the photographer. He'll develop the film, mark the pictures with the grid coordinates and push the data up the line. Anything else?"

Oliver stood up. "No, sir."

"Get over to Ops and fill out the hit report. Oh, and it might be a good idea to buy that photographer…"

"Spec Five Underwood," supplied Oliver, helpfully.

Fox looked annoyed. He didn't like being interrupted. "Whatever. Buy him a drink for losing his cherry."

Oliver smiled. "In the officers' club…"

"Good point. Have the crew chief buy him a drink. Now, go away before I think of something else to yell at you about."

After leaving the commanding officer, Oliver returned to the aircraft to inspect the damage. There was a bullet stuck in the skid, two through the skin just behind the crew chief's position and three through the tail boom. None of the rounds had hit anything vital. It was all cosmetic.

Behr approached and pointed at the bullets. "Just what in the hell did you do?"

"Just flying along minding my own business and must have flown over some VC or NVA. No big deal."

"Sometimes I think you're the magnet," said Behr.

"Just because I got shot at today doesn't make me the magnet."

"It just seems that if there is a shot fired at the flight it hits your aircraft. Nobody else seems to get hit as often."

Oliver shrugged. "What can I say?"

"Let's head to the club and I'll buy you a beer."

Oliver was going to ask if he had any luck finding a suitable location but realized they shouldn't be talking about it. Then he thought he should try to find Underwood and see how he was holding up. Finally, he thought he should take him a beer rather than buying him one in either the officers' club of the NCO club.

To Behr, he said, "I'll meet you there. I've got to fill out the hit report which is probably a waste of time. Can't see where writing down the location of the hits is going to do anything important. Some analyst, sitting in Washington with nothing better to do will look at the data and draw some poor conclusions about the situation here."

"I'll meet you at the club." Behr turned and walked off.

Oliver went to operations, filled out the paperwork that asked no relevant questions and then walked back into the Orderly Room. He asked the sergeant there if he knew where the photographers were billeted. He then walked to the officers' club, bought a single can of beer and made his way to the enlisted side of the company area. He found the hootch where Underwood was billeted and entered.

One of the crew chiefs saw him and said, "You're not supposed to be here." He grinned as he said it.

Oliver looked beyond him and called, "Hey. Underwood. Come here for a moment."

Underwood came forward slowly, looking slightly trepidatious. "You wanted to see me, sir?"

"I have a quick question to be sure that I understand the situation. You've never been shot at before today?"

"I normally work in Saigon and stay on our compound. I don't get out in the field all that much."

"Then today was the first?"

"Yes, sir."

Oliver reached into the pocket of his jungle fatigue jacket and pulled out a can of beer. "Well, then, it is incumbent on me to welcome you to the club of those who have been shot at and were missed." He handed Underwood the beer.

Underwood looked puzzled. "Am I supposed to have that here, in the hootch?"

"Special circumstance calls for special consideration. That means you can certainly have a single beer here because of today's mission."

There was a moment of silence in the hootch and then someone shouted, "Hey, I never got a beer the first time someone shot at me."

"That's because it was some outraged husband protecting his wife back in the World. You didn't deserve a beer for that."

There was an explosion of laughter and then applause. When that died down, Oliver said, "Some of you veterans should take young Specialist Underwood to the NCO club and see that he is properly initiated into the organization of those who have been shot at but were missed."

"Yes, sir. But shouldn't you buy the first round?"

"This is what I get for trying to be a nice guy. Buy one beer and the next thing I know; I'm having to buy the bar."

"It's only fair, sir."

Oliver pulled out his wallet, took out a twenty-dollar MPC and handed it to Underwood. "Specialist Underwood, I am entrusting you with this military payment certificate in the amount of twenty dollars for the express purpose of buying the bar in the NCO club. That should cover a drink for everyone in there at the time. This is a one-time offer and will not be repeated."

"Thank you, sir."

The crew chief, who was standing with an amused smile on his face, said, "I don't believe it's fair that you have to buy the bar without a chance to participate in that activity. If you'll lose the jungle jacket, why I think we can sneak you into the club to have a drink with us."

"Why thank you. I would be delighted to participate in this ritual, as long as you don't tell the others that I did it."

"No, sir. We wouldn't want to get in trouble for sneaking you into our club. It's a very special place that only the elite can see."

CHAPTER 9

The planning for the full-scale rehearsal had taken nearly ten days. Corley had spent some of the time creating the master plan for what was now thought of as a patrol base rather than a fire support base. The difference was in the size and the mission.

An infantry company had already been deployed, though here, in Hawaii, that deployment had been by truck rather than helicopter. They simulated a combat assault with ten trucks carrying ten or twelve soldiers each, along with the company commander, RTO and first sergeant. Once they reached the landing zone, they jumped from the trucks with several squads running to specific points to begin security.

The company commander, along with the first sergeant, scanned the area and began to deploy the rest of the soldiers. The plan was to control the access to the raised area that commanded a view of the surrounding terrain. The elevation was only five or six feet, but it was high enough for them.

Gerber and Fetterman had accompanied the soldiers as observers. They had no role in the defense or the structure of the security. Their role more closely matched that of the Special Forces advisors in Vietnam. They would provide guidance if needed, but it seemed that the company commander knew what he was doing.

Once they were set, the next flight landed, which were also in trucks. This was an engineer company with Major Joshua Corley leading. Rather than standing around, they spread out, kneeling. They would support the infantry if there was an attack. Corley had vetoed the idea of a force to simulate a VC response because that would detract from the rehearsal.

He, along with a squad, pounded an eight-foot-long spike into the ground. There was a long rope attached to it, with a large bag of powdered lime with a hole in the center. Corley ran out the rope to its limit and began a slow walk around what would become the perimeter of the base. With that finished, they marked out the dimensions of a dozen bunkers spaced evenly around the perimeter.

With that finished, the rest of the engineer company unpacked the charges they had brought with them. Then, at opposite sides of the perimeter, they set the charges to excavate the bunkers. Corley had calculated the blast radius, which, given the nature of the charges, wasn't very wide because they were shaped to excavate the bunkers as they had done with the preliminary test.

"Fire in the hole! Fire in the hole!"

Corley looked around, saw that the area was clear and detonated the first of the charges. A moment later, he heard, on the opposite side of the circle, "Fire in the hole!"

There was a second detonation. As soon as the dust cleared, both teams moved clockwise and excavated their second bunker. They stayed with it, moving quickly until all the bunkers had been excavated using the high explosives.

Corley was on the radio. "Execute Part Four. I say again. Execute Part Four."

They had been unable to requisition enough Chinooks to bring in all the pallets at once, but they did have two. They had set up the pallets half a klick away so that it would be almost the same as having the necessary number for the plan.

Within minutes the Chinooks appeared, flying low, the pallets hanging beneath them. One of the loads seemed to be swinging more than it should, but it wasn't endangering the aircraft. Engineers popped smoke and tossed the grenades into the bunkers where they wanted the pallets. Guides, on the ground, directed the pilots and once the loads had been dropped, the Chinooks took off to their second loads.

"Get to it," ordered Corley.

With that, engineers dropped into the excavations nearest the pallets. Others broke open the loads. There were unfilled sandbags on top of the beams and flooring that would be used in the bunkers. They began filling the sandbags from the dirt in the bunker, tossing the finished sandbags to the side.

Corley turned to the engineer company commander. "That's what we need, but maybe rather than piling them up, just toss them up along the sides, where they'll be used. It'll save a little work."

The engineers squared the sides of the bunkers and then bought in the flooring beams. They wrestled them into place but it was a difficult task. The bunker wasn't quite wide enough for the beams and the engineers dug into the side of the bunker to make them fit. Once that was done and the beams leveled, the flooring planks were installed and the vertical beams were erected in the corners. Then, using strapping, horizontal beams were fastened to the uprights and more planking was laid over the top to create the roof.

While that was going on, the soldiers on the outside were stacking sandbags to create walls. The floor was about three feet below ground level and the sandbags were erected to a point about seven feet from the floor. At the same time, sandbags were laid across the planking on the top of the bunker. PSP was placed on the sandbags and then more sandbags on top of the PSP. The theory was to detonate the mortar shells on top of the bunker. The explosion would scatter the shrapnel up and away. The mortar round wouldn't penetrate the protection on the top. Of course, over the next several days, the soldiers would have the opportunity to reinforce the protection on top of the bunker.

Gerber strolled over to Corley and watched as one of the bunkers was nearly completed. "We've been here about two hours. They're making good time."

"We'll be completed by nightfall, or rather, we'll be in a better defensive posture by nightfall."

"We could use another company about now. Spell the guys working in the bunkers and put them on security," said Gerber. "Give them a rest."

"I was thinking the same thing."

"We need to think about getting them something to eat. We've got C-rats for lunch and we have some tea and Kool-Aid for hydration."

Corley turned to look at Gerber. "In the field, meaning, I suppose, in Vietnam, will we be left alone to erect the camp?"

"I think," said Gerber, "that it will be nearly impossible for Charlie to mount any sort of operation against the camp during the first day. There might be some mortar fire or a bit of a probe the first night, but nothing very heavy. It'll take them sometime to mount a proper attack. Charlie doesn't assemble a strong force until it's needed."

"Will they do that?"

Gerber grinned. "We're doing here and now, basically, what I did months ago in that general region. Set up a base in a place where there hadn't been one. I suspect that this was the reason that Sergeant Major Fetterman and I were called in. We'd done it a little differently, but we'd done it before. We're the resident experts."

"Will it work?"

"With a properly placed base, inside the range of our artillery from fire support bases, and close air support from the Army and a little heavier support from the Air Force, it'll work."

"I hope you're right."

Colonel Larson sat in the air-conditioned comfort of his office, a cold can of Pepsi close at hand. He was reviewing, for the fourth time, the after-action reports from Gerber's little Vietnam adventure. Larson was sure that there was a flaw in the report somewhere because there were always flaws in the after-action reports. Sometimes it was just a matter of perception, sometimes it was just a simple error, and sometimes it was a matter of deceit. Larson didn't like Gerber and he didn't like elite, Special Forces soldiers. He was now in a position to do something about that and he planned on finding the area of deceit even if he had to invent it.

He looked at the list of names of the soldiers who had been involved with Gerber. He had spoken to a dozen or so and thought it was a waste of time to contact the others. Those guys in the Special Forces stuck together. But Larson also knew that he couldn't just give up because it might be the last man on the list who would provide a clue or a lead that would allow him to dig a little deeper and get to the final answer which had to do with a raid into Cambodia.

"Wilcox?"

Larson's assistant appeared at the door. "Yes, sir."

"Let's make a few telephone calls."

"Well, sir, that might not be necessary. I found one of the soldiers here in Hawaii. He wasn't Special Forces. Just a grunt who was involved in the defense of the camp. Major Gerber did use some straight legs to bolster the defense force."

"And you know where he is?"

"Yes, sir. I didn't bother his first sergeant with any information because I thought that might complicate the issue."

Larson chuckled. "You're a good man, Wilcox. Take another stripe out of petty cash."

Wilcox wasn't sure what that meant and asked, "Am I being promoted?"

"Let's see how this works out and I'll go to the general. We can maybe get you promoted a little early." He then asked, "What's on the schedule?"

"Nothing that can't be pushed back, sir."

Larson stood up. "Well, get me the contact information for this soldier and then I'll be out of the office for a little while."

Wilcox wrote the man's name and unit on a slip of paper and handed it to Larson. "Aren't going to call first?"

"And tip them off. No. I get a better response when I show up in my colonel suit. I will, of course, stop by the commander officer's office first and ask to see —" he glanced at the paper — "Spec Five Jennings."

"If the general calls?"

"I'm out of the office on official business. Anyone else, get a telephone number and tell them I'll get back to them."

Larson had no trouble finding Jennings' company orderly room. He walked in, to the surprise of the company clerk and the first sergeant, who sprang to his feet. "How may I help you, sir?" He read Larson's nametag and looked at the awards and decorations over his left pocket, noting that Larson apparently had never heard a shot fired in anger. But then there were the eagles of a colonel on his uniform.

"I'd like to chat with Specialist Jennings, if that isn't too much trouble."

"Yes, sir. Can you tell me what this is about?"

"Is the company commander in?"

"Yes, sir. In his office." The first sergeant walked to a closed door, knocked twice, and opened it. "There's a Colonel Larson here, sir."

Without waiting, Larson entered the room and sat down. He was telling the captain that he, Larson, was in charge and that was all the captain had to know about it.

The captain didn't have a chance to stand, so he remained sitting in a breach of military protocol, but then Larson had done the same thing. Since Larson wasn't in his chain of command and wouldn't be writing his OER, the captain didn't much care. He'd been around the Army long enough to know that he could, if he wanted, cause Larson some trouble for showing up unannounced. But it was something that the battalion commander could handle if it came to that.

"I would like to have a word with Specialist Jennings, if that would be convenient." Larson could see no reason to be rude.

The captain raised his voice and shouted, "Heywood."

The first sergeant appeared at the door again. "Yes, sir."

"Have young Specialist Jennings brought to the orderly room."

"Yes, sir."

The first sergeant turned and disappeared back to his desk.

"Colonel, while you're waiting would you care for a cup of coffee?"

"No."

The captain sat staring at Larson and then asked, "What is this all about?"

"Between you and me and the fence post," said Larson, "Jennings was involved in an operation in Vietnam and I have some questions for him about that operation."

"He's a good soldier. Bright and always willing to lend a hand. Doesn't drink," the captain smiled, "well, not to excess anyway. I think he'll be a staff sergeant by this time next year."

Larson nodded but didn't respond. He found that silence was a weapon. Most people could only stand the silence for a short time, a minute or less, and then had to say something, anything. It was just too awkward to remain quiet. The company commander apparently had the same information because he said nothing.

Larson finally spoke. "Is there a quiet, somewhat secure room, that we can use?"

The captain raised his voice again and called, "Heywood. Clear the dayroom and make sure the door is unlocked. Colonel Larson will have use for it for the next hour or so."

Ten minutes later, Jennings arrived wearing sweat-stained jungle fatigues. He also looked as if he could use a shave. He entered the commander's office without knocking since the door was open, walked up to the desk and saluted. "Specialist Jennings, reporting as ordered."

The commander returned the salute. "This is Colonel Larson. He wants to have a word with you."

Jennings turned, saw Larson and said, "Yes, sir."

Larson got to his feet. "If you'll follow me... On second thought, I'll follow you to the day room. We'll have a little chat."

Jennings looked thoroughly confused, and then said, simply, "Yes, sir." He waited, but when no one else said anything, he said, "If you'll follow me, sir."

They left the orderly room, turned right, and walked along a gravel path bordered by white painted rocks. Jennings opened the door and was surprised that it was empty. He didn't know that the first sergeant had cleared it for Larson.

Once inside, Larson said, "Grab a seat, Jennings."

Jennings sat down and then looked at Larson. He had no idea what was going on. He just knew that anytime he was involved with a senior officer; it didn't end well.

Without much in the way of preliminary discussion, Larson said, "I believe that you were part of an infantry unit that was deployed to a reconstituted base in western Vietnam, south of Tay Ninh during your tour in Vietnam."

Jennings nodded. "If you're referring to Xa Cat, then yes, sir. I was there for a little more than two weeks."

"Just what was your job?"

"We were providing infantry support. The base had Green Berets running the show and there were a couple of hundred ARVN there as well."

"What did you, specifically, do?"

Jennings scratched his ear. "Filled in on guard duty, assisted in some of the construction. We patrolled with the Green Berets sometimes, but never very far from the base. I think they took us along for the experience. They taught us some of the things they had learned."

"I notice you have a combat infantry badge, but you say you were only there for about two weeks. Regulations require a longer period for eligibility for that award."

"Well, yes, sir, but I was involved in other operations while in Vietnam that added up to more than thirty days."

Larson waved a hand suggesting that it wasn't all that important. Instead, he asked, "Were you involved in a cross-border operation?"

"No, sir. As I said, the patrolling we did was to the south and east of the camp, staying away from the border. We never patrolled to the west and certainly not into Cambodia."

"You hear any rumors?"

Jennings looked down at the floor. "I heard things, of course, but they were just rumors."

"So, you're saying that there was a cross-border operation?"

"Sir, I think that one of the Vietnamese officers organized something. Captain Gerber sent out a blocking force that included some of the American soldiers, but they remained in South Vietnam as far as I know."

"Did you go out with that blocking force?"

"No, sir. I was ordered to stay with most of the infantry soldiers and a few of the engineers. We were on the perimeter, waiting for a rumored assault. It never came, but we did hear shooting from the direction of the ambush. Hell, Colonel, we were in a combat zone. We heard artillery fire all the time and even arc lights."

"Arc lights?"

Jennings grinned. "B-52 bombers dropping bombs through thirty-three thousand feet. If you were close enough you could feel the ground shake and if you were too close, the shockwave would kill you."

"Tell me about that ambush."

"There's nothing for me to tell. Captain Gerber and the Green Berets went out on it. We had officers from other camps there, off and on, and I think some of them were in on it but I really don't know. As I said, I just stayed back, on our base, on orders from my first sergeant. We were waiting for some sort of ground probe that intelligence said we could expect."

Larson decided to try a different approach. "You understand, Jennings, that you're not in any trouble here. On the night of the cross-border raid, the night that Gerber ambushed the VC or NVA on the Vietnam side of the border, you were at the camp. You didn't participate. You had no role in the planning and were not consulted."

"Is Captain Gerber in trouble, sir?"

"All I'm doing here," said Larson, "is gathering information about a possible cross-border operation. No one is in trouble."

"I was just a Spec Four at the time, sir. They didn't confide in me. Just told me what to do. I heard some rumors, but you know how that is. People talk, but it's all rumor. We used to joke that if you haven't heard a rumor by noon, it was time to start one."

Larson realized that Jennings had nothing to add to his investigation. He had been there but he hadn't crossed the border. He'd been there and engaged the enemy when they attacked the camp, but the camp was in South Vietnam, close to the border. But it was still in South Vietnam.

"Okay, Jennings. That's all I need."

Jennings stood up. "You'll tell the first sergeant that I didn't do anything wrong, sir? You just had some questions about that base in Vietnam?"

"Yes, I'll him that you assisted me in my investigation. But tell him and your platoon sergeant, if it comes up, that you're not to talk about the nature of this discussion."

"Yes, sir." Jennings bolted for the door.

Larson sat there for a minute and thought to himself, *Well, that was thirty minutes I'll never get back.*

It was nearly dusk when the trucks returned. Gerber, Fetterman and Corley were in the last group to be picked up. They had erected the camp during the daylight hours. There were a dozen bunkers arranged in a circle with short sandbag walls erected between them, a fire control tower brought in under a Chinook set in the center of the camp and a tactical generator protected by a sandbag revetment, that was powerful enough to run the electrical equipment. Some of the cables from the generator were unprotected, but that wasn't a real problem.

As they walked to the trucks, Corley said, "We got it done."

"There are some problems. Some weaknesses that need to be addressed, but if there was an attack in the night, we would have a good defensive position."

"What would you do differently?" asked Corley.

Gerber shook his head and stood back as Corley climbed up, into the back of the truck. "That's what the debriefing is for. Sergeant Major Fetterman and I have to discuss this and put our thoughts down on paper."

"Just give me a hint."

"There is nothing specific. Just little things that we could do to make this whole thing more efficient."

Corley sat down on the wooden bench across from Gerber and Fetterman. He took a last look at the camp in the fading sunlight. He thought there weren't enough sandbags on the roof of the bunkers and maybe the fifty cals could be sited better. He couldn't see anything wrong, but then he didn't have the experience that Gerber and Fetterman had.

"You like to meet us for dinner? About seven?" asked Gerber.

Corley hesitated and then shrugged. "Where?"

"Certainly not at the officers' club. That would leave Tony out. Thought we could discuss what we're going to say to the general tomorrow."

"I have nothing better to do. If they serve alcohol at this mysterious restaurant of yours, I'll buy the first round," said Corley.

"Just at the hotel. And remember, they do serve cocktails."

As the trucks pulled into the drop-off point, Gerber said, "See you at seven."

Since they wouldn't be discussing anything that was classified, Gerber invited Robin to dinner. She'd spent the day on the beach, waiting for him to get off duty, so she had earned the invitation. Plus she could be trusted to keep her mouth shut if they strayed into sensitive matters

Both Gerber and Fetterman were dressed in the unofficial uniform of the off-duty soldier which consisted of a blue sport coat and khaki trousers. Morrow opted for a long sleeve blouse, short skirt and knee-high boots. It might be thought of as the unofficial uniform of the young, professional woman who was heading out on a date and wanted to leave the office behind her.

Together they walked down to the restaurant. They were surprised to find Corley already there, but he hadn't gotten the memo. He was wearing a dark sport coat and darker trousers. He looked more like a traveling salesman who wasn't all that good at the job than he did a field grade officer in civilian clothes.

Corley was surprised to see Morrow and raised an eyebrow in question.

Gerber shrugged. "Robin has been with us in Vietnam and knows the score. We're not going to discuss anything classified, and if we do move into that arena, she'll excuse herself. So, just relax."

For a moment it looked as if Corley was going to leave. He didn't like the way Gerber and Fetterman allowed a civilian to sit in on some of these discussions. But then Gerber had been trained by the Green Berets and understood operational security. He wouldn't violate that. If they strayed into an area that shouldn't be discussed, he could say something then.

He nodded, and waved them into the main dining room. "It is always nice to dine with a pretty woman."

Once they had been seated and ordered drinks, Morrow said, "One of my friends, a reporter who has contacts here, wondered if I was here working on a story. He said that he had heard a rumor there was an investigation into a group of Green Berets who had run an unauthorized cross-border op several months ago. He wondered what I might know about it or if I had heard anything about it."

"I don't like the sound of that," said Fetterman. "Your friend know anything more about this investigation?"

"Said it was a rumor, but there were some people interested in it. I knew, of course, that it referred to you two and I wondered why you had been sent here for this … planning session."

"The reason we were given was that we had reopened a base in a VC stronghold, so that we had some experience in this sort of thing," said Gerber thoughtfully. "We understood some of the problems of doing that and in this case, speed was more important." He saw the question on Morrow's face and added, "Meaning speed in erecting the base and not necessarily that they had some plan in mind."

"This is a repeat of your operation, then?" asked Morrow.

Gerber glanced at Corley. "We have talked about the logistics of setting up that base, and about a properly authorized ambush we ran within a klick or two of the Cambodia border."

Morrow saw the question on Gerber's face and realized she shouldn't have mentioned it here. But the call had come in just as Gerber had knocked on her door and he hadn't given her a chance to mention it. She hadn't known that Corley was going to be there, complicating the issue.

"It's a different problem," Gerber continued. "We want to test the plan to build a base where there was none. To put it up rapidly. There is a tactical advantage to that because it would interrupt the enemy lines of communication. This seems to be more experimental than practical."

Corley looked uncomfortable. Gerber was close to revealing classified, tactical information. He was about to say something when Morrow asked, "What's next then?"

Gerber grinned. "Well, if I understand the system, we'll produce a final report and by final report, I mean Major Corley will produce the final report because he seems to be the project officer here. Tony and I return to Vietnam and slide back into our assignments there. Corley will head back to his unit as well and the report will be filed to be used in some distant land in another conflict."

Morrow took a drink of water and set the glass down carefully. "When do you leave?"

"Don't know," said Fetterman. "Maybe in a couple of days, which we could stretch into a week if we play our cards right."

"Before we order," said Corley, "is there anything of real importance we need to discuss here? I mean, if you're finished with the discussion of our exercise."

"I thought we might go over what we learned today while we eat. That way you will be ready when we meet the general, whenever that is."

"I learned that it's really all a matter of bringing in the soldiers and the supplies in the proper order. The infantry company and an engineering platoon should be on the first lift. And I wondered about some earth-moving equipment, maybe a small excavator to speed up the process of finishing the bunkers. I'll have to see what is in the inventory, but there must be something that could be brought in by helicopter. It's a matter of setting up a schedule for the various lifts and equipment resupply. I had a preliminary TO&E worked out and will probably take about an hour to modify it."

"I think Tony might be able to help with some of that," said Gerber. "You need to be sure you have a strong enough security force."

"We can meet in the morning," said Fetterman. "I'm getting hungry."

"So am I," said Morrow. "You boys can work all this out later."

CHAPTER 10

Colonel Larson sat behind his desk, a folder in front of him. He looked at the document again and knew there had to be something in there. He knew, absolutely knew, that Gerber had led the raid into Cambodia. He just couldn't prove it. Bocker knew it, but the old NCO was too smart to fall for any of the interrogation tricks Larson had used. Bocker had probably used them himself as a Special Forces soldier. He wouldn't fall into the trap.

Tyme was the same. He might not have the experience that Bocker did, but he had been around long enough to know how to protect a secret.

Larson had thought that Jennings would be easy to crack. He was a youngster, who didn't have the training of the others, but Jennings hadn't known much, other than Gerber and Fetterman had ambushed the NVA or VC on the Vietnam side of the border. Everyone knew that as well, and there was documentation for the legality of the ambush.

To himself, he said, "But I know they were there. I know it."

He thought about going to the general and pointing out the coincidence of the ambush within an hour or two of the attack in Cambodia. He reread the after-action report but there was no clue there. It said nothing about the fight in Cambodia, only that Gerber had set up an ambush in Vietnam to stop the infiltration of enemy soldiers into the area. And it did make some sense, given the history of the region, but he was sure that the NVA were there because of the attack.

His chance to get Gerber was slipping away. He told himself that he had nothing personal against the Special Forces officer.

It was the violation of the neutral country and the unprovoked attack on a military facility in that country. Officers were not allowed to invade foreign lands. Officers should not skirt international law because they thought they knew more than the leadership of the military, both the general officers and the civilians. Just thinking about it infuriated him and he was going to do something about it.

And then there were the lies. Gerber was lying about where he had been and what his role had been. Officers do not lie. They tell the truth, even when that truth is harmful to them. Gerber was everything that was wrong with an officer, but he thought he could get away with it because he was a Green Beret. Gerber would become an example to rein in the rest of the Special Forces. They did not understand what it meant to be officers and soldiers.

There was a knock at the door and Wilcox said, "Major Gerber is here, sir."

Larson flipped the folder closed and put it in his desk drawer. "Send him in."

Gerber entered and walked toward the desk. He stopped short before coming to attention. Flipping Larson a salute, he said, "Major Gerber, MacKenzie K., reporting as ordered."

Larson stared at him, as if he was surprised that Gerber remembered the proper way to report to a superior officer. He returned the salute. "Thank you for coming in today," he said. "Have a seat."

Gerber sat down. "I was a bit surprised by the summons."

"I thought we should chat about the practice mission yesterday."

"Corley is preparing the after-action report for that. We didn't find anything wrong with the op order. I think we need to tweak the order of battle and have a security force in the first lift."

"Order of battle? Isn't that a bit dramatic for this?"

"Probably, but we need to move the men and the supplies in the right order for maximum efficiency."

Lason waved a hand and said, "I didn't ask you here to talk about that. We'll get to it at this afternoon's debrief. I had a couple of other questions for you about operations in Vietnam."

"I thought there might be something else going on," said Gerber warily.

"Frankly, Major, I'm a little disturbed by your attitude."

Gerber smiled and said, "I'm not surprised."

Larson felt his anger bubble to the surface. "Now, what's that supposed to mean?"

Gerber leaned forward, his hands on the arm of his chair. "I've noticed a hint of hostility in our interactions. You seem to be less than thrilled with the involvement of Special Forces in this project and I've wondered why we were ordered here. It didn't seem to be necessary."

Larson stared at Gerber and said, "You were brought here because of your expertise in this sort of an operation." He tapped the folder sitting on his desk. "Your own after-action reports suggest a certain expertise."

"Come on, Colonel. I know why I'm here, in your office, today and it has nothing to do with the current operation or the creation of these mobile bases."

"You're nearing the line toward insubordination, Major. Remember where you are. You're not surrounded by your Special Forces cronies now." When Gerber failed to respond, he said, "Did you hear what I said?"

"Certainly."

"I wanted to ask you about the ambush you conducted near the Vietnamese border…"

"You just said you have the after-action report and you have the testimony of two of my NCOs who were there."

Larson was surprised by that response. "Just how do you know that?"

"We all talk. We all share information. We look out for one another. They told you that we ambushed an enemy force on the Vietnamese side of the border just as it says in the after-action report. Evidence in the field, collected independently, proved we were on the Vietnamese said of the border. They told you nothing more than what was in those reports."

"You don't control everyone who was there that night. You had support from a regular Army infantry company. I've talked with some of them and I know what you did."

Gerber had to laugh. "I seriously doubt that you learned anything from them. Those soldiers were at the base camp with a company or two of Vietnamese strikers. We had another company of strikers with us."

"You just made a mistake, Gerber. You didn't have that many striker companies at your camp."

"No, sir. Sure didn't. But there were two other Special Forces A-Teams close enough to provide the support we needed. We brought in a company for support on the camp and took our strikers out for the ambush. It was all coordinated through B-Team headquarters in Nha Trang and with MACV-SOG in Saigon."

"This is becoming tiresome, Gerber. I know the truth."

"I'm fairly certain that you don't know the truth. You may suspect something, you may think you know something, but you've come up with nothing positive."

"How would you know that?"

"Your leak to the press. You've hinted to reporters about a cross-border op run by American Special Forces. Your hope is that a civilian reporter who is less than thrilled with our operations in Vietnam might dig deep and find something incriminating."

"Are you denying that you led an assault on an NVA or VC compound in Cambodia?"

"I can tell you that I did not lead any assault on an enemy compound in Cambodia."

Larson realized that he was letting his emotions control the conversation. He took a deep breath and rubbed his forehead with his hand. "You deny you were there?"

"No, sir. I deny that I led it. The raid was an operation led by the commander of one of the striker companies."

"You led it," accused Larson.

"No, sir. I advised it, as I was supposed to do."

"You admit that?"

Gerber shrugged. "Why not? It's what I'm paid to do."

"You know that I'm going have to advise the general about this? The after-action report does not include any information about that aspect of the battle. It says nothing about a cross-border operation."

"The after-action report contains the relevant information, as required. I did not embellish it or include information about the operation of the striker company because it was the striker company commander's job to write his own after-action report."

"Let's stop screwing around, Major. I know you lead this and that's what I'm going to tell the general."

Gerber stood up. "Then I guess we're through here."

"I'll tell you when you're dismissed. Sit down."

"What are you going to do? Send me to Vietnam?" Gerber walked to the door.

Larson sat there, stunned, and then said, "This is not over."

Gerber and Fetterman walked down the hallway toward the conference room.

"So, Larson knows? He told you he knows?" Fetterman asked.

"He suspects. I told him I was there as an advisor, which was the truth but not the whole truth. Your name never came up."

"What do you think will happen?"

"I don't think this will go much further," Gerber said. "I think the general understands that sometimes you have to be a little bold for the mission. Given this was months ago and given that there and have been no international repercussions, I think we're in the clear."

Fetterman had more questions, but before he could speak Gerber said, "We'll have to talk about this later. I don't want to go into it in the hallway here."

Fetterman looked at him and then shrugged. "I'm not worried. We've been down this road before."

The armed guard was still stationed at the door. They showed their ID and he allowed them to enter. Corley sat at one end of the conference table, while Bocker, Douglas and Williams had chairs on the side. Gerber took his normal seat but Fetterman remained standing.

An instant later, the door opened again, and the MP announced, "Gentlemen, General Jones."

Everyone got to their feet as Jones entered, trailed by Larson. The newcomers took their places at the table. As the general sat down, he said, "Be seated."

Once there were all seated again, Jones said, "Major Corley, you have the floor. Let's have it."

Corley got to his feet. "Yesterday, we simulated the creation of a small base, now designated a patrol base. It took us about thirteen hours to accomplish it, but before it was dark we had the base erected, the weapons sited and were prepared for an attack, if one was launched. I suspect that an NVA regiment might be able to overrun it, but it would cost them dearly."

"Explain."

Corley launched into a report giving the facts and figures of what they had learned, suggestions to improve the mission and ways to speed up the construction of the base. He was able to provide exact figures about the manpower needed, the best weapons for the first night, and improvements to the construction of the bunkers.

"If we had a small excavator or backhoe," Corley went on, "that would make building the bunkers go faster. The men could be diverted to other activities."

"How would you get the backhoe in there?"

"Either as a sling load, or loaded in a Chinook. We don't need a huge backhoe and there are models that could be carried in the Chinook."

"Anything else?"

"I haven't talked to the cannon cockers, but some artillery would strengthen the base defense. Ninety-millimeter recoilless rifles and sixty or eight-two-millimeter mortars would fit the bill. The base is too small for howitzers but by strategic placement, 105s and 155s at other fire support bases can be brought to bear if needed."

"That works?" asked Corley.

"We just have to fire registration, which is simple enough, and we can always call in artillery as needed, not to mention gunships and fighters. Artillery and close air support is always close at hand with a little pre-planning," said Gerber.

Jones looked at Douglas and asked, "Helicopter gunships are that close?"

"Yes, sir. Depending on the situation and the location, gunships could get there quickly. The last thing each day is to refuel and rearm so that they'll be available as needed. They can be hot started in about forty seconds, assuming that pre-flight has been accomplished, but in an emergency, it is assumed that the aircraft that was flyable the day before is still flyable. Not an ideal situation, but one that is sometimes necessary given the problems of combat operations."

Jones nodded. "Seems as if some of this is pre-planned, meaning that we can lay the missions of the specific units on for security, so that the base has as much defensive capability as possible in a matter of hours."

"And given the situation," said Gerber, "it is doubtful that the VC or NVA would be able to mount an attack that first night. Maybe a harassment raid, intermittent mortar or rocket fire, but not a full-scale assault."

"You're sure of this?" asked Jones.

"Yes, General. This is a good plan that will interrupt the enemy lines of communication."

Corley nodded. "It's the fire support base concept reduced to its minimum size so that it can be erected in a day."

"Okay," said Jones. "Get me a complete report on this, Major Corley. I think we need about a week to wrap it all up. We'll keep everyone here for another couple of days in case you need some additional specifics and then everyone returns to their normal assignments. That work?"

He looked around the table at the assembled officers. All nodded their agreement. "That's it for today, gentlemen. Make sure that we know where you are at all times, even at the hotel or on the town. Thanks."

As Jones stood up, Larson said, "A minute of your time, General?"

"Walk with me, Colonel."

As Jones and Larson left the conference room, Fetterman turned to Gerber. "What do you think that was all about?"

Gerber turned to the others and said, "Give us a moment and then let's go eat."

"We'll meet you in the parking lot." Corley said as they stepped out into the hallway and closed the door behind them.

"Well?"

Gerber poured himself a glass of water. "As I told you, Larson couldn't prove anything. Bocker and Tyme wouldn't tell him anything and he found one or two of the grunts who basically told him nothing."

"So, there's no problem."

"Tony, you've been around the Army long enough to know that a full bull colonel with a stick up his ass can always cause trouble. I told him that I had been along as an advisor but the plan was all Vietnamese. This really isn't about that raid, but something deeper. I don't know what he's after."

"And he believed that?"

"If he did, he's dumber than I thought. I don't think there are going to be any repercussions given that it was so long ago and with the regime change in Cambodia, the guise of neutrality has slipped away. A lot is going on in that corner of the world."

"Well, I wasn't exactly ready to retire," said Fetterman, "but I would guess it might be an option for me. You're screwed, of course, but I'm just a lowly NCO, led astray by a college boy officer."

"Your sarcasm is not appreciated."

"Since when?"

"I've been meaning to talk to you about it for some time."

Fetterman grinned. "So, what do we do now?"

"Go to the beach, hang out there for a while, and wait and see what happens next." He fell silent for a moment, then said, "Maybe I'll call General Perkins at Camp Mackall and see what he has to say. Find out if he has heard anything about a probe into that mission."

"Why not talk to Robin and see what she knows about all this. Might be illustrative."

Gerber nodded. "She could give us the press angle on this. Couldn't hurt."

Brigadier General Jones sat down behind his desk, looked at the message slips lined up on it as if they were on parade, and then over at Larson. "Okay, Jim, what's on your mind?"

Larson realized that he had not been invited to sit and military protocol required him to stand in the presence of a general officer until invited to sit down. Even though the air in the room was frigid, he felt the sweat pop out on his forehead. This was one of those make or break a career moves.

"Major Gerber," he said by way of preamble. "I've been looking at the documents about his activities in Vietnam."

"Why would you do that?"

"I found some gaps that are problematic, General. I think we should look into that base he established close to the Cambodian border."

"Why in the hell would we do that?" asked Jones. He leaned over, pulled out the bottom drawer of his desk and propped his feet up on it. He still did not ask Larson to sit down.

"It's not so much the establishment of the base, sir, but the rumors that he led a raid across the border into Cambodia which would be in violation of international law."

"How is that our concern? How is it *your* concern?"

Larson wanted to pulled out his handkerchief and mop his face with it, but feared it would send the wrong message. Instead he said, "That would be the invasion of a neutral country and an overt act of war."

"Granted, but isn't that the responsibility of MACV and General Abrams? He's the theater commander there now."

"He might not be aware of the illegal operation carried out by the Special Forces, General, especially if it was kept at a low key."

"Let's cut to the chase. What do you have to support this allegation?"

"Gerber admitted that he was there. He said a South Vietnamese officer was in charge and that ARVN troops were involved. He said he was there only as an advisor."

Jones took a deep breath. "Doesn't that absolve him of responsibility? He was not the officer in command but a military advisor doing the job he had been assigned. He had no authority to tell the Vietnamese that they couldn't carry out their mission. He might have objected, he might have advised against it, but in the end the ultimate decision was left up to the Vietnamese."

"He led it and you know it, General."

Jones dropped his feet to the floor and leaned forward, elbows on his desk. "Don't tell me what I know, Colonel. And don't tell me what you think. You have any evidence and I might, and I stress *might*, be inclined to carry the allegation up the chain of the command. But it is going to take some real evidence and not just your suspicions."

"He admitted he was there," said Larson, somewhat lamely.

"Being there, as an advisor, doing the job he was assigned without interfering in ARVN military operations is different from leading the mission. Just what do you have here?"

"He was in on the ambush of the VC —"

"In South Vietnam. He was fully authorized in engaging the enemy at that point. There is no evidence of any sort of war crime or violation of international law by Gerber. Don't you think that had something as serious as this occurred it would have been investigated by now?"

"You've looked into this, General?"

"Of course I have, after I heard the allegations. I even had a telephone call from a reporter looking for more information. But I know of nothing that would suggest that Gerber did anything illegal or in violation of his orders."

Larson ran his hand over his face and them wiped his palm on the front of his khaki shirt, leaving a ragged stain.

"Just what do you have against this officer, Colonel?"

"He has a bad attitude. He thinks he's better than the rest of us and can get away with anything because he has a green beret."

"Unless you have something more substantial than these rather nebulous allegations, Colonel, I would suggest that you concentrate on your duties here. Is that clear?"

"Yes, General. But don't you think we have a responsibility to investigate war crimes?"

"War crimes? *War crimes?* Are you aware there was a regime change in Cambodia recently and that changed the dynamic of the situation in South Vietnam and in Southeast Asia? It could be argued that the Cambodian government asked for some help in clearing away these enemy camps that had been established there illegally. That the Vietnamese government had authorized the raid."

Larson said suddenly, "I would like to request thirty days leave, General. I have more than seventy days accrued and I believe that it would be a good time to take some of that leave."

Jones raised his eyebrows. "Do you know what you're doing?"

"Yes, sir. I just need some time off."

"Submit the paperwork and give it to my aide. If there is nothing pressing on your schedule, you can probably have your thirty days. It'll take a few days to process the paperwork so be sure that you have your schedule cleared so that nothing of importance can fall through the cracks. When you've done that, you can take off."

Sensing that the conversation had ended, Larson said. "Is that all, sir?"

Jones waved a hand at him. "You're dismissed."

Larson returned to his office and searched his desktop for the note with the reporter's name on it. He didn't worry about how the reporter had gotten his name. There was just a note that he had called and wanted to talk about matters pertaining to Vietnam, which explained nothing. In fact, the reporter might have been looking for information about a thousand different things.

He hadn't returned the call because of a natural distrust that many military officers had for members of the press. He stared at the telephone number for a long time, trying to decide what to do. He knew that most dealings with the press turned out bad. They had a way of twisting the facts to their point of view, and often spoke as experts in fields in which they knew nothing. They were sometimes duped by plausible-sounding information because they didn't know enough about the subject to realize when they were being led astray.

There were times, however, when reporters were useful, and Larson finally decided that this was one of those times. He could feed the man some information about Gerber without saying much at all. A hint here or there and let the reporter ferret out the information for himself. Larson picked up the phone and dialed the number. When a voice on the other end answered, he asked, "Is this Chuck Tatum?"

"Yes. Who's calling please?"

"Never mind that. I have some information about a cross-border operation in Vietnam that you might find interesting. I can't go on the record or even be quoted as a high-level source, but I can point you in the right direction. I have the inside information that you'll need."

"I'm listening," said Tatum, cautiously.

"Have you heard anything about a cross-border operation in the last year or so?"

"That's not how this works," said Tatum. "I must ask the questions, but I can't tell you much about what I know or don't know because that could be thought of as priming the pump. It would be seen as leading the witness or the discussion and could invalidate anything that I learn."

Larson thought about that for a moment. He was surprised to hear a reporter talk of ethics in that way. He thought they would do anything for a story, even if it involved deception. All was fair as long as there was a good story at the end of the trail.

"You still there?" asked Tatum.

"I'm thinking," said Larson. After a few moments, he said, "There are three people here, in Hawaii, you need to talk to. They were involved in some fashion."

"How do I know that you're telling me the truth?"

"You'll know once you talk to these people. You have to move fast while they are still in Hawaii. They might be returning to their regular duty stations soon. Within days they'll be scattered all over the world."

"Okay. Who are they?"

"A major named Gerber, a sergeant major named Fetterman, and a specialist five named Jennings. Gerber and Fetterman are staying in a hotel here but Jennings is assigned here." Larson supplied the name of the hotel and Jennings' unit.

"You say they were in Cambodia?"

"Unless I miss my guess, Gerber led the raid. He's Army Special Forces and those guys are always doing crazy stuff."

"You say, 'guess'?"

"Poor choice of words. I know that Gerber crossed the border. I know the date of the operation."

"And what did you say your name was?"

Larson wasn't going to fall for that. "I'll be in touch after you've had a chance to check on this. Maybe point you to some paperwork that will provide more evidence. This could be a big story if you handle it right."

Larson hung up and as he did so, he wondered if he had done the right thing. Gerber and the others were fellow soldiers and he had put their military careers at risk. Fetterman had his twenty years in and could retire before anything happened to him, at least that was what Larson believed. It was the bigger picture that interested him and he didn't believe that he was driven by his distaste for these special, elite troops who seemed to operate in a different world.

He pulled open his desk drawer and reached for the folder he had placed there. Inside was a map that showed the location of the camp and the NVA base on the other side of the border. The two weren't separated by all that much. The only logical conclusion was that the raiders had come from Gerber's camp and Gerber had suggested the operation.

Gerber was sitting in Robin Morrow's hotel room, watching Morrow as she typed a story that was more feature-oriented than hard news. The phone rang and without thinking he picked it up. "Hello?"

"Is Robin Morrow there?"

"Hang on a minute." Gerber covered the mouth piece and said, "Who knows you're here?"

"Couple of friends. My editor. I take it the call is for me?"

Gerber handed her the phone and she said, "Morrow."

She listened, and then asked, "Are you sure? Thanks."

She handed the phone back to Gerber. "That was a pal of mine working in the bureau here. He just had a call from another reporter, Chuck Tatum, who has somehow gotten your name and a suggestion that you were in Cambodia. He's looking for you to talk about a cross-border operation and thought I might know how to find you, seeing as I have contacts with the Green Berets."

Gerber stared at her for a moment and then rubbed his face with his hand. "This Tatum is looking for me?"

"You and Fetterman."

"What else did he say?"

"Apparently, Tatum knows you're staying in the hotel. I think he was looking for some background on you before he attempts to interview you. He thinks he'll have a leg up if he knows more than just your name."

Gerber turned and picked up the phone. When it was answered, he said, "Tony? We have to get out of here."

Morrow, surprised, asked, "Why?"

To Morrow, he said, "Because if we're not here, then he can't find us. I think we need to head back to Vietnam before this Tatum finds us."

To Fetterman, he said, "How fast can you get packed?"

There was a response on the line and Gerber nodded. "Okay. We'll check out in twenty minutes." He hung up and turned to Morrow. "I've got to go pack. I'll let you know when we're ready to leave." He walked to the door and paused. "Sorry to cut this short."

As he entered his room, the phone rang. He hesitated, wondering if Tatum was calling. Finally, he picked up the receiver. "Hello?"

It was General Jones. "Is that the proper way to answer a telephone, Major?"

"When we're in a hotel, playing at being civilians, then yes, sir, it is."

"I want to see you within the hour."

"Yes, sir."

Without another word, Jones hung up. Gerber then called Morrow. "The general now wants to see me."

"It have anything to do with Tatum?"

"I don't know. Seems to me that someone leaked some information that should have been a better kept secret. I guess he wants to know what I know about that. I want to get Tony and me checked out. I was going to suggest that you stay here, but if Tatum is smart enough, or one of the clerks overly talkative, that could tie you directly to us here in Hawaii and that isn't an ideal situation."

"Why don't you just take me to the airport," she said. "Then it won't be a problem."

Gerber shrugged helplessly. "Yeah. That works. Doesn't seem fair somehow."

"Let me pack. You can drop me at the airport and then go see the general. What about, Tony?"

"I'll take him with me. He can wait in the car or find some way to amuse himself while I'm talking to the general."

CHAPTER 11

Fetterman pulled into the parking space marked for staff. As he turned off the engine of the rental car, he asked, "Do I come in with you?"

"How about you wait fifteen minutes," said Gerber, "and if I'm not back or haven't sent for you, you find something interesting to do?"

"I'll go read a newspaper at the snack bar. Can you get a ride over there?"

"I'm sure I can." Gerber got out and walked up the steps.

As he opened the door, the general's aide, Captain Jonathan Harker, came forward. "The general is expecting you."

Gerber thought about saying something sarcastic about that but none of this was Harker's fault. He was just doing his job. Instead he said, "Lead on, McDuff."

They walked down the hallway until they came to an outer office. Harker walked to a closed door, knocked, and then opened it. "Major Gerber is here, General."

"Send him in."

Gerber entered the office, surprised to see Jones in a Class A uniform complete with all his awards and decorations. It was an impressive display, including awards for valor and meritorious service, but then one didn't achieve flag rank without having done a few things right in his career, unless he had a specialty such as medicine or law.

Before Gerber could follow normal protocol, Jones gestured at one of the chairs. "Sit down, Mack."

As he sat, Jones told Harker, "Find us some coffee." He then looked at Gerber, "Or maybe a soft drink?"

Gerber, surprised at the offer, said, "Pepsi, if you have it. A water if you don't."

"I'll have a coffee," said Jones.

As the aide left, Jones turned to Gerber. "I have been hearing some very bad things about you, Major."

Gerber grinned. "I'm not surprised, given the sudden press interest in me and Sergeant Major Fetterman."

"Then you know that reporter, Tatum, is looking for you?"

"Yes, sir. When you're in the Special Forces you have to know these things."

Jones leaned back in his chair. "Any truth to the rumors?"

"Oh, yes, sir. There is a great deal of truth in the rumors."

"You're not going to deny that you participated in an unauthorized cross-border operation?"

"I told Colonel Larson I had been there. He seemed to think that there was something nefarious in taking the war to the enemy."

"Major, I'm a little surprised at your candor here," said Jones.

"I might have been a little more reluctant if I hadn't seen the awards you have earned during your career. It suggests to me that you understand what being a warrior is all about. If nothing else, you have earned the respect of the soldiers around you."

"You can save the soft soap. Tell me about this mission."

"As you know, General, we had established a base camp within a stone's throw of the Cambodian border. The idea was to restrict the flow of military equipment and supplies for those who were fighting the South Vietnamese and our forces. I wanted to flip the provenance from one of reluctant support of the VC and the communists to, at best, a neutral position or possibly one of support to the Saigon government."

Jones tapped a document on his desk. "I have the after-action reports, including the top-secret investigation into what happened. There are several documents here that I don't believe you've seen, including testimony from several grunts who were dragged into your little adventure."

Gerber hadn't known that there had been any investigations beyond those made in the days that followed the fight in Cambodia and the ambush on the Vietnamese side of the border. He then wondered if General Crinshaw had been pulling strings. Crinshaw didn't like the Green Berets in general and Gerber in particular. Anything that Crinshaw drafted would have been biased and probably filled with half-truths.

As there wasn't much to say about that, Gerber merely said, "Yes, sir."

"I had you assigned to this mission of ours because of that little adventure of yours. It seemed to be the type of thinking that was required for what I, among others, wished to accomplished."

"Frankly, General, both Sergeant Major Fetterman and I wondered if this wasn't some sort of fact-finding mission with this quick-built base as the cover. We wondered if they, well, you, were attempting to learn more about our operation in Vietnam."

"In a sense it was," said Jones. "We were trying to find a way to interdict the supplies and manpower crossing into South Vietnam. We wanted to find out why you were successful when others were not. This cross-border rumor was not important to me — to us. What I want to know now is if you did move into Cambodia."

Gerber collected his thoughts. "I'm not sure who first suggested it. We were having a meeting that involved the leadership of the strike forces assigned to us, some of the officers from other A-Teams, and the problem of that enemy base came up. We developed an attack plan from there."

"Did you take a leadership role in this?"

"That's hard to say. My guidance was sought as the planning was underway. I made suggestions, as did Sergeant Major Fetterman and some of the senior NCOs with us. Our mission was to advise the South Vietnamese as they worked to pacify the area."

"Did you lead the mission?"

They had reached the moment of truth. To this point, Gerber had not lied about the mission. He had shaded the truth and had not volunteered additional information. If a question was not asked, he could avoid revealing too much. Finally, he said, "Technically, no."

"Meaning?"

"Captain Minh and the Vietnamese were technically in charge. If I made a suggestion, Minh and the others considered it an order. We all wanted the same thing. Eliminate the threat."

"Even one in Cambodia."

Gerber snorted. "I was not bound by invisible lines on the ground. We could reasonably claim that the territory was in South Vietnam. There have been disputes with the drawing of the borders for decades so that it might be said that we didn't cross the border."

"So, you went into Cambodia?"

And at last, there was no further dodges. "Yes, sir."

"Okay. You're going to have to get out of Hawaii as soon as possible."

"I had planned to see you about that today. I was going to suggest that our job here was done and we were no longer needed. Major Corley had drafted the after-action report, and I provided a few notes. But then this thing with the reporter came up and I thought that it might be a better for us to get out before we bumped into him."

"Where's Sergeant Major Fetterman now?"

"Either sitting in the car outside or at the snack bar drinking ice tea and reading the newspaper."

Jones raised his voice and called, "Harker?"

The aide appeared at the door. "Yes, General?"

"Track down Sergeant Major Fetterman and have him join us. He'll either be in the car outside or at the snack bar."

"Yes, sir."

Jones turned to Gerber. "Once Harker is back, I'll have him get in touch with the travel office and arrange a flight out tomorrow. The sooner we get the two of you out of here, the better we're going to be."

"I'd rather go commercial. I'm not thrilled about riding in the back of a military aircraft."

Jones smiled. "Well, I'm not particularly interested in how you'd rather travel, but in this case, you're in luck. We have flights transiting here on their way to Vietnam. Commercial jets that are chartered to the Army. The only difference is the meals served are not as good and the movies, if they have one, are not the best."

Harker returned with Fetterman. Fetterman saluted but didn't say anything.

Jones returned the salute and said, "You ready to leave Hawaii?"

"Anytime, General."

"Tomorrow, then. I'll have Captain Harker call later with the flight details. Anything else?"

"No, sir," said Fetterman.

Gerber stood and for some reason said, "By your leave, General."

"Get out of here," Jones said with a grin. "And try to stay in South Vietnam this time."

They saluted and headed for the car. "What was that all about?" asked Fetterman.

"He knows we went into Cambodia, but I think he's running interference for us so there is nothing to worry about."

"Sure. That's what the scouts said to Custer just before he rode down into that valley."

Colonel Larson was sitting in his apartment, a one-bedroom affair that was off post and away from the noise of the BOQ. Since he had been a second lieutenant, he'd had an aversion to living on post. His wife had elected to stay in Michigan when he had been transferred to Hawaii and he didn't blame her. Things hadn't been all that great between them for the last year or so anyway. Larson thought that a separation, caused by the Army, was just the thing, so he had opted for the small apartment with a view of the Pacific. It beat looking at the parking lot from a BOQ window.

He picked up the telephone and called an old friend at the Pentagon, Colonel Miles Porter. They had served together twice during their careers. First, they had been in Europe for a three-year stabilized tour, and then in Korea on a shorter tour. They had worked together, had the same basic beliefs about the Army and who made the best officers, and they had participated in an investigation about the loss of a piece of strategic equipment that resulted in jail time for two officers and a senior NCO.

They had celebrated the triumph and both had been among the first to receive Meritorious Service Medals to be awarded by the Army. That had cemented their friendship and they had stayed in touch as they were reassigned and separated: Porter to the Pentagon and Larson to Hawaii. Each thought the other had gotten the plum assignment.

Larson managed to track Porter down at home for the evening. He didn't want to think about the cost of the telephone call, which he could have made for free using the Autovon System that connected Army telephones to one another throughout the world. But using the Army system would create a record, and Larson didn't want that. He was on a somewhat unauthorized fact-finding mission.

When Porter answered the telephone, in the proscribed matter for off-quarter telephone calls, Larson said, "Miles, you old reprobate."

"There's a voice from the past. Are you in town?"

"I'm still in Hawaii, but I'm on thirty days leave."

"What did you screw up?"

Larson laughed. "Nothing. I asked for some time off because I wanted to investigate some troubling rumors. I think I might have found evidence of a war crime and the violation of the neutrality of Cambodia."

"You found this in Hawaii?"

"You have a few minutes for an off-the-record conversation? I'm just following up on those rumors, but I don't want it to get out that I'm looking into this. The trouble might go all the way into MACV and maybe even back into Washington."

"Let me get something to drink and sit down before we get too deep into this."

"Make it snappy. I'm paying for this call so that there is no official record of it. If it turns out to be wrong, then no harm, no foul. On the other hand…" He let that hang in the air.

Although it took only a minute, to Larson, it seemed longer. Finally, Porter said, "I'm ready. Do I take notes?"

"You might have to write down a name or two, but nothing too extensive."

There was the sound of ice cubes rattling in a glass and Porter said, "Fire."

Larson began to lay out what he thought he knew about Gerber's cross-border operation, making it clear that he had seen the after-action reports, a couple of classified documents, and an assessment that suggested the whole operation had been run by the Vietnamese.

"Just what do you want me to do?" asked Porter when he had finished.

"My thinking is this, if there was just such an operation, then there might be some classified documents addressing what happened and the legality of what happened. There might be something of a cover because those Special Forces boys protect one another and after Kennedy made them the darlings of the Army, it was almost as if they could do no wrong."

"You have a vendetta against these guys?"

"I'm looking at the bigger picture. If Gerber went rogue on this and there is a cover up, we'd better find out. There is some real pressure because a reporter here, in Hawaii, has been chasing the story. If he gets it, then the Army will have some embarrassing questions to answer."

"How in the hell did a reporter in Hawaii get onto a story about a clandestine operation in Vietnam, and one that is so far removed from Saigon and the press there."

Larson hesitated and then said, almost truthfully, "There seems to be a leak here. Not a big one, but big enough so that this reporter started nosing around."

Porter drained his glass and Larson heard him set it down. "What do you want from me?"

"Just what I said. Find out if there is a classified assessment of this operation and if anyone is doing anything about it. Find out what you can and let me know. That way I can head off the reporter's questions and we'll come out of this smelling like roses."

"I don't know, Jim. This sounds like something way above my pay grade. You've got two problems. One is finding out if Gerber led the raid and the second is to plug the leak. If classified material was compromised, then someone is going to jail."

Larson decided it was time to be creative. "I'm on a thirty day leave so that there is no paper trail here. You can't be touched because there is no official record that we ever talked about this, and if someone asks, it was just two old friends chatting about good times."

"I'll see what I can find out," said Porter, "but don't expect too much. I think you need to talk to someone at the Special Warfare Center. If Gerber is Special Forces, they'll know what he's been up to."

"And they might be the ones doing the covering," said Larson. "I want to stay away from them until I know a little more."

"You going to be in Washington anytime soon?"

"Depends on what you find and what I find and where the trail leads."

"Well, I don't like this. The whole thing smells. I'll see what I can find out, discreetly, but I'll have to be careful."

"Thanks, Miles. I'll be in touch." Larson hung up, pleased with himself. He had enlisted the aid of an ally in the Pentagon. That should get the ball rolling.

Gerber, Fetterman and Morrow had arrived at the airport early. They had nothing else to do after they had checked out of the hotel and eaten breakfast. Gerber had suggested they head out to the airport to wait for their flight as he figured reporters were less likely to be looking for them there. No one had objected.

They were sitting in a small coffee shop, watching the airplanes take off and land. The weather was clear, the sky a deep blue. It was a perfect day for flying, at least in the vicinity of Hawaii. The weather over the Pacific Ocean might be different, but at that moment, they didn't care.

Morrow carefully setting her coffee cup on the table. "I can probably get assigned to Vietnam in a couple of weeks."

"Why would you want to do that, Robin?" asked Gerber.

"Well, you'll be there, and the story is there, or rather, there are many stories there and I don't like San Francisco all that much. It's a crappy place."

Fetterman interrupted before Gerber could reply. "Would you believe that General Jones and his aide are here?"

Gerber kept his attention focused on Morrow and said, simply, "No."

Jones, dressed in civilian clothes, as was Harker, spotted them and walked up to the table. Both Gerber and Fetterman stood up but they didn't salute. They were all in a public place and not on a military reservation.

"Thought I would come to see you off," said Jones.

"Unnecessary," said Gerber.

"Let's sit," said Jones. "It isn't a completely friendly gesture on my part. I have an amendment to your orders. Rather than heading to Nha Trang, you're to report to MACV Headquarters in Saigon for a special in-country briefing."

Gerber smiled. "I don't believe we need an in-country briefing. We've been there before. Besides, we're assigned to the Special Forces Group in Nha Trang."

Harker handed a stack of papers to Gerber. "These are your new orders."

"I believe that these orders will be of more interest to you," Jones said.

Gerber glanced at the top sheet. It was a standard set of orders telling him, and Fetterman, that they were still assigned as temporary duty to Jones, and by extension, to his counterpart in Vietnam. They were authorized commercial air travel, but that had already been arranged.

"Captain Harker has checked with the airline and you are manifested through to Tan Son Nhut with a stop in Okinawa for refueling. You'll be in Vietnam before you know it."

"Our weapons are with the armorer in Nha Trang," said Fetterman.

"They have weapons at MACV," countered Jones.

"We have not zeroed them and I don't know what condition they're in. Those hot dogs in Saigon don't take good care of their weapons," protested Fetterman.

Gerber glanced at Fetterman. "We can get our weapons sent to us from Nha Trang. It's not a big deal."

"I don't like this, Major. Sorry, General, but this horsing us around makes me nervous. I don't know these people in Saigon and I don't know what's going to be expected of us."

Jones looked at Morrow and raised an eyebrow.

"There is nothing that you can say here, at this airport, that Robin can't hear," said Gerber.

Jones ignored that. "Everything will become clear when you get to Vietnam. Now, if there are no questions, Captain Harker and I will be on our way."

As the two of them left, Morrow said, "What was that all about?"

Gerber shrugged. "I suspect it had to do with the briefings that we were here for."

"And nothing to do with that camp you established?"

"Sometimes, Robin, you know more than you should. I can't get into that now. Not here, and especially not with that reporter, Tatum, breathing down our necks."

"Tatum doesn't know anything of importance," said Morrow.

"See that he doesn't," said Gerber.

Anger flashed in Morrow's eyes. "Just what does that mean?"

"It means that sometimes reporters know more than is good for them. Sometimes they should be aware of the ramifications of what they print."

"We have a job to do," snapped Morrow. "An important job. We keep the people informed about what the government is doing. We have the right to publish everything that is relevant."

"And sometimes," said Gerber, "all that publishing is not in the best interests of the military."

Fetterman looked from one to the other. "Do you really want to get into this here?"

"I'm just explaining to Robin that there is a time and a place for some of these stories and once the soldiers are engaged in combat operations, a little restraint is a good thing. We shouldn't have to worry about reporters looking for a byline and how that might affect us in Vietnam."

"The First Amendment to the Constitution provides for a free press," said Morrow coldly.

"But there are limits," said Gerber.

"No, not really."

"You can't yell fire in a crowded theater," countered Gerber.

"You can if the theater is on fire," Morrow shot back. "In fact, you can yell fire if you want. There might be legal consequences for doing that, but you have the right to yell."

Fetterman held up a hand. "Why don't you two think of something else to talk about?"

"We have a reporter breathing down our necks and we know the coverage is going to be biased and unfair." Gerber said. "Bad American soldiers doing things that are not nice."

"Oh, come on, Mack, that is just stupid."

"But you know that it's true."

Morrow stood up. "I'm going back into town before this gets completely out of hand."

Gerber rocked back in his chair and stared at her. He suddenly realized that she wasn't angry about their argument. It had nothing to do with the Constitution or freedom of the press, but everything to do with Gerber heading back into a combat environment and Morrow remaining behind. It was her way of dealing with the coming forced separation without some of the pain associated with that separation.

Just then, their flight was called over the airport PA system.

Gerber got to his feet. "I've got to go."

Morrow smiled weakly. "I know."

Before dawn, Colonel Larson was pacing around his small apartment. He wasn't interested in early daytime TV, had read last night's newspaper, and turned on the radio only to turn it off almost immediately because the sound of it hurt his ears. It was too early for Porter to have learned anything of use, even if he tried. Porter had to be careful because of the circumstances and knowing Porter, Larson was sure that he would be careful.

Finally, he sat down next to the telephone, picked up the receiver and dialed. At the other end he heard, "Tatum. Talk to me."

"I was wondering if you had learned anything of interest?"

"I heard that some Green Berets set up a camp near the Cambodian border and I heard that the brass made them move. I haven't heard anything but a couple of rumors. Gerber is not in his hotel room and neither is Fetterman. Clerk said there was never anyone by those names registered there, but I think he lied to me about it."

Larson sighed. He knew that both Gerber and Fetterman were leaving Hawaii. He didn't know exactly when they were leaving, but he knew they were going soon. He said, "You know this could be big story."

"I know that I haven't had any luck. I did talk to that Sergeant Tyme, but he played dumb. I think those guys are trained to deny everything and act like they know nothing."

Larson realized that this was not going anywhere. Tatum just didn't have the connections needed to penetrate the inner wall of the Special Forces. He was about to hang up when a thought struck him. "Try Brigadier General Thomas Jones. He might be able to tell you something."

"Where is he?"

"Here in Hawaii." Then he hung up.

He sat there for a moment, staring at the telephone. There had to be something else he could do, but he couldn't think of it. He had the redacted file. He'd nearly memorized the content. He knew the names of the Americans involved, or rather all of the Green Berets involved, but only the officers and senior NCOs of the other regular infantry units.

He was sure that there was a classified after-action report, but that would be filed at the Special Warfare Center in North

Carolina. Even if he traveled there, he doubted they would help him out because he would be outside their chain of command. He would just have to wait on Porter for that.

The key might be Master Sergeant Bocker. Although Bocker was Special Forces and therefore reluctant to provide details, Larson might be able to learn something that would help him. Since Gerber had admitted to him that he had been on the raid into Cambodia, and if he mentioned that to Bocker, then Bocker might be more willing to help. A second source would be valuable and since Bocker was here, in Hawaii, Larson could arrange for Bocker to meet Tatum. That might crack this thing open.

He learned that Bocker had checked out of his hotel and had arranged for the shuttle to take him to the airport. Apparently, he had missed Bocker by only half an hour. If he hurried, he might be able to catch him at the airport. He grabbed the phone and told Tatum there was a soldier at the airport that he might want to talk to. Once Tatum had agreed to meet him the airport, Larson turned off the coffee pot, grabbed his keys and headed for the door. He hadn't considered that he would be exposing his real identity to Tatum. At the moment, he just wanted Tatum to talk to Bocker.

It was early enough that there was little traffic and he made good time. He left the car in short-term parking, hurried into the terminal, and then wondered where to go. Without a destination, Larson wandered by the ticketing agents, glanced at the departure boards, and checked the coffee shops. By accident, he spotted Bocker in one of the newsstands, looking at the row of hardback books.

He approached Bocker, who was traveling in civilian clothes, and said, "Master Sergeant, quite the coincidence."

Bocker turned, looked at him as if he didn't know him and then said, "Colonel?"

"Heading home?"

"Yes, sir. Back on my leave. Going to visit my parents and see some old friends."

"How about I buy you a cup of coffee?"

"No, thank you, sir. I've had enough coffee while I've been here, in Hawaii, that I don't need any more."

"Then an orange juice or a Coke."

Bocker realized that Larson wasn't going to leave him alone, so he nodded and said, "I suppose a Coke, though I really don't need the caffeine in it either."

As they headed toward one of the snack bars, Larson asked, "What did you think of our little plan?"

Bocker looked at him, surprised he would mention it out in the open, but then there was nothing in the question that violated the classified status of the meeting. It was just a generic question.

"Interesting plan."

"Yes. Well. I have a friend. A reporter who is interested in the latest strategies employed in Vietnam. Wondered if you might like to talk with him."

"I'm about to fly back to the World in the next couple of hours. I won't have time."

"You could give him a call. Just a chat. Off the record."

Bocker stopped walking. "To what purpose, Colonel?"

"Frankly, Sergeant, we've been getting too much bad press lately. This would be an opportunity for a little positive reporting. Let them know what is really happening in Vietnam."

Now Bocker laughed. "Why would you think I know what is happening in Vietnam? I'm just a team sergeant and all I know is what I've been doing. There is nothing interesting in talking about radio communications."

"I'm just trying to change a few minds," said Larson. "This reporter, Chuck Tatum, is looking for a good human interest story. I thought by putting the two of you together he could get that story. A soldier home on leave from the rigors of war."

"I don't think so, Colonel."

"Well, let me buy you that Coke anyway." The military protocol seemed to demand that he allow Larson buy him the Coke, even thought he was off-duty, on leave, and in civilian clothes. Larson was still a colonel, even in his civilian clothes.

As they approached the snack bar, Larson saw Tatum, recognizing him from this picture in the newspaper. He altered his path to intercept him. He didn't see Robin Morrow, who knew both Bocker and Tatum, walking toward the exit.

CHAPTER 12

Together Gerber and Fetterman boarded the aircraft. About midway down the aisle, there were two seats together, one on the aisle and one in the middle. Gerber headed that way and Fetterman followed. When they reached them, Gerber said, "Middle suit you?"

"Couldn't care less."

As they sat down, Fetterman said, "You know, this is getting out of hand. We're summoned here for what seems to be a preliminary planning session that nearly any competent Special Forces officer or NCO could handle. We don't have any special knowledge that requires us to be here. Young Douglas isn't even twenty and he's brought in as the expert in airmobile operations. They bring in Bocker for some reason that I don't understand and now we're sneaking out of town in the dead of night."

"Mid-morning is hardly the dead of night, Tony."

"You know what I mean. Then Jones shows up here and hands us a new set of orders so that we go to MACV rather than Nha Trang. I don't like any of this."

Gerber sighed. "There is nothing we can do about it."

"And to top it off, we have that reporter trying to find us to ask about our experiences in Vietnam."

"All we can do is our job as best we can. Besides, the reporter is staying in Hawaii and we're not."

"I don't trust Colonel Larson. He's running around asking questions that don't relate to anything other than a cross-border operation, and you told him that you were there. That's going to inspire him to keep pushing."

"Tony, you remember what George Patton said?"

"Don't take counsel of your fears, more or less."

"Exactly. At this point there is nothing that we can do. I think Jones got us out of Hawaii so that Larson couldn't talk to us. Jones doesn't seem to care what we did or didn't do on our last tour. That is in the past. He has something else in mind for us."

Fetterman settled back in his seat. "There are a lot of people who were there and one of them is bound to talk out of turn. There is always someone who spills the beans whether he means to or not."

"They're scattered all over the world now. They're in Germany and Africa and South America, or out of the Army and at home enjoying civilian life."

"Being out of the Army is no protection. They can be recalled for special duty under the Uniform Code of Military Justice."

They felt a lurch as the airplane began to move.

"Well, we're on our way. Can't get us now," said Gerber.

"No, but they can grab us in Okinawa."

Lieutenant Colonel Robert Cornett was not in a good mood. It had nothing to do with the Army or Vietnam, and everything to do with running the battalion. Too many soldiers were unhappy with their lot in life, thinking that there must be a way to beat the system, but sometimes the system fought back. The report from the CIC was sitting on his desk and he couldn't believe one of the names that was on it.

He yelled, "Sergeant Major."

Sergeant Major Clifford Sparks, a burly man who had spent his whole adult life in the Army, appeared in the doorway. He was dressed in starched jungle fatigues that were sweat stained but still looked as if they had been starched. He had little hair, but that was because he kept as short as possible and he avoided facial hair because the Army prohibited beards and discouraged mustaches. He didn't like that many of the pilots opted for mustaches and knew that some of those who didn't wear them were incapable of growing them. Age got in their way, but that didn't stop them from trying.

"Yes, sir?"

Cornett pointed at one of the papers on his desk. "What in the hell is this?"

"I'm afraid I don't know, sir. Which document is that?"

"Anderson had a run in with an MP while he was in Saigon."

It was a statement rather than a question and Sparks couldn't help but smile.

"Yes, sir, he sure did. I take it that Anderson was minding his own business when some MP who has never gotten outside of Saigon decided that his uniform was not properly pressed and his boots not glossy enough. Stopped him and gave him a DR. Anderson then slowly shredded the document, showered the MP with it and walked away. At least he didn't punch out the MP. I think it took them this long for the discrepancy report to find its way to us."

"Was Anderson's uniform and boots that bad?"

"I think the problem is that the MPs have been told to discourage the soldiers from wandering around in Saigon in their jungle fatigues. With the press there, not to mention so many brass hats, they believe their jobs would be easier if we swine from the hinterlands remained, well, in the hinterlands."

Cornett rubbed a hand through his hair. "I'm not going to deny our soldiers a little in-country R and R because someone doesn't think their uniforms rise to the standards of those in Saigon. If they're clean, then I'm happy."

"Yes, sir. Is that all?"

"No. Send Anderson in for a little chat. I'm just going to let him know that we have received the DR and I will respond that the proper administrative action has been taken."

"Which is?"

"I'm just going to tell him not to shred the DR and shower the MP with it, if it happens again. Accept it with a smile and deposit it in the first trashcan he finds. We don't want him littering the streets of Saigon."

"He's in the field at the moment, watching some trail near the Cambodian border."

"Again? I thought we'd let him stay here for a few days?"

"He volunteered to go and his company commander thought it was a good idea. Anderson is one of the best on these sneak-and-peek missions."

"When is he due back?"

"There are several teams out on the sneak-and-peek missions. I believe they are all due back with a day or two. Their schedule is staggered because we don't want to give anything away."

Cornett tapped the papers on his desk again. "Let me know when he returns. Have his company commander alert you."

"Yes, sir."

"What's the movie for tonight?"

"You're not going to believe it. *The Green Berets.*"

"Gotta love that John Wayne. Remakes *The Alamo* as a Vietnam War movie. I think I'll give it a pass."

"I can call the club NCO and see if he can get us something else? Maybe a nice murder mystery or a western."

"Forget it. If I feel the urge, I'll watch John do on film what we're not allowed to do in real life."

"Yes, sir. Anything else?"

Cornett shook his head, glancing down at his desk, and then changed his mind. He'd just read the next document in the pile. "We need to extract Anderson ASAP."

Robin Morrow sat in her hotel room not wanting to pack, not wanting to leave Hawaii but having no reason to remain. Gerber, along with Fetterman, had taken off for Vietnam, and she had a job waiting in San Francisco. She didn't have a story idea, though there had been hints of something interesting about to happen in Vietnam. She thought about attempting to convince her editors to send her to Vietnam, but they were reluctant to do that, even though she had been there previously and had established good contacts throughout the Army chain of command.

The television was on in the background but she wasn't paying attention. It was some mindless gameshow. She just wanted the background noise, which was almost as good as having someone in the room with her. She wasn't ready to be alone, though it had happened often.

The telephone rang, startling her. Only her editors knew where she was and she didn't think they'd be calling. She picked up the receiver and said, "Hello?"

"Robin Morrow?"

"Who is this?"

"Chuck Tatum, Robin. We've met a couple of times. Once in Saigon."

Although she was tempted to tell him that she didn't remember him, she did. He was as a pompous ass who wasn't above changing the dynamics of a story to make it sound better. He added details that weren't true or that were more rumor than fact if it improved the human interest of the story.

She didn't like him because she thought he gave journalism a bad name.

"What do you want, Chuck?"

"I have been chasing a story that deals with the Green Berets and I thought you might be able to give me some guidance. I know that you are tight with a couple of them and have been out to their camps in Vietnam."

She didn't like the implication, though it was true. "I'm not sure that I can help you."

"I have come across a rumor that the Green Berets have been running cross-border operations in violation of DoD directives and international law."

"That could potentially be a big story," she said noncommittally.

"But I've sort of run into a brick wall. I do have one name and wondered if you knew him."

Morrow felt her blood run cold. She knew the name he was about to mention. It explained why Tatum had been at the airport talking to a man dressed in civilian clothes that she suspected was an Army officer.

"It's unlikely that I know him," she said. "There are a lot of Green Berets."

"Can we get together for lunch or drinks or something?"

"I'm about to leave Hawaii," she said.

"We can meet at the airport."

"I'd rather not. Flying is a little more stressful than I care to admit and I'm not in the mood to talk about Green Berets at the airport."

"When do you leave?"

"I'm not sure that's any of your business."

"Listen, I just need a little help on a story. I'm not looking to horn in on anything you might be doing. I have a lot of contacts in the States, and I might be able to return the favor at some point. Sort of a quid pro quo."

She was about to refuse and hang up, but then she wondered what Tatum might know and if it had anything to do with Gerber.

"I'm busy packing," she said. "What do you want to know? Make it fast."

There was a sigh at the other end, and she knew what he was thinking. It was better to interview a subject in person. Facial expressions and body language were indicators of the truth and you couldn't see them over the telephone. She too preferred meeting in person rather than talking over the telephone, but she had no desire to meet Tatum.

Finally Tatum said, "I have it on good authority that a Green Beret officer, a captain by the name of Gerber, was involved in a cross-border op several months ago."

"What makes you think that I would know anything about that?"

"I thought you might know this Gerber, and how I might find him."

"If he's a Green Beret, I would suggest that you call the Special Warfare Center at Fort Bragg. They know where their soldiers are assigned. But I doubt they'll tell you anything without a good reason to do so. They'd be afraid they might compromise a clandestine mission and put lives at risk."

"You seem to know a lot about this."

"I was with some Special Forces soldiers in Vietnam. I wrote some stories about them." She was immediately sorry she had said that. One of the oldest tricks in the book was to keep the subject talking because you didn't know what he or she would say. Now, if Tatum had half a brain, and if he knew where she worked, he could pull her clips and learn that she knew Gerber.

"I didn't think about the Special Warfare Center, though I probably would have gotten around to it eventually. You have a number or a contact there?"

She did, but she wasn't about to share it with Tatum. She wanted the Green Berets to think of her as a friend. Rather than lie, she said, "I'd rather not burn my sources."

"Nothing to burn. They don't have to know where I got the information."

"Why not just call the public affairs officer and talk to him? He could direct you on this."

"I think I would get the runaround unless I had a name to drop or a contact there."

"Listen, Tatum, I really don't have time for this. I have to finish packing and catch a flight. You understand?"

"I understand that you're hiding something…"

Without another word, Morrow quietly hung up and then began packing quickly. She didn't want Tatum turning up at her hotel room door before she could leave.

The plane taxied off the runway and jerked to a halt on the tarmac at Tan Son Nhut. A member of the flight crew opened the doors at the front of the plane as mobile steps were pushed against the fuselage. The heat and humidity of Vietnam flooded into the interior, overpowering the air-conditioning. As he stood to exit, Gerber shivered from the sudden change in temperature and then felt the sweat pop out on his forehead and trickle down his sides.

With Fetterman following him, Gerber shuffled forward until he reached the door and then blinked in the bright, afternoon sunlight. He had expected someone to be waiting for them at the terminal, but when they reached it no one was there. Fetterman said, "So, what do we do now?"

"I guess we make our way over to MACV."

"Before finding a hotel room and getting a shower?"

"Before," Gerber confirmed.

They left the terminal and walked toward the MACV compound. Saigon hadn't changed in the time they had been gone and then Gerber realized that it hadn't been all that long ago. The GIs still walked along looking for female companions, the hustlers were still trying to sell anything they could to the gullible, and the beggars still sat around with their hands out. Gerber ignored them all.

The armed MP at the gate to Pentagon East, the MACV Headquarters, checked their ID and they climbed the concrete steps to the large glass doors of the main two-story building. While the compound itself was neither as large as the Pentagon, nor pentagon shaped, it was made up of a series of separate buildings that were connected with open, central areas. The trouble was that it was difficult to defend if attacked.

They walked through the main entrance and were stopped by another MP who asked for their identification and then asked for their reason for being there.

"Orders," said Gerber.

"May I see a copy of your orders, sir?"

"VOCO from General Jones."

"We don't have a General Jones assigned here."

Fetterman decided to take over. "We received those orders in Hawaii and were told to report here upon arrival in-country. We need to speak with someone in the Studies and Observations Group."

The MP consulted a clipboard. "Are you Major Gerber and Sergeant Major Fetterman?"

Gerber couldn't help himself. "You just checked our ID. You know who we are."

"Yes, sir. If you'll wait here, I'll find someone to escort you to the conference room."

Gerber merely nodded. It didn't take more than a minute for a lieutenant colonel to appear. "Major Gerber, I take it?"

"Yes, sir. With Sergeant Major Fetterman."

"Didn't expect you so soon. I'm Colonel Mark Rogers. If you'll follow me, I'll take you to meet with the general."

They walked down a series of corridors with prints of historic U.S. Army battles on the walls. There were representations of the various shoulder patches worn by the soldiers in Vietnam. Gerber wondered about the wisdom of that, but decided that the enemy probably already knew what units were deployed in Vietnam and what their patches looked like. All Charlie had to do was have some spy watch the evening news in the World and report on what he learned. Probably some college kid without a brain in his head believing he was doing something for democracy.

The conference room was smaller than they had expected. Six chairs had been placed around a table in the center and all were vacant. There was nothing on the table, no visible screen and nothing to suggest that a meeting was going to be held there.

"Take a seat," Rogers said. "The General will be with you in a moment."

"Thank you," said Gerber as Rogers shut the door. He dropped into a chair. "Fly halfway around the world so that we can sit in a tiny conference room..."

"At least it's air conditioned."

The door opened again and a general entered, followed by his aide. As Gerber and Fetterman rose to their feet the general said, "Keep your seats. This won't take long." Then he grinned. "And you will be annoyed when we're through here."

The general took the chair at the head of the table. "I'm Major General Douglas Whitney and I'm the intelligence officer here." He held up a hand to forestall any questions. "I'll be brief. This is not your last stop. A chopper is waiting to pick you up at Hotel Three to take you to the staging area at Tay Ninh. There you will meet the rest of the force that we have assembled —"

Gerber interrupted him. "General, we have no idea what you're talking about."

"Our weapons are at Nha Trang," added Fetterman.

"First, you have just returned from a special assignment in Hawaii to plan to establish what we are now calling a patrol base. That force, including the engineers and the infantry companies, are standing by at Tay Ninh."

"They've had a rehearsal already?"

"No, Major. The rehearsal took place in Hawaii and you were there. That's one of the reasons you are not going to Nha Trang from here but to Tay Ninh. There is an engineering platoon there that was at the rehearsal. The soldiers assigned know how to dig a fox hole and most of them have participated in erecting bunkers. They have done it here before."

Gerber didn't like what he was hearing. It sounded like a boondoggle. The Army was famous for boondoggles, though the Special Forces attempted to keep those at a minimum. Sometimes they inherited the boondoggles from other military units.

To Fetterman, Whitney said, "Second, we have your weapons here."

"They've been out of our hands, handled by others. I'd like a chance to zero them again and inspect them."

"That can be done at Tay Ninh." Whitney took a deep breath. "The mission is not something that the Special Forces would normally be involved in, but you two were involved in the planning, which makes you the subject matter experts. Just makes sense for you to be there now. You both have the expertise and your experience is a valuable asset to the overall mission. Once you're at Tay Ninh, you'll be brought up to date by Major Corley and the infantry battalion commander whose name I have forgotten…"

At that point the aide spoke up. "That would be Lieutenant Colonel Arthur Philips. He's on his second tour and commanded a company on his first. He knows what he's doing."

"Thank you, Travis," said Whitney. "If you have no other questions, I'll have your weapons brought to you and you can then head over to Hotel Three where the chopper is waiting."

"With all due respect, General," said Gerber, "we could have been told all this by your aide."

"Yes, but we thought you'd be a little more impressed if I delivered the orders. At least that's the theory."

Fetterman nodded. "It works. I tend to listen to generals."

Whitney stood and the others followed suit. "Good luck, gentlemen," he said as he moved toward the door, then added, "You'll understand the push for speed soon. It's not just the latest fad here at MACV."

"Yes, sir," Gerber said.

As Whitney left, two soldiers appeared carrying the weapons. Fetterman took his, cleared it, looked at the serial number to ensure it was his and then inspected the rifle. When he was finished, he said, "It is cleaned and lubed."

Gerber went through the same ritual and then picked the Colt .45 1911A1 pistol off the table. He dropped the magazine, worked the slide to ensure it was unloaded and asked, "Ammo?"

One of the men set a couple of pouches on the table that held loaded magazines for the pistols and then handed out the bandoliers with magazines for the M-16s. He said, "Standard load for both weapons."

Gerber picked up one of the pistol belts and buckled it around his waist. "I guess that covers it."

"You need to sign the hand receipt for the weapons, sir."

"Of course."

CHAPTER 13

The terminal building at Hotel Three was a small, one-story structure with a dirty plywood floor, some battered chairs and sofas, and a scheduling board behind a makeshift counter. Some pilots had entered their projected flight departures on the board, along with their destination. Some just announced that they would take anyone who needed a ride to a specific place. It was something of a free-for-all with a chance for a ride that might not pan out for hours.

As Gerber and Fetterman, now legally armed and carrying their duffel bags, wondered how, exactly, they would find the pilot who would take them to Tay Ninh, Fetterman spotted Corley. He nudged Gerber.

"Our ride is here."

Corley strolled up, grinned, and asked, "Need a ride, soldier?"

"I will assume," said Gerber, "that you know where we need to go and that you have access to aerial transportation."

"Follow me."

As they left the terminal, Fetterman asked, "How in the hell did you get here before us, sir?"

"General Jones arranged it. I had a direct flight with midair refueling. While you were crawling across the ocean in a slow commercial aircraft with a long stop in Okinawa, I flew here with no stops or layovers."

"I'm not sure that makes sense," said Gerber. "I thought you needed to finish the after-action report."

"A verbal debriefing by the general and I was off to Vietnam."

There were several Huey helicopters sitting on the ground at Hotel Three. One had the rotors spinning and Corley led them to it. "Toss your crap back there and we'll get going."

Gerber moved forward and climbed into the cargo compartment. He shoved his duffel bag out of the way, sliding it under the red troop seat. Then he sat down and buckled himself in as Fetterman and Corley followed suit.

Over the noise of the turbine and the popping of the rotor blades, Corley shouted, "Takes about an hour."

Gerber nodded as the helicopter lifted off the ground and turned slightly. They climbed out slowly until they were at fifteen hundred feet. Below them, the ground was fairly flat. To the south Gerber could see a swampy area that didn't have much in the way of terrain features. There were a few small villages that were little more than a cluster of hootches, but it seemed they all had a soccer field.

Gerber closed his eyes and leaned his head against the gray padding of the cargo compartment. He listened to the whine of the turbine and the snapping of the rotors. He felt them swerve once but he didn't bother to open his eyes. There was nothing that he wanted to see and nothing that he needed to see. He was out of the action, waiting for the game to begin.

Corley finally yelled, "We're getting close."

Gerber could see Nui Ba Den, the Black Virgin Mountain, one of high points in Three Corps at over three thousand feet. The top of the extinct volcano was used as a basse by both the South Vietnamese and American forces. It was said that the VC and the North Vietnamese controlled the sides of the mountain. No one bothered anybody on the mountain.

Beyond the mountain was the city of Tay Ninh, and beyond that was the American base camp that housed thousands of American soldiers. Gerber and Fetterman had been to the base several times, especially when they were operating in the vicinity of the Cambodia border.

The helicopter turned, entered the traffic pattern, and landed on the south side of the base, where there was a temporary tent city. Corley, yelling, explained that those involved in the project were housed there to keep them away from the soldiers stationed at Tay Ninh, and away from the hundreds of Vietnamese workers who daily entered the base camp as required by the status of forces agreement between the US and the South Vietnamese government.

As they touched down, Gerber, Fetterman and Corley, carrying their weapons and duffle bags, leapt out. Gerber held up a hand to let the pilot know he appreciated the lift and watched as the helicopter turned and hovered off to one of the revetment areas. The sound died as the aircraft departed and Corley said, "We'll get you settled. There'll be a formal briefing tomorrow for the officers and senior NCOs. We anticipate commencing the operation in twenty-four to forty-eight hours. We have the logistics in place and we have the aviation assets dedicated."

Fetterman looked at the tents. "Not exactly the sort of accommodations I require."

"I understand that it will be a hardship, but look at it this way," said Corley. "In a day or two, you'll see the tents as luxurious."

"I think not," said Fetterman.

Gerber shouldered his duffle bag. "Show us to our tent. Do you really think this keeps our soldiers from mingling with the others? Don't they have PX privileges? What about showers, hot meals, and some entertainment?"

"When their duties are completed, they're on free time though we want them to stay in the immediate area. The PX here isn't all that great, and we set up movies in the evening."

Their tent was set away from most of the other tents. Gerber wasn't thrilled with that. There was no air conditioning.

"I haven't heard you complain this much in years," said Fetterman.

Gerber grinned. "That was before I was a field grade officer. We, of such high and exalted rank, expect something a little better than a hot tent with no electricity."

"Oh, we have electricity from tactical generators, which are rather noisy. We don't use them during the day. We have field lighting in the tents but as you can imagine, the generators have a tendency to run out of fuel at the worst time."

Gerber, still holding his duffle bag said, "Well, if this is the best you can do, who am I to complain. It can't get much worse."

But, of course, he was wrong.

Colonel Larson was more than a little annoyed. Chuck Tatum had failed to learn much about Gerber and the cross-border operation, and Porter had failed to call. Larson had expected some sort of response from one of them rather quickly. He had not expected a complete blackout from both.

While it was midmorning in Hawaii, it was late afternoon in Washington, D.C., which meant that Porter would still be in his office. He wanted to use the Autovon instead of his private phone line because the cost of calls was becoming prohibitive. But that would have required he go to his office and he didn't want to do that. He told the secretary who answered the phone that he needed to speak with Colonel Porter and was put through.

"Miles? Jim. Thought I would touch base with you."

"Let me close the door," Porter surprised him by saying, then, "I'm not sure that I want to talk to you."

"What's happened?"

"If you plan to ever wear the star of a general officer, you need to drop your inquiry and pretend that you never asked the questions."

"What did you learn?"

"First, those Special Forces boys operate in another world. They engage in unconventional missions and asymmetrical warfare. They have a lot of latitude in those clandestine operations and nearly all of the operations are authorized at the highest levels."

Larson felt his anger build. "They're not allowed to go rogue. They are governed by the same rules of land warfare and the same regulations that we are."

Porter chuckled. "That's not entirely true."

"Are you telling me that Gerber had approval?"

"Let's not use names. And yes, I'm telling you that there is no one looking into this. It is a dead issue."

Larson fell silent, unsure of what to say or ask.

"I will tell you," said Porter, "that my boss was not happy to learn that I had even asked what I thought of as a fairly benign question. He grilled me about my interest in this to make sure that I had not been exposed to classified information to which I had no need to know, and then he told me to forget about it. I *have* forgotten about it."

"I was hoping that —"

Porter interrupted. "No, Jim. If you wish to remain on active duty and not retired at a lower grade than you now hold, then you need to drop the inquiry."

"I'm not in your chain of command," said Larson, a little sharper than he intended.

"It doesn't matter and I'm not giving you an order, I'm merely stating a fact as it was put to me."

"They said I would be retired?"

"You misunderstand, Jim. Not you. Me. And there were questions about retiring as an oh six, but at a reduced grade which means a smaller check. I extrapolated that you would face the same outcome because you were the one who initiated my involvement and if I am asked a specific question, I will answer it truthfully."

"Good God," said Larson. He felt the blood drain from his face and was suddenly light headed.

"I think you're beginning to get the picture. This is none of my business and none of your business. There is something else going on and I'm not going to ask any more questions about it."

"Okay, Miles. I get it."

"I hope you do. Let's just forget this whole thing." With that, Porter hung up.

Larson felt the sweat bead on his forehead. He was suddenly hot in his air-conditioned apartment. He'd spent his adult life as a soldier and it was all he knew. He couldn't afford to throw that away because of one major he found to be arrogant and unmilitary.

But he just couldn't let it go. Maybe there was a way to push Gerber out without having any mud splashed on him. Although he had met him once in the airport, Tatum didn't know his name or that he had leaked the information to him. He supposed that Tatum could make an educated guess, but that's all it would be. He picked up the phone again.

When he finally reached Tatum, he said, without preamble, "You get the dirt on this Gerber?"

Tatum responded, "I know who you are."

That surprised Larson. "No, you don't."

"Colonel James Larson, what is you beef with Major Gerber?"

For the second time in less than twenty minutes, Larson felt as if he had been punched in the stomach. "Does it matter if the story is good?"

"The story is dead. Gerber is in Vietnam. The Special Warfare Center doesn't know who he is, if we're to believe that, and I can find no corroboration for the claim he illegally violated the neutrality of Cambodia."

"Surely you have sources that can provide corroboration?"

"No, Colonel, I don't. I tried to talk with Robin Morrow. According to her bylines on various articles, she knows Gerber, but she won't talk to me. Frankly, I don't blame her. She's gotten some good stuff from Gerber and she probably doesn't want to burn that bridge. I have nothing, other than one colonel who apparently doesn't like one major and that's about all I have."

"Then our relationship is over?"

"Colonel, we don't have a relationship. You provided, or tried to provide, a story that, if I could verify it, would be a good one. But without you on the record — and I assume that you won't go on the record — and without verification from other sources, there is nothing to write."

"Then I guess we're through here."

"If you find anything else, some documentation, or some way to prove that Gerber acted on his own, then let me know. I'll keep my eyes open, of course, but I don't know where else to go."

"Thank you," said Larson, though he didn't know why he said it. He hung up the phone and sat staring at it. In the space of thirty minutes, he'd seen the whole thing unravel. Porter had warned him off and Tatum couldn't verify the story.

He had reached the end of the rope. Now there was only the fiery plunge into the volcano.

The meeting was held in what was known as the headquarters tent. It was set up at one end of the area that had been designated for use by Lieutenant Colonel Arthur Philips. It was larger than the squad tents being used by the soldiers, had a tactical generator for continual electrical power, and a variety of chairs that looked as if they had been discarded. It was not a military formation of similar chairs lined up in neat rows, but it would do for now.

Philips stood at the front of the tent, or what he had designated the front of the tent, beside an easel covered by a large cloth to hide the map underneath it. Guards were posted around the tent, twenty feet away so that they would not overhear what was being said. They would prevent anyone approaching the tent once the briefing started and listening to the classified information.

He watched as the officers and senior NCOs entered the tent. The men from each unit stayed together, though there was no order given for them to do that. A few looked for refreshments, coffee, water or maybe a doughnut or sandwich. There was nothing like that available.

At ten, Philips nodded once and the flaps on the tent were closed. Philips knew that it would heat up rapidly but he didn't want the meeting to last long. If the men were uncomfortable, they would be less inclined to ask questions or engage in useless speculation. It was a management technique he had discovered years earlier and had employed often.

When all the flaps were closed, Philips said, "We have assembled this team from several units, several areas of expertise and from those who have the appropriate combat experience. I will now turn this briefing over to Major Corley who is one of those who inspired us."

Corley, looking tired and wearing sweat-soaked jungle fatigues, stood up and moved to the easel. "To recap, we are going to erect a camp where there is none in a matter of hours. We will land a company of infantry at beginning morning nautical twilight, or about the time there is enough sunlight available to see fairly well on the ground. By the end of the day the camp will be ready to repel a ground assault."

There was no real response because those in the tent knew the basics of what was about to happen. They were there for the specifics.

"The first order of business was where to site the camp. To that end, LRRP teams were sent in to recon the area. Sergeant First Class Sam Anderson led one of those teams. In consultation with him, we have found the best available site. Sergeant Anderson will explain where we'll be going and the criterion we used to make the choice."

Anderson, wearing what looked like a brand new uniform, pulled the cloth off the easel and picked up the pointer. "We wanted to find a location where Charlie felt comfortable and unafraid. We wanted something along his lines of communication so that we could disrupt the flow of arms, supplies and personnel into South Vietnam."

He pointed to an area southwest of Tay Ninh. "This is a somewhat open area, away from jungle, but with enough cover to allow for the infiltration of the enemy without much worry of being spotted. There is another area, here, that rises to about ten or twelve feet above the plains. It offers an outstanding view of the surrounding environs. Given that it is raised, all the advantage goes to us. We'd be in a position to spot the infiltrators as they try sneak up on us."

"You know this how?" asked someone.

"My team and I stayed there for about forty-eight hours watching the enemy and they never saw us."

Anderson pointed to a second site. "This area isn't quite as good, though it is close to a jungle infiltration route. That route is more difficult to transit, meaning that Charlie has trouble along it and the numbers are smaller than those at the first site."

"What is the terrain like?"

Anderson looked to Corley, who stood up. "It's solid. Not marshy or soft so that we'd have a solid foundation for the bunkers. Water table is low enough that we don't have a water problem. Rainfall will drain to the south when the monsoon begins." He sat back down.

Anderson put the pointer back on the easel. "Any questions?"

When there were none, Corley said, simply, "Aviation?"

Major Fox half stood and said, "I'll defer to Mister Douglas, who has been involved in this from the beginning."

Douglas was about to say that he had nothing to add, but then stood up. "We'll be using our standard combat assault tactics. There will be multiple lifts by slicks, we'll have gun cover, and the Chinooks will bring in the pallets once the perimeter of the base is established. Flight time to the location is about fifteen minutes or a thirty-minute round trip. We can get everyone in without having to refuel. Once all the infantry is moved to the base site, we'll be on standby."

"We're getting a little ahead here," Corley said.

"There isn't really much that I can add," said Douglas, ignoring him. "I guess you have all participated in combat assaults before. We'll get in, unload, and get out, heading back to the next load. The itinerary, I guess, will be security force first, reinforcements second, along with the engineers. Then Chinooks and more infantry."

Douglas stopped talking and looked around the tent. He spotted the man he wanted. "Captain Racine can address the Chinook operations."

As Douglas sat down, Racine stood up. "Our only job is to bring in the pallets and the rest of the engineers. Just pop a smoke and have a guide where we can see him, showing us where to position the pallets." Racine sat down.

Gerber, who had remained silent, spoke up. "I've looked at the op order and the sequence of events has been laid out there. Each soldier will have a basic load of ammunition, two C-rats, and two canteens with water. Everything else will be brought in on the pallets."

"If I might interrupt, Major," said Corley. "I think everyone here has sat in on a meeting or two discussing all this. We're talking about some of the things that we have already resolved. We have four infantry companies for security and for erecting the bunkers. Duty will rotate so that no one company only builds bunkers and only one is patrolling while the third is deploying the concertina wire. Are there any questions that we haven't answered?"

"How long are we going to be deployed at this base?"

"I can't say right now."

"It seems to me," Gerber said, "that the order should be the security company with the engineering platoon, then the Chinooks, and then the last two lifts of infantry. That keeps the number of people on the ground to a minimum while the engineers are using explosives. The security company will be off the hill and away from the area of detonations. The security force should be big enough to handle anything thrown at us at first."

Corley looked at Fox and said, "Is that a problem?"

Fox shook his head. "Just have to change the op order scheduling. It really doesn't matter to us which company is landed when."

"Okay," said Corley.

"What about close air support from the Air Force?" someone asked.

Corley sighed. "That has been coordinated. Fighters were will on alert at Tan Son Nhut and can be on station is less than thirty minutes."

He covered the easel then and said, "This has been laid out in the op order. We ran a rehearsal in Hawaii and all the engineers here were involved with that rehearsal. They know what needs to be done and the order in which we need to do it. There is nothing in the task that an infantry soldier didn't learn in AIT." He paused, and then said, "Infantry?"

"It's getting awfully hot in here," said a voice in the rear of the tent.

Philips ignored the comment and stood up. He could feel the sweat dripping. "You all have been briefed on your portion of the mission. To recap, Captain Jordan, you're up."

Captain Robert Jordan was the senior company commander. He'd been in Vietnam for nine months. Having served his six months in the bush, rather than take a job at a base camp, he'd opted to stay with his company. Although he didn't think of himself as a lifer, he was moving in that direction.

"I'll take the first lift in as the security force," Jordan said. "I have designated the platoons with their assignments, including a roving force off the hilltop, and moving close to the jungle to keep Charlie away from those erecting the base." He grinned and sat down.

Philips said, "If I am not on hand, Captain Jordan, as the senior captain will assume command over all the infantry companies on site." He looked around and saw one of the other company commanders. "Captain Smith?"

Smith, a younger man than Jordan who had been in Vietnam for only three months, stood. "I've got the third lift. We'll have base security, meaning that we'll be on site but won't be engaged, at first, in the construction of the bunker line or the placement of the crew served weapons. I think of our role as a quick reaction force if someone shoots at us and Captain Jordan is engaged elsewhere." He sat down.

Philips looked around the faces in the tent. "Captain Lasco? Ah, there you are."

Captain Larry Lasco was a stocky man in sweat-soaked fatigues. He stood and ran a hand over his head. "I've got the first duty of assisting the engineers in the construction of the bunkers. My company has been issued additional pioneer gear. We'll work to fill additional sandbags, straighten and square the bunker walls, and help get the tops of the bunkers placed. We're more of a construction company for the first couple of hours and then we'll relieve Captain Smith, who'll take our position."

When Lasco sat down, Philips asked, "Major Gerber, do you have anything to add?"

Gerber stood up. "Sergeant Major Fetterman and I will be on hand to observe and advise. We were present in Hawaii for the engineer rehearsal so we have a good idea about the sequence of events. We'll be there to assist where necessary, but the command functions will remain with Colonel Philips and Captain Jordan."

Corley looked at the men. "You all know what you have to do. Are there any relevant questions?"

When no one spoke, Philips took over again. "Be ready to go by zero five hundred tomorrow morning. In that time I would suggest you get to your units and get your equipment checked. We're having a special meal brought in, so be back here by sixteen hundred. That's it."

As the soldiers left the tent, Gerber walked up to Philips. "Sergeant Major Fetterman and I believe that we should go with the first lift of the day."

Philips considered. "If you think that's best."

"We want to ensure that the security company is deployed in the best fashion possible."

"You don't believe that the company commander is capable of deploying his men adequately?"

"No, sir. We just believe that, because of our experience, we might see something that he does not."

"Major Gerber, it has been made clear to me that you are operating outside my chain of command here. You certainly don't need my permission to accompany the first lift. That is entirely up to you."

"I wasn't asking permission, sir. I was explaining our thoughts on the matter."

Philips almost laughed. "You people think you know it all."

"No, sir. We're just experienced in this sort of thing."

"Suit yourself, Major." Philips turned and walked away.

Fetterman watched him go. "What's his problem?"

"He's afraid that we'll find something wrong with this operation and he'll look bad. He firmly believes that when he's told we're here to help, it means that someone has lost faith in him."

Fetterman shook his head. "That's the trouble with the ground pounders."

Brigadier General Jones studied the note that had been placed on his desk and then looked up at his aide. "When did this come in?"

"Twenty minutes ago," replied Harker. "Took the commo boys a few minutes to decode it and then they brought it to me."

Jones sighed. "I just don't get it. What is Larson's problem?"

When Harker started to answer, Jones waved him to silence. "That was a rhetorical question. I didn't expect an answer. Do you know where Colonel Larson is right now?"

"He's still on leave, but I think I saw him in his office an hour ago."

"Would you see if he's still in the building? If he has trouble with coming here, immediately, pick up the phone and call me. I'll make the order clear to him."

"Yes, sir."

Harker returned a few minutes later with Larson, who marched into Jones' office, stopped three feet short of his desk and although dressed in civilian clothes, saluted as if he was on a parade ground. "Colonel Larson, James T., reporting as ordered."

"Cut the crap Colonel and sit down."

Larson didn't move until Jones returned his salute. He then sat down in one of the two leather chairs in front of the desk.

"Jim, I have here on my desk a communication for the Pentagon. Believe it or not, it is marked 'Flash.' Someone in the Pentagon with more rank than me thought this was important enough to send the message with the highest priority."

Larson realized that Jones was waiting for a response. "Yes, sir," he said.

"Somehow they have learned that you have been asking questions about Major Gerber and his last tour in Vietnam."

The color drained from Larson's face. "Yes, sir."

"I'm not going to ask you about the apparent vendetta you have against a fine and highly decorated officer with multiple tours in Vietnam. I don't care. I do want to know who you have been talking to."

"I'd rather not get a fellow officer in trouble for doing me a favor."

"One that he clearly had to know was outside of channels. One that he had to know was unauthorized and could compromise a mission in the planning stages."

"I don't believe that he knew about any mission in the planning stages that could be compromised, but he did know we were out of channels."

"I won't ask you his name, though I suspect those in Washington know who he is. I mean, for it to have come to their attention, they would have to know who was asking the questions."

"As I said, General, he was doing me a favor."

"I do have to ask you a couple of questions, however. Who have you talked to about this?"

Larson realized that he was now in real trouble. Chuck Tatum knew that he was the leak, and Tatum was outside the control of the Army unless there was a national security issue. That would be difficult to prove because it could be there had been no international repercussions. To prosecute him for the leak would open that can of worms. But they could let him know that his career was basically over. He could retire quietly, pension intact, or they could reduce him to his permanent rank and see that he was kept busy counting mess kits at some small Army post in an out of the way area.

"There are two reporters," he said.

"Shit. Don't you have a brain in your head?"

"They approached me," said Larson, realizing that he had just lied.

"Who are they?"

"Do we have to go down that path?"

"I have to know how far this has gotten so that I might assess the damage you have done."

"I don't see what damage I have done," said Larson.

"That's the trouble, Colonel. Let me tell you a little story about a man who claimed to have escaped from the Viet Cong not all that long ago. He was bragging how his interrogators were asking about our Order of Battle. He said that he belonged to General Custer's Seventh Cavalry stationed near Tay Ninh. He thought it a great joke, but the problem is that the Seventh is now part of the First Cavalry Division which is, in fact, at Tay Ninh. Now, if he had been a real POW, he would have just given the enemy information that was absolutely true. Custer was no longer the commander, but who cared? That liar had burned the Seventh. The point is that this alleged POW didn't know enough about the situation and thought he was being clever. Fortunately, as I said, the man was lying about his POW status, but it is illustrative."

Jones took a pen out of its holder and pulled a legal pad closer. "Who are these reporters."

"Robin Morrow and Chuck Tatum."

"Morrow's not the problem. I don't know this Tatum."

"I spoke with him earlier. He has nothing. He was trying to find a second source on the story…"

"Who was the first source?"

Larson realized that he had again said too much. He believed that Tatum would not burn a source, especially for no real reason, so he said, "I don't know. He was looking for a second source. That's all I know."

"Okay, Colonel. Get out of here and I'll try to piss on this fire. I fear it's not over yet, but I'll do what I can."

Larson stood up. "Yes, sir. Thank you, General." He spun and got out of the office as fast as he could.

Jones yelled at his aide. "Harker, get me General Harrison in Washington."

A moment later, Jones picked up the telephone and said, "I think the problem is contained. I don't believe there will be repercussions."

"What are you going to do about your big mouth colonel?"

"Haven't decided yet, but I doubt he'll ever find himself on a promotion list for brigadier general. He'll be forced to retire in about two years when the clock runs out on him."

"Keep an eye on him."

"I planned on that."

CHAPTER 14

First Lieutenant Albert Wyeth, a twenty-three-year-old graduate of both OCS and helicopter flight training, sat in the cockpit of his helicopter. He was sitting perpendicular to the other aircraft so that he could see them as they joined the formation. As they hovered into position and touched down, in a trail formation, Wyeth turned his aircraft to the right, taking his position as lead.

Wyeth keyed his mike and said, "Six. Lead."

"Go, Lead."

"We are lined up and ready."

"Roger. Troops on the way."

Although he heard nothing more from Major Fox, who was in the command-and-control aircraft flying somewhere to the south of Tay Ninh, Wyeth knew that the ground mission commander, Lieutenant Colonel Arthur Philips, had issued an order to one of the infantry companies to board the helicopters. Wyeth looked over toward tent city, where the infantry soldiers were now moving toward the aircraft, ducking low under the spinning rotors. They scrambled on board in seconds.

As the last of the soldiers climbed in, Douglas, flying trail, was on the radio. "Lead, you are loaded with ten."

"Roger. Lead is on the go."

They took off, the lead chopper lifting gently into the brightening sky. Wyeth dumped the nose and began to pick up speed and altitude. The aircraft raced toward the bunker line, flying past the refueling point, and then began a rapid climb.

Through the windshield Wyeth could see the lights of Tay Ninh City twinkling like a hundred thousand stars, despite the threat of a VC mortar or rocket attack. To the right, toward Cambodia, there was nothing but darkness.

"Lead, you're off with ten."

"Roger. Flight come up in a staggered right."

Wyeth climbed to fifteen hundred feet where the air was cooler without the humidity on the ground. Slowly the other aircraft caught up and then fell into position behind him. Douglas, about to join the flight, said, "Lead. You are joined with ten."

"Lead is rolling over."

As Lead said that he was on the go, Fox, in the C and C helicopter orbiting at three thousand feet, turned toward the proposed landing zone. Over the company fox mike, he said, "Gun Team Leader, do you have me in sight?"

Two short clicks over the radio signaled his response.

The gun team leader turned his aircraft in the direction of Tay Ninh to intercept the flight. On seeing them, he made another hundred-and-eighty-degree turn to lead them to the LZ.

Following the gunship, the flight began their descent. There was now enough sunlight that they could see the open hilltop and the ground around it. There was no movement anywhere. The gunship, flying close to the ground, raced over the open area. A yellow smoke grenade tumbled from the helicopter, landing near the edge of the high ground.

"Lead. Land twenty yards from the smoke."

"Lead. Roger."

Sitting in the fifth helicopter of the first lift, Gerber could make out swamps, rice paddies and clumps of palm trees.

Hidden in some of them were hootches. These were separated from the LZ by half a klick or more, and there was no movement and no lights near them. The helicopter flared for landing, Gerber charged his weapon. Those around him, following his lead, did the same thing.

As they touched down, Gerber leaped out, ran fifteen or twenty feet from the aircraft and then knelt on the ground, his eyes sweeping the horizon. The timing couldn't have been better.

The helicopters lifted off, almost as one, climbed out and turned back, toward the base camp where the second lift waited. Fetterman appeared and stood looking down at Gerber. "You want to get going, Major?"

"Company commander is in charge here, Tony."

"Just thought we might want to watch him in action, in case he needs some advice."

"I've talked to him and he's been in-country for a long time. This isn't his first combat assault. He knows what to do. Besides, I discussed this with him last night. He should be getting a patrol out to sweep around while the rest of the company forms something of a perimeter."

Fetterman grinned. "Just checking. Haven't worked with this many grunts in a long time."

Gerber saw that they were standing on what was the crest of the slight rise where the camp would be erected. It wasn't much of a panoramic view, but it did command the area out to four or five hundred meters. It didn't look as if the grass was very tall, so that there wasn't much concealment for Charlie if he was out there. The location was perfect for the base.

The company commander, Captain Jordan, trotted up but didn't salute. He knew better than to do that in the field. All that did was identify the officers for any enemy sniper who happened to be watching. It was the same reason that the officers tried to stay away from the RTO. Made them a high value target for that sniper.

"Got a twenty-man patrol heading out," Jordan said. "They'll work their way in a circle about half a klick out, near the edge of the jungle."

"It's your show, Captain," said Gerber. "If I see something strange, I'll let you know."

Gerber wondered why the man felt it necessary to report on the obvious, but let it go. Instead, he turned his attention to the engineers who had come in with them on the first lift.

Major Corley, using an engineer stake driven into the ground in the center of the rise, was already marking out the perimeter of the base. With a hundred-and-thirty-foot rope, tied to the stake, he drew the bunker line. The engineers then marked the four cardinal points of the compass so that the circle was now quartered. The main bunkers would be created at those points with supporting bunkers and berm running from them.

With the location secure, or at least as secure as they could make it given the situation, Corley called in the Chinooks with the palletized loads. The engineers had spread out, one standing in front of the area designated for the bunkers. Dropping the loads close to the location where they would be used would speed up the process.

The timing was such that one Chinook would hover in, drop its sling load and then land so that the soldiers it carried could be deployed. When that was done, the next one would come in until there were twenty-four pallets sitting in front of each bunker.

On each of the pallets were the shape charges to be used to excavate the bunkers. As soon as all the pallets were dropped and the aircraft clear of the area, the engineers pulled the explosives and set them up using the detonators they had brought in with them. When all the charges had been placed, and with all the soldiers on security outside the blast danger zones, one of the engineers yelled, "Fire in the hole!"

A moment later the charges set for the first bunker detonated, showering the surrounding area with dirt and debris. Before the dust had settled, another shout went up. "Fire in the hole!"

As the last of the charges were detonated, the soldiers brought in by the Chinooks began to square the bunkers. They used PSP for the floor and began to stack sandbags on the ground directly in front of the bunkers, which were roofed over with wooden planks and more sandbags. Construction of the base was well underway by midmorning.

After transporting the security company, Douglas and Williams, along with the rest of the flight were shut down near the tent city. Their job was to take the second and third infantry company into the area once the Chinooks had delivered their loads and the engineers had excavated the bunkers.

Douglas sat on the troop seat, a paperback science fiction novel in his hand, waiting for the appearance of the soldiers and the order to crank. He figured he had about thirty minutes to relax. Had it been later in the morning, and had they had a longer time shut down, Douglas would have stretched out on the troop seat and tried to sleep.

Before Douglas had read two pages, Williams appeared. "Lead wants us up and running."

There were no soldiers around, but if the flight was cranking up, then the soldiers wouldn't be far behind. Douglas slipped the book into one of the side pockets of his flight suit and jumped out of the cargo compartment. He opened the door on the left side of the Huey and climbed up, into the cockpit. As he waited for Williams to get settled, he turned and looked back into the cargo compartment. The door gunner and the crew chief were now sitting in their wells, behind the M-60 machine guns, helmets on and plugged into the intercom system.

Satisfied, Douglas yelled, "Clear," heard both the crew chief and door gunner respond and pulled the trigger on the underside of the collective. The turbine began to whine. He checked the instruments and then slowly rolled on the throttle, watching the gas producer gauge to make sure that the temperature didn't move out of the green.

Soldiers hurried towards the aircraft, their heads bowed, and climbed in. Douglas watched as they loaded the aircraft. The second lift was as uneventful as the first. The only difference was that they could now see the outline of the base. There were holes in a circular formation. Engineers were in some of them, working to square the sides and clear the dirt from the center.

Rather than land in the center of the base, the flight landed on the north side. As they touched down, the grunts leaped out and took up defensive positions until the flight took off again. Douglas radioed Lead to tell them they were ready to go.

Back at Tay Ninh, the soldiers were lined up in a staggered trail formation. The helicopters landed near each of the loads. As the skids touched the ground, the grunts scrambled into the cargo compartments.

Before he was on the ground, Douglas could see that most of the other aircraft were ready to go. He said, "Lead, you're down with ten and loaded."

"Roger. Lead's on the go."

They lifted off, with Douglas still flying in the trail position. When the formation came together, he said, "Lead. You're joined."

"Rolling over."

Williams said, "This is getting monotonous."

"Better than having someone shooting at us."

"I don't know. A little excitement might brighten the day."

"I think I'd just as soon have the monotonous day — listen to some tunes on the ADF, build my flight time and check another day off my short timer's calendar."

Just as he said that, Douglas thought he saw a green tracer. Then he heard the machine gun firing. Over the Fox Mike he said, "Trail's taking fire on the left."

Over the intercom he shouted, "You see where that came from?"

The crew chief had already swung him M-60 machine gun around and was busy firing his weapon into the jungle below.

There was a sudden series of explosions. The crew chief was on the intercom. "Guns on the attack."

"You see anything else?"

"Negative. I just put some rounds down in the trees hoping to keep Charlie's head down until we were clear."

"I'll bet it was just one guy," said Douglas. "One or two."

They continued the descent to the LZ. As the helicopters landed, men leaped from the cargo compartments, crouching in the grass, their weapons pointed outward.

"You're down and unloaded."

"Lead's on the go."

Williams said, "Not much of a combat assault with that one guy."

"Golden BB, my man," countered Douglas. "Golden BB."

"What in the hell is a golden BB?"

"I can't believe you haven't heard the term. It is the single shot fired at the flight that kills someone. A fluke shot that should have been wild and missed by a mile. You can just never tell."

Douglas keyed the mike. "You're off with ten."

"And we're through for the day," said Williams.

"I wouldn't count on that. These guys might not need us for a few hours, but there is plenty of time for another mission. Can't just be sitting around when there is a war on. Major Fox will find us something to do."

Corley walked over to where Gerber was standing. "Flight took some fire in-bound."

"So, I heard."

"Shouldn't we send someone out to take a look?"

"That would be up to the ground commander," said Gerber.

Corley smiled. "That would be me, at the moment."

"Wouldn't that be Philips? Or, if you want the guy on the ground, Jordan?"

"Philips will be coming in with the supplies at noon, I think," said Corley. "He's flying around in the C and C."

"Then he would be the ground mission commander and the senior officer here, other than you, me and Jordan. But, of course, one of the company commanders on security could certainly send out someone to look for the enemy. We just have to let everyone do his job and not micromanage the situation."

Almost before Gerber had finished talking, an RTO approached. "Major Gerber? Colonel Philips would like a word."

Gerber took the handset. "This is Golf Bravo Six."

"How about a patrol out to where the flight took fire?"

"We were just about to do that."

"We're circling in the general vicinity at three thousand feet."

Gerber grinned. The C and C was way out of small arms range. "Roger that. Patrol is on the way."

"You going?" asked Corley.

"Why not? Fetterman and I haven't been doing much to contribute here so we might as well go with the patrol."

Gerber spotted Jordan and waved him over. "Sergeant Major Fetterman and I would like to accompany the patrol, if there are no objections."

"You'll be taking charge?" asked Jordan.

"No. Just going along as observers. Looking out for anything that might prove to be of intelligence value. Something that might be overlooked by infantry soldiers who have other things on their minds."

"You're a major so if you want to go along…"

"And you're the senior company commander here. If you'd rather we didn't accompany the patrol, then say so."

Jordan looked at Gerber as if trying to make up his mind. "I can't see any harm in that. Sergeant Jacobs will be in charge of the patrol."

"It's his show," said Gerber, "unless he does something really stupid."

"He's been in-country for seven or eight months. He knows how to run a patrol."

"I'll meet with him," said Gerber.

"He's over there, sir. Tall guy with the ace of spades stuck on his helmet."

Gerber laughed. "Does he know that in some parts of Vietnam that would make him a target?"

"He knows. That's why he put it there."

Gerber walked over to Jacobs, who was standing with his back to him. "Sergeant Jacobs?"

The sergeant turned, saw the major's leaf on Gerber's collar, and said, "Yes, sir."

"Sergeant Major Fetterman and I will be accompanying the patrol. Captain Jordan doesn't mind us tagging along with you. You'll still be in charge. We'll just be there to observe."

Jacobs didn't look pleased with that. He glanced at the ground and then back up at Gerber. "I assume you've been on patrol before?"

"This is not my first tour, Sergeant. I've been on a patrol or two."

"Yes, sir."

"This isn't going to be a long one. Just weapons, ammo, and water if I might be so bold as to suggest that."

"Yes, sir. I know, sir. I don't need help doing my job."

Gerber sighed and said, "My apologies, Sergeant. Old habits die hard. When do you plan to move out?"

"Just as soon as I brief the patrol on what we're going to be doing. If the information I have is correct, we're going to be only a klick or two from here. Under that circling chopper."

"I'll ask Sergeant Major Fetterman to join us."

"Yes, sir."

Gerber walked back to Fetterman and said, "I do not believe I have thrilled the patrol leader."

"You have that capability."

"Let's do this. I'll hang back with the tail of the patrol, and you find a place near Jacobs."

As Gerber and Fetterman approached the patrol, Gerber noticed that each man had two canteens attached to his pistol belt. One man was armed with an M-60 machine gun and another had an M-79 grenade launcher. They all had additional belts of 7.62 ammo slung over their shoulders. Gerber wondered about all the firepower and thought, given the circumstances, it wasn't needed. But it was better to have it and not need it, than to need it and not have it.

Jacobs moved among the men, checking their equipment. When he was satisfied with all that he saw, he said, "We'll make our way to the point of jungle off to the right." He nodded in that direction but didn't point, telling Gerber that Jacobs had been around for a while. "We'll want to be well spread out as we cross the open ground and then close it up as we enter the trees. Nathan, you've got the point and Jeffords, you've got the rear. Any questions?"

There were none and Jacobs said, "Then let's go. Nathan, move out."

The patrol walked across the rise, and down toward the finger of jungle. Nathan, proving that he had been in Vietnam for several months as well, avoided the rice paddy dikes. Instead, he walked in the soft mud of the paddy itself, but avoided stepping on the young rice plants. It made it harder to maintain the pace, but it didn't annoy the farmers because he wasn't killing the rice.

The others followed him. They wound their way around a swampy area, sticking to the rice paddy. As they crossed one of the dikes, no more than eighteen inches high, Gerber saw a shallow depression and wondered if it was a booby trap. If it had been properly planted, he wouldn't have seen it. Had he been walking along on the dike, he would have stepped over it. He thought about marking it but knew the farmers all knew where it was.

They reached the tree line. The jungle wasn't as dense as it was up the in Two Corps. This was not triple canopy. The trees weren't as tall and the undergrowth not as thick. There was a trail that looked as if it was made by humans rather than animals, but Nathan avoided it as well. He was ten or fifteen meters to the left, following the path but staying away from it.

Glancing up, Gerber could see the orbiting command and control helicopter. They were nearing the point where Charlie had fired at the helicopter and as they did, there was a subtle, but real change in the patrol. When they had been in the open area, the men had had a more relaxed attitude, like taking a stroll through a park. There had been no signs of an ambush and nowhere for the enemy to hide. There had been nothing to suggest a mechanical ambush other than the depression that Gerber had seen. There had been no trip wires or dead vegetation that might conceal a punji stake trap. Just open rice paddies and swamp that didn't lend itself to any sort of a sneak attack.

Now, in the trees, the pace slowed and Gerber saw the men checking the area around them, searching for any sign of enemy action. They held their weapons at the ready, with their thumbs on the safety. It was now a professional patrol and no longer an afternoon stroll.

At the front, Nathan held up a ball fist, and everyone stopped moving. They crouched where they were, facing in opposite directions so that someone had eyes on the whole area. They were quiet, careful, and waiting.

Nathan looked back, pointed at Fetterman, and signaled him forward. Quietly, Fetterman moved up to the point. They were nearly under the C and C now and there was evidence that both rockets and machine guns had been emplaced there. Trees were blown in half. The ground was torn up by the miniguns on the helicopter gunships.

Gerber worked his way forward until he could see what Nathan had found. Three men lying on the ground, all dead and all dressed in the black pajamas that marked then as VC rather than NVA. One had half his head blown off. There was only a single weapon, and Gerber knew that if the gunships hadn't killed them all, the survivors would have taken the weapon with them.

Fetterman approached the closest body. He rolled it over. Just a young man who might have been VC or might not, given the single weapon.

Fetterman checked the pockets for wallet or papers, but found nothing of intelligence value on any of the bodies. Gerber was waiting for Nathan or Jacobs to signal their return to the camp when he heard something moving toward them. He crouched again, staring off into the trees and bushes when he caught movement. Without a word, he signaled Fetterman, who nodded his understanding.

Jacobs looked at the rest of the patrol, then pointed at the available cover. He set the patrol up, facing the movement while he stayed back, looking to the rear to make sure they weren't ambushed from that angle.

Gerber saw one man; he was carrying an old SKS semi-automatic rifle. It was chambered for the 7.62, but had a shorter cartridge than that used in the American weapons. Gerber slowly raised his rifle, got a clear sight picture, but didn't fire. He wanted to make sure they had all the enemy spotted before he alerted them.

Someone else fired first. When he did, Gerber pulled the trigger and the man dropped without a sound. Firing erupted all around him and Gerber saw more men fall. There had been no return fire from the enemy.

Gerber heard Jacobs on the radio, explaining they had run into a small VC unit and had annihilated it. He gave the handset back to the RTO and said, "We're to fall back."

"We should check the bodies first," said Gerber.

"And grab the weapons," said Fetterman. He held an AK-47 in one hand and his M-16 in the other.

Once the weapons were collected and the bodies checked, the patrol slipped back into the jungle, working their way back to the base.

Gerber was surprised at the progress that had been made to the base while he had been with the patrol. Several of the bunkers looked as if they had been completed. About four feet of the bunker had been dug into the ground, and another four feet were heavy sandbag walls. There was a firing port in front and a staggered entrance at the rear so that the back wasn't completely open. The L-shaped entrance provided some protection if the enemy penetrated the perimeter.

A small bulldozer was hard at work creating a berm around the perimeter of the camp. Others were piling sandbags on top of the berm, adding to its height and protection for the defenders. Gerber figured that the bulldozer had been brought in while he was out with the patrol. It was a nice touch.

There was also a water buffalo, a large canvas and plastic container erected on a tripod to hold drinking water. It wouldn't taste all that great, but there was enough of it to resupply each man throughout the day. With the rising temperature and humidity, heat stroke and dehydration were a real concern. Next to it was a stack of boxes that held C-rations. Lunch had arrived, even if it wasn't the greatest meal ever contemplated.

Corley was standing near the engineer's stake in the center of the camp. He watched as the engineers and the soldiers worked to finish off another of the bunkers. Gerber approached him. "Going according to plan?"

"Better. I think the grunts want to get out of here before dark."

"The fire control tower will be in the center?"

"Right where we are standing when it is brought in. That's not scheduled for another two hours."

Gerber chuckled and said, "I feel about as useless as it can get. You've got everything covered and the infantry commanders are taking care of security. Jacobs ran a top-notch patrol."

"How did that go?"

"I think we found the bodies of the VC who shot at the flight and we ran into a small patrolThey're all down."

"There going to be more of that?"

Gerber shook his head. "I don't think so. Our roving patrols might find someone, but they're out about a klick. Shouldn't affect us here."

"We should be ready by sixteen, seventeen hundred tonight. We can then fine tune this tomorrow. Let's go take a look at one of the bunkers."

The one that Gerber thought of as on the north wall had been completed and the engineers had moved on to another. Gerber and Corley entered and dropped down. The floor was made of wooden planks and there might have been PSP under the wood. There were four by fours in each corner, holding up the roof, which was made of reinforced PSP with two or three layers of sandbags on top.

It wasn't quite what Gerber expected. "I thought there was going to be wooden planks overhead."

"I thought PSP, sandbags and then the planks would offer more protection from mortars."

Gerber moved forward so that he could peer out of the firing port. It gave a good view of the open ground between the camp and the tree line that was five or six hundred meters away. That was a long way to run under heavy machine gun and small arms fire. He saw soldiers stringing concertina wire about twenty-five meters in front of the bunker, while others were planting new claymore mines.

"How many claymores are there?"

"We've got about a hundred and fifty, but we'll have to double that number tomorrow," said Corley. "I upped the number from the last plan you saw."

"Looks like we have goods field of fire."

"Anything you think we need to change, just point it out."

"There's nothing obvious. The guys stringing the concertina might want to use some tanglefoot, but I don't think the problem is Charlie trying to sneak in. There will be a rocket and mortar attack and they'll come swarming out of the trees with bugles blaring. There will be nothing subtle about the assault."

"You think we're safe?" asked Corley.

"Oh, hell no. Charlie is going to have to attack us. He can't allow us to put up a camp in his front yard. He'll throw a couple of battalions, maybe a regiment if he can get one together, to push us out."

"When?"

Gerber rubbed his chin. "I don't think it will be tonight. Too soon. Assembling the force will take him some time. Maybe tomorrow and certainly the day after. We can expect some mortar or rockets here tonight."

"Can we repel him?" asked Corley.

"Even if all the infantry remains here, which won't happen, I'm not sure we could stop a concentrated effort. But we have heavy artillery support from the base camps and fire support bases around here, and we'll have air support. Both fighters and helicopter and maybe a Super Spooky. We've got a lot of air power on call."

"I'm not looking forward to that," said Corley.

"Neither am I," said Gerber, "but it's why we're paid the big bucks."

CHAPTER 15

It had been dark for an hour when the first mortar round fell, erupting into a dense fountain of yellow-white sparks that was reminiscent of fireworks on the Fourth of July. Gerber heard the round detonate and although he didn't see it, he knew exactly what it was. He turned in the direction of the explosion. The round had landed between the first two rows of concertina wire and caused no damage. Gerber heard nothing to suggest that the shrapnel had come close to him or anywhere else for that matter.

He trotted to the nearest bunker, ears straining, but he didn't hear another round fired. He dropped in and asked the two men inside, "Anyone see where that came from?"

"No, sir. Just heard it hit."

"It didn't pass over the camp. I think it came from the jungle out in front of us here."

"We weren't really watching, sir," said the ranking man. "We didn't expect anything for another couple of hours. Our CO said that Charlie likes to attack about two in the morning when everyone is getting really tired."

"Well, he's right about that, but there is always the unexpected. Why don't you crank up that fifty and put some rounds into the trees out in front."

The man grinned. "Yes, sir."

Gerber plugged his ears as the man worked the bolt on the machine gun, loaded a live round and depressed the butterfly trigger. The weapon fired with the slow chugging of the heavy machine gun. Gerber looked out through the firing port and watched the tracers disappear into the trees. One of them hit something, spun upward and then burned out quickly.

The gunner moved the weapon around and fired another short burst with the same results. There was no return fire and Gerber figured that the enemy, after launching the single mortar round, had broken down the tube, picked up the base plate and run.

"Hold you fire," Gerber ordered. "Keep your eyes open and if you see the flash, engage immediately."

"Yes, sir."

Gerber climbed out of the bunker and saw both Corley and Fetterman running toward him. "You see the flash?" Fetterman asked.

"No. Just told the gunner to fire into the trees in front of us. Figured the round was fired from there but I doubt they hit anything."

"Maybe we should get up in the fire control tower."

"I was just on my way," said Gerber. "I told the guys in the bunker to fire if they saw the flash. It's more suppressive fire than pinpoint target shooting, but it might discourage Charlie."

As they walked to the fire control tower, Corley asked, "Can we expect more of that?"

"There might even be a probe of our defenses. Sort of a scouting mission to see if they can spot any weakness to exploit."

"Tonight?"

Fetterman took over. "I doubt it, Major. I don't think they can have assembled a force yet."

Once they were up in the sandbagged tower, Gerber unpacked the AN/PVS-2 Starlight Scope that was designed for use with the M-14, M-16 and the M-60 machine gun. It was a passive system that gathered the ambient light and seemed to magnify it so that the user would see a green landscape that was bright enough to pick out enemy soldiers if they were moving around outside the base. The problem was that it weighed about six pounds, but since Gerber was in the tower and not carrying it through the jungle, the weight made no real difference to him.

He slowly scanned the trees, looking for any sign of movement. It was difficult to make out much of anything in the strange green light of the Starlight Scope. Then he caught a bright flash of light. He slowly tracked back, saw it again, but couldn't identify it. There was something just inside the tree line that was metallic and reflecting light.

The patrols made during the day had failed to find any civilians in the area. They had all moved out or been drafted by the VC to join in the fight against the Saigon puppet government and their American, imperial masters. It didn't matter what the locals thought or what they believed, they were dragged off to fight for the VC and Uncle Ho up in Hanoi.

Gerber picked up the handheld radio which was the only communications between the tower and the main bunkers. A land line would be created in a day or two, but radios worked just fine for the moment. He said, "Bunker one, FTC."

"Go ahead, tower."

"Got something directly in front of you, just inside the tree line. Not sure what it is. Put a few rounds from Ma Deuce into the woods."

An instant later, there was a short burst from the .50-caliber machine gun. The tracers flashed out to the left of the target.

"Adjust to the right a degree or two."

This burst hit the right spot and Gerber, using the artillery term, said, "Fire for effect."

The gunner fired three more short bursts as Gerber watched from the tower. He said to Corley, "You see anything?"

"Other than our tracers, nothing."

Gerber said over the radio, "Cease fire."

Corley asked, "What'd you see?"

"Not sure. Just a bright flash in that area. It's gone now. Could have been Charlie moving something into position, but the fifty chased him away. Could have been a reflection that had nothing to do with Charlie. We can find out in the morning."

Gerber continued to scan the trees in front of them, but there was nothing going on. He handed the Starlight Scope to Fetterman. "Tell me what you see."

After a moment, Fetterman said, "Nothing of importance."

There was a distant crump and Gerber knew that another mortar had been fired. He turned his attention to the left, searching for any sign of the mortar tube. "Anyone see the flash?"

The rounds landed; this time closer to the bunker line but too far away to do any damage. Gerber thought they might have cut the concertina wire in one or two places, but that could be fixed in the morning.

Gerber just couldn't get excited about the mortars. They weren't coming close to him in the tower. The second round had landed farther away, which, for the moment, meant that he wasn't the target. It might be they were trying to hit the bunkers.

"Looks like a sixty millimeter," he said.

Fetterman nodded and said, "Two tubes, I think. Maybe just one, but probably two."

"That's what I thought," said Gerber. "You see the flash?"

"Might have been to our southwest, just a little closer to the border."

"They're not doing any damage," said Corley.

"That's not the point. They're just harassing us. Keeping us awake. Most of the soldiers have been in a mortar attack or two in the past. If the rounds even woke them, they're doing the same thing we are. Assessing where the rounds are landing, deciding if they were moving toward them or away, and if away, probably going back to sleep."

"Maybe we should send out a patrol," said Corley.

"Nah," said Gerber. "We would just be exposing our guys to an unnecessary risk. We'll wait for first light when the advantage shifts back to us."

"Counter mortar," said Fetterman.

Gerber thought for a moment and then said, "I don't like the risk there either. At worst, it's two, maybe three tubes and they're long gone by now, or they certainly will be before a helicopter gunship can get here."

"Just a thought," said Fetterman.

It was just after two when Gerber, using the Starlight Scope, spotted enemy soldiers coming out of the trees. He nudged Fetterman and handed him the Starlight. "To our left. At the trees."

"Got 'em."

"How many?"

"Fifteen, maybe eighteen. Not many."

"They're not moving in military formation. Too close together, and they're not using the terrain or the vegetation to disguise their movement."

"I think they're checking to see how alert we are. Seeing how close they can get before we open fire," said Fetterman.

"I'm going down to the bunker. We'll take them out when they get closer to the wire. Pop the claymores there and give them a surprise."

"You want me to stay here?"

Gerber nodded. "Keep your eyes open to make sure that this isn't a diversion. We don't want a company to hit the other side of the line."

Gerber climbed down from the tower and then jogged to the bunker. He dropped in and saw that one of the men was at the firing port, watching the enemy. "Where are the firing controls for the claymores?"

The man pointed to a board, to which the firing wires were attached. The mines could be detonated all at once, or fired in sequence, depending on what the situation demanded.

"Where's the first mine?"

"White post about two hundred meters directly in front."

"Fire them in sequence," Gerber ordered. "We'll replace them in the morning."

The soldier picked up the firing mechanisms and triggered them in rapid sequence. There was a series of bright flashes as the mines detonated, sending seven hundred deadly steel ball bearings at the enemy and shredding them.

Firing erupted from the bunkers, with both M-60 machine guns and the M-2 .50-caliber shooting into the trees. In seconds the firing died and there was no movement in the wire.

"That's got it," said Gerber.

"Body count, sir?"

"We'll check tomorrow morning, when we'll be in better shape to avoid any casualties on our side."

"Charlie might try to drag the bodies away."

"I don't care," said Gerber. "I'm not going to lose a man trying to count bodies. We'll check in the morning. But keep your eyes on that area and if you see anyone move, kill him."

"Yes, sir." The soldier was enthusiastic in his response because there was nothing ambiguous about the order.

Gerber climbed out of the rear of the bunker and walked back to the fire control tower. He climbed it rapidly, hugging the ladder in an attempt to obscure his shape in case there were any enemy snipers searching for a living target. No one shot at him.

As he climbed over the sandbags at the top of the tower, he asked, "What'd you see?"

"Watched about twenty VC attempt to get through the wire without making any noise," said Fetterman. "Then a series of flashes and all the enemy were down. Didn't see anyone try to get away. All were wounded if not killed. Should be interesting in the morning."

"It's been interesting already," said Gerber.

"They going to try anything else?" asked Corley.

"Maybe a few more mortar rounds or maybe some small arms fire. Nothing to really worry about. I don't think they'll try another probe of the wire. They'll want to know more about what we have set up."

They didn't hear the discharge, but both Gerber and Fetterman ducked as one round flew overhead.

"That was close," said Fetterman. He crouched on one knee and peered over the top of the sandbags. "And no, I didn't see the muzzle flash."

"They going to keep this up all night?" asked Corley.

"Probably," said Gerber. "They think it will disturb our sleep and make us careless the next day. A few rifle rounds fired at us isn't going to do the trick. Mortars might, but I think most of our guys are veterans. Unless something happens, they'll sleep through it."

"With one man in each bunker awake and watching, as we will be up here," said Fetterman. Then he thought about it and said, "You know, we all don't have to be awake."

"If you're sleepy, Tony, go crash in a bunker. I'll wake you at dawn."

"Then I bid you good night, Major."

Captain Harker had been awakened early by a call from the communications center. There was a flash message for the general. Although the standing orders were to wake the general for any flash messages addressed to him, Harker was the first call to ensure that the message required the general's immediate attention. Flash messages were the highest priority and required an immediate response. Jones had delegated that duty to Harker because, frankly, that was what aides were for and not all flash messages were as important as the senders believed them to be.

Harker was carrying the flash message in a leather folder. There was a top-secret cover sheet on the message, though that was concealed in the leather folder. He had read the message because he had a top-secret clearance and was authorized to review nearly everything sent to the general. Having read the message, he knew that there was no immediate response to be made. It was an informational flash message rather than one that needed attention.

He waited until zero six hundred and then drove to the general's quarters, knowing that the general would now be awake and eating his breakfast. He knocked on the door and an NCO who was charged with preparing the general's meals answered. Although there was no requirement for Harker to say anything, he told the sergeant, "I have a message for the general."

The sergeant stepped aside and asked, "Would you like some breakfast, sir?"

"Eggs, over easy, toast and orange juice," said Harker, "if that's not too much trouble?"

"No, sir. Coming right up."

From the other room Jones yelled, "That you Harker?"

"Yes, sir. Flash message."

"Well don't just stand there, bring it to me."

Harker walked in but didn't salute. The general was in a bathrobe with the remains of his breakfast on the table in front of him. He was reading the newspaper but put it aside.

Harker handed over the leather folder and watched as the general lifted the cover sheet and read the message. He frowned. "Rather cryptic, isn't it?"

Harker looked around and saw the sergeant standing at the stove, cracking the eggs into the skillet. Given that he worked in close proximity to the general, he was required to hold a top-secret clearance. If he wasn't cleared, they would have to chase him from the room every time something of a cryptic nature was discussed. Even so, Harker lowered his voice. "Base was established in less than twelve hours."

Jones closed the folder and set it aside. "Was there ever any question that it couldn't be done? We had the rehearsal that proved it. The only difference, that I can see, is that they did it in a combat environment in Vietnam, but they still had access to all the assets they needed."

Harker sat down at the table and the sergeant set a plate of eggs in front of him. Harker picked up his fork but before he took a bite, the telephone rang. He got up and answered it.

"General Jones' quarters. Captain Harker speaking. How may I help you?"

He listened and then hung up. "Another flash message."

"Finish your breakfast. We can pick it up on the way in."

"Yes, sir."

When Harker finished eating, they left the general's residence and drove to the communications center. While the general waited in the car, Harker went in, signed for the message, and came back out. He handed the document, with the top-secret cover sheet, to Jones, and started the car.

"They're reporting they were attacked."

"When?" asked Harker.

Jones looked at his watch and realized that was useless, since the attack happened at night. "Started about two in the morning. Just a few mortars. Nothing substantial."

"I didn't expect anything so quick, sir."

"When we get to the office, get the intel officer in for his assessment."

"Yes, sir. Just intel?"

"For now. That information must be hours old. I don't think Corley and Gerber have access to a commo center. Has to go through a couple of layers of bureaucrats to get to us."

"They in trouble?"

"Not yet. A few mortar rounds is not much of an attack. A little early, but nothing to worry about."

As they entered the building, they saw Sergeant Major George. He said, "We have some pastries and Colonel Blum is waiting."

"Forget the pastries." Jones turned and saw Blum standing there. Blum was a slight man who had served in a variety of support positions, had only commanded a company early in his career and then found himself on what he thought of as the "staff officer" track. He was too good at that sort of thing to be wasted doing anything else. It was an unfortunate situation. Good staff officers were hard to find, but it slowed them down. The emphasis was always on command and those were favored over the staff officer.

Jones waved at him and said, "Come into my office, Colonel."

As he sat down behind his desk, Jones asked, "What can I do for you?"

Still standing, Blum said, "This is a little difficult. I don't want to be a snitch, but I have to report that Colonel Larson has been in communication with a reporter. I believe he is leaking classified information to the man."

Jones looked up at Blum. "What makes you think that?"

"This is the difficult part, General. I overheard a conversation in the club last night. Larson was on the telephone talking to someone about a mission run out of this office concerning some sort of operation in Vietnam."

Jones sat quietly for a moment and then said, "Have a seat, Colonel, and tell me what you know. Consider the fact that, if you are wrong, you could potentially damage a fellow officer's career and, if you are wrong, you're going to have some problems with your own."

Blum dropped into one of the chairs. "I didn't mean to listen, but Larson was a bit agitated."

When he finished, Jones raised his voice and said, "Harker, get in here. We might have a problem."

Although he wanted to accompany the patrol out to where the enemy bodies lay, Gerber knew that he had to stay inside the compound. There was too much to do and the patrol, while it would always be in sight of the camp, would be outside the perimeter.

"I can go with them, Major," Fetterman volunteered.

"I was going to say, make the count, look for anything of intelligence value and pick up the weapons, but you already know to do that."

"And we might even follow the blood trails."

"No, Tony. Don't do that. I think we need to restrict everyone to the base today, or at least within sight of the base. I don't want any engagements until we have the fine details completed here and are ready to repel any attack."

Gerber accompanied the patrol to the gate. He watched as they left the compound and worked their way through the concertina wire, toward the bodies. He thought about going up to the tower where he'd have a better view but decided to stay where he was.

Corley approached and asked, "What should I do about the wire?"

"Wait till Fetterman gets back. If there are no problems, then send out the teams to restring the wire. Use as much tanglefoot as you have. I don't think we're going to do much patrolling in the next several days."

"Shouldn't we be searching for Charlie?"

Gerber laughed. "Why? Charlie knows we're here now and he's annoyed. He'll come to us. I don't think we should expose our guys when we don't need to. We just hunker down here and let him make the move."

"I thought the best defense was a good offense?"

"In most cases I would agree. But the other side of that coin is that the attackers must have a three to one advantage for success, and you have to remember we control the air. We can have gunships here in minutes and fighters not long after that. Changes the odds in our favor. It would take a couple of regiments to push us out or overrun us and Charlie doesn't have the manpower to do it."

"You're awfully confident," said Corley.

"I've been here before and I understand asymmetrical warfare. Normally, we'd be chasing the enemy. We don't have to do that. If he sends a large force against us and we defeat it, then he is badly crippled. The best strategic move is for us to wait right here."

"I don't mean to be pessimistic," said Corley, "but if he overruns us…"

"We'll cross that bridge when we come to it." Gerber studied Corley's face for a moment and then said, "But we're not going to be overrun. That just doesn't happen."

"I've heard about Lang Vei," said Corley.

"That is the only example, and it was only because they didn't get the promised relief and it was the NVA who had tanks. Had the LAW rockets worked as advertised, it would not have happened."

"We don't have any LAWs."

"No. But we're going to have ninety-millimeter recoilless rifles and we have the fifties with armor-piecing rounds. Charlie isn't going to have tanks, and if he does, we have dedicated air support. We won't be overrun."

Gerber watched as Fetterman and the patrol reached the enemy bodies. A moment later he heard the muffed pop of a mortar. Fetterman hit the ground while those around him stood an instant longer. The round hit far short of them and to the right.

Gerber sprinted for the fire control tower and scrambled up the ladder. A sergeant he didn't recognize was up there. Gerber asked, "You see where that came from?"

"No, sir."

Gerber wasn't surprised. The flash would be difficult to see in the daylight and if the crew had done anything to conceal it, it might be impossible. Gerber picked up one of the pairs of binoculars and scanned the tree line for any hint of enemy activity.

He glanced down and saw that Fetterman and the soldiers with him were heading back to the camp. They were carrying extra weapons, which they had recovered from the dead.

Gerber turned to the sergeant. "Keep scanning the trees and if you see anything suspicious, get some fire put on it. Fifty caliber at least."

"Yes, sir."

He climbed back down the ladder, and met Fetterman as he came back in. "What'd you see, Tony?"

"I counted fifteen dead and saw a blood trail or two. I think we got most of them because there were still weapons left. Interesting thing was that they weren't carrying any spare magazines for the Aks, but most of the weapons were those old SKSs. These were not front-line troops."

"What are you suggesting?"

"I think it was a test of our capabilities. Wanted to see how we would react."

"So, you're telling me that they were sacrificed to gain a bit of intelligence about us?"

"Yes, sir. That's exactly what I'm saying ... and, I'll say that it was meant to keep us busy while they gathered a force to attack us. I didn't have a chance to look for documents, but I doubt if they'd have any. No sign of rank, but one guy had a pistol, which I think made him the leader. I don't know if he was an officer or a senior NCO. The rest of them didn't look like they were NVA. Just VC and not very well trained."

There was a sudden burst of firing. Some of the soldiers around them dropped to the ground, but Gerber recognized it as outgoing rather than incoming.

"So, what's our next move?" Fetterman asked.

"I'm going to see if we can't get a recon flight out to look for that mortar tube."

"You think it's still there?"

"No. I think they've broken it down and gone into hiding, but an aircraft overhead will keep them in hiding, which is the next best thing for us."

The flight was shut down near the tent city and parallel to the runway. They were far enough from the tents that their rotor wash wouldn't knock down any of the tents or throw up clouds of dust and debris to make things miserable for the waiting grunts.

Douglas, as he did almost every morning after the first flight or the movement of the aircraft to their standby positions, climbed into the back of the Huey and lay down. It seemed that he had trouble sleeping when he was off duty and that wake up always came long before he was ready, but once the first lift or mission was out of the way and they were back on standby, he could sleep. It never occurred to him that these naps might be the reason he couldn't sleep at night. He just knew that he was tired in the morning.

Flight Lead, Warrant Officer Damon Matthews, walked back to the trail aircraft. Matthews was twenty-one and had only been one of the flight leads for a month, but he was comfortable in the role. He looked into the cargo compartment and saw Douglas asleep on the troop seat.

"Douglas, you have a mission."

He waited, and when Douglas didn't respond, he grabbed the toe of his boot and shook it. "You have a mission."

Douglas opened his eyes and said, "I heard you the first time."

"Then why didn't you say anything?"

"I was hoping you'd give up and assign it to someone else."

"You're trail. You get the follow-on missions. You need to fly a recon over the camp."

"Isn't that something for the guns to do?"

"They requested a slick. I'm thinking they're attempting to downplay the belligerent role."

"That makes no sense," said Douglas, sitting up. He rubbed his eyes, which felt as if they were filled with sand.

"Guns will be orbiting somewhere to the east, out of sight. They can be on target in a minute or two, if needed. You'll need to contact the camp at six four decimal five when you are about five minutes out. He'll give you precise instructions. Monitor the Company Uniform."

Douglas climbed out of the cargo compartment and opened the door on his side of the aircraft. He said, simply, "Got it. See you."

Douglas watched as Hampton climbed in and strapped himself into the co-pilot seat. He then looked around, yelled, "Clear," out the window and pulled the trigger on the collective. There was a whine as the turbine began to wind up and the rotor blades began to slowly rotate, picking up speed as the noise grew to a roar. As he slowly rolled on the throttle, he saw both the crew chief and the door gunner running toward the aircraft. Over the intercom, he said to Hampton, "Knew this would get their attention."

Once the crew chief and the door gunner were strapped in and ready to go, Douglas pulled up on the collective, lifting the chopper to a three-foot hover. He requested permission from the tower for takeoff and when cleared, pushed the cyclic forward as he pulled in more pitch. He climbed out over the base camp defenses and turned to the south.

CHAPTER 16

Brigadier General Jones was smoking a cigar and looking out the window. He thought it would be nice to have a view of the beach rather than the wall of another building, but then, beyond that, he could see a hint of the ocean. It was certainly better than the view from many of the other offices, and he had taken this one because it was twice as large as most of them. The privilege of rank and long service, which those at the other end of the command chain never understood. He had been at that other end once, and understood the resentment. He sometimes wondered if he should attempt to explain it to them, but he knew that they just wouldn't get it until they had been around long enough to have earned some of the same privileges that he now enjoyed.

Just as Jones set his cigar down in the ashtray, Harker tapped on the open door. "Latest flash message, General."

Jones waved him in and held out a hand. Harker gave him the message. Jones lifted the top-secret cover sheet and read it over. "You read this?" he asked.

"No, sir."

"Says that there was a probe last night. Reliable report of fifteen dead, a couple of blood trails and several weapons captured. They mention a single casualty on our side. Minor shrapnel wound."

"Probably going to be more tonight," said Harker, and then thought about it. "Or maybe about now, given the time difference."

Jones changed the subject. "Do you have eyes on Colonel Larson?"

"I believe he's in his office now that his leave has been cancelled."

"Have him join me."

"Yes, sir." Harker turned and left the office.

Jones picked up the cigar, took a puff and blew out smoke rings. It was to be the last relaxing thing he did for the next hour.

Larson knocked on the door and Jones waved him in. Larson stopped three feet in front of Jones' desk, saluted, and said, "Colonel Larson reporting as ordered."

"Take a seat, Colonel."

"Yes, sir."

"Let's have a bit of a chat. I had suggested that you not speak with members of the press about our work in Vietnam. You remember that?"

"Yes, sir. I think you mentioned one man in particular."

"I also suggested that you forget about Major Gerber and Sergeant Major Fetterman. Their activities on their last tour in Vietnam were of no concern to us and certainly no concern to you. You do remember that?"

"Yes, sir."

"Then why have I received a telephone call from the commandant at the Special Warfare School wondering why we are interested in those two Green Berets?"

Larson sat quietly for a moment. Finally, he said, "I believe that they were involved in a war crime and I saw it as my duty — our duty — to ensure that the laws of land warfare and Army regulations had not been violated by them."

"Maybe I didn't make myself clear before, Colonel. It is not our duty to investigate alleged war crimes when we do not have the jurisdiction to do so and when there is no evidence that a war crime has been committed. That was investigated at the time by competent authority in Vietnam and it was found that the operation that moved across the border was not American-led and that there was approval from both the Vietnamese and the Cambodian governments for that operation. I do not understand your obsession here."

"We have an obligation to follow the rules of land warfare, General —"

Jones interrupted him. "I do not need a lecture from you on the rules of land warfare. But here's the question for you. Did it ever pop into your head that I had checked all this out before bringing in Gerber and Fetterman?"

That surprised Larson. He started to speak, stopped, and then said, "Why didn't you mention this?"

"Because I am not obligated to explain my decisions to you. I understand that we, as the American Army, should hold ourselves to a higher standard. We are not supposed to violate the rules of land warfare. We are supposed to treat our prisoners of war with humanity. We find ourselves caught in asymmetrical warfare and that changes the rules slightly, but we do our best to adhere to them."

"I was just trying to ensure that we were," said Larson.

"Bullshit."

"Sir?"

"You heard me. You continued your contact with that reporter in violation of the lawful order that I gave you."

"General, I tried to break it off with him."

"Too little, too late. I think it's time for you to find yourself another career path. That is all."

"Sir, if I might explain."

"What could you possibly say that would alter the situation? The call from the commandant said that you contacted his organization just hours ago. After we'd had our little chat.

After Gerber and Fetterman had returned to their duty stations in Vietnam. After no one but you believed there was any sort of crime committed."

Larson's mouth hung open for a moment, then slowly closed. "Am I dismissed?"

"You may clean out your office in the next hour or so. I'll arrange for your transfer to another assignment, somewhere on the mainland where I won't run into you by accident."

Larson stood and turned to leave. He hesitated at the door, as if there was something else to be said, but thought better of it. He then continued out, toward his own office.

Jones raised his voice. "Harker. Get me the G-1 on post. I'll have a word with him, now."

"Yes, sir. What about the reporter?"

"He has no business on post. Have the MPs stop him at the gate and turn him around if he tries to enter. We are not obligated to allow unauthorized personnel on post, even if they hold press credentials."

"That could cause a problem, sir."

"I'll handle it," said Jones. He picked up the cigar and puffed on it, creating a cloud of blue smoke.

"Yes, sir," said Harker.

As they approached the camp, Douglas contacted them on the designated frequency to say that he was about five minutes out.

"Land on the north side of the camp. We'll throw smoke."

Over the intercom Hampton said, "I see red."

Douglas, over the radio, said, "I have the red smoke in sight." He lowered the collective and began the descent, aiming to put the nose right over the red smoke grenade.

Douglas flared out and set the aircraft down. As the skids hit the ground, four men, all carrying M-16s, hurried to the waiting chopper. They had barely climbed aboard when the aircraft took off again, climbing out through the billowing red smoke.

Over the intercom the crew chief said, "They want to circle to the south side of the camp, over the jungle there. They said that there was a mortar crew in there."

Douglas leveled off at fifteen hundred feet and turned to the south. He flew over the jungle heading to the west, toward Cambodia. He then reversed course, slowing to sixty knots, watching the ground below him.

From the rear of the aircraft, Gerber watched as they gained altitude. Looking down from the cargo door, he noticed that the open ground leading to the jungle showed that someone had been moving through it. He leaned close to Fetterman to shout over the roar of the Huey's engine, the pop of the rotors and the wind through the cargo compartment doors. "See the trails?"

"Looks like a platoon?"

"Maybe less," said Gerber. "Heading toward the middle of the jungle." He looked around at the door gunner. "Can you have the pilots fly more to the south, and then turn back to the east?"

Although he didn't hear the request repeated by the door gunner, the helicopter banked around and then flew directly over a small clearing. He saw what looked like evidence that a mortar had been set up there.

Out the other side of the helicopter, Gerber saw movement in the trees. A couple of men wearing black, though neither appeared to have any weapons. But they stared up at the helicopter. Gerber knew that the farmers and the civilians rarely looked up. They were afraid of drawing fire, but the young men, the VC or the NVA, stared defiantly at the aircraft.

Gerber moved around and tapped the co-pilot on the shoulder. He started to shout something when the pilot pushed his helmet microphone around to pick up this voice. Gerber said, "Can you fly back to the west, to near the border?"

"We can't get too close," Hampton shouted in response.

"We need to see if we can spot an infiltration route from Cambodia."

Hampton looked at Douglas, who said over the headset, "Tell him we'll get as close as we can, but there are heavy anti-aircraft emplacements all along the border."

Hampton relayed the message and Gerber nodded. "Get as close as you can. We just need to get a look at that area."

As Douglas banked the aircraft, Gerber moved back to Fetterman. "We need the grid coordinates."

"I wish we'd had time to register the artillery," said Fetterman. "Using the grid coordinates is a little sloppy."

Gerber marked his map where he thought the clearing was located. There were no landmarks to make it easy and he had to estimate the distance from the camp. If that was the launching point of the mortar rounds, then he knew the maximum range of the 60mm mortar was just over two miles and that one had been fired much closer. He marked the approximate location on his map. He and Fetterman could compare notes later.

The jungle thickened as they flew closer to the border. Gerber knew that the jungle provided cover as the enemy crossed the border. Once in Vietnam, then they could disperse as they reinforced the military units and resupplied them.

There was nothing obvious below them. There were a few hints of trails, but that was meaningless. Farmers and animals used the trails as well as the enemy. Through the tops of the trees, Gerber saw the sparkling of a spring. The flashes of sunlight almost looked like the muzzle flashes of rifle fire. He knew that no one was shooting at them.

The pilots changed course, turned to the north, giving Gerber a better view of the terrain back toward Cambodia. But there was nothing that he could see that suggested enemy activity. He knew that the enemy was down there, somewhere, but they were well hidden. He wished he could get a handle on the strength of the enemy units. That advantage went to the NVA.

They made a hundred-and-eighty-degree turn, now flying south. Fetterman had the view to Cambodia and Gerber was looking back, into Vietnam. But it was just more jungle and then open fields of rice paddies and swamp. There was nothing down there that looked out of place.

Finally, Gerber signaled to the crew chief and yelled, "Let's head on back."

The crew chief relayed the message and the pilots turned to the northeast. They flew over that finger of jungle and then turned again, toward the camp. They touched down a few moments later in about the same place. Gerber unbuckled his seat belt, jumped out of the cargo compartment and then stepped up on the skid so that he was looking into the cockpit. "Thanks for the lift."

Douglas nodded and yelled back, "Glad to do it."

As soon as Fetterman and Gerber had stepped back, away for the helicopter, it lifted and began to climb out. As the sound faded, Gerber said to Fetterman, "You get anything interesting?"

"Just some trails and that small open area. Looked natural but I wonder if someone didn't cut back a few of the trees."

"They would have had to do that recently because there would be no reason for it until we arrived."

"I have it marked," said Fetterman. "Maybe we can get the artillery to drop a few rounds there."

"It's a little close to us," said Gerber. "I think I'd rather wait until we have a reason to do it. We don't want to give away too much."

"You think they'll hit us tonight?"

"Your guess is as good as mine, Tony, but it'll probably be a recon in force tonight with the main thrust tomorrow."

"Yeah, that's kind of what I thought."

Gerber, Fetterman, Corley and Captain Jordan were in what was now considered the command bunker. It looked out over the open field, toward the jungle that would provide the best cover for the attacking force. The enemy would still have to cross about five hundred meters of open ground and then get though the six strands of razor-sharp concertina wire that now circled the base. A disciplined force, with the right equipment, would be able to penetrate the wire with relative ease, but it would slow them down.

The bunker contained the main radios, had communications with the other bunkers, and two M-60 machine guns at the firing port with two M-2 .50-caliber guns, one on each side of the bunker. It also had direct communication with the fire control tower. It was the only bunker connected to the tactical generator, other than the bunker used as the field kitchen. No meals had been prepared there. Food was either flown in, or the soldiers ate C-rations. Not exactly gourmet meals, but some of the C-rations were quite good. The problem was the ham and lima beans. No one wanted those.

Corley led off the meeting by saying, "I think we're as prepared as we can be for tonight. The concertina is all strung. We've put out around three hundred claymores. Each of the

M-2s is backed up by two M-60s. Radio communication and antenna have all been checked and we have good commo with the surrounding fire support bases, the aviation units on standby at Tay Ninh and the fighters in Saigon."

"Are we set for a half alert tonight?" asked Gerber.

"Meaning that half the soldiers are awake at all times?"

"Yes. I recommend four-hour shifts, starting at eight tonight."

"We can do that."

Gerber started to say something, stopped, and cocked his head to the side. "Incoming," he said calmly.

Corley dropped to the floor but none of the others moved.

"Just a mortar round," Gerber said. "Shouldn't penetrate the bunker if it hits us."

There was a detonation. Fetterman chuckled, "You know, I thought about dropping to the floor, but it seemed too dirty."

Gerber got on the radio. "Anyone see where that came from?"

"The jungle. Saw the flash."

"Who is this and where are you?"

"Jepson. Southside of the camp, well southeast side."

"If you saw the flash, you should engage."

There was a moment of silence and then Gerber heard the slow chugging of a fifty, followed by both M-60 machine guns and M-16 personal weapons firing.

"That a good idea, Major?"

Gerber looked at Jordan. "We have plenty of ammunition and I know of no civilians in that area. The area is deserted. Pass the word that any evidence of enemy activity is to be engaged immediately. I don't want the men afraid to fire their weapons because one of us may get angry about it."

"Of course," said Fetterman, "they should maintain some semblance of fire discipline as well."

The firing slowly tapered. "I guess they ran out of targets," said Gerber.

"Or a competent NCO told them to cease fire."

"Is there anything else that we should be doing now?" asked Corley.

"I'm going to the fire control tower," said Gerber. "That's the best place for watching our perimeter and about the only thing I can think of at the moment."

"Major," said Fetterman, "isn't there something else to be said?"

"Oh, yes. Pass the word that we should go to full alert about two. Charlie likes to attack about that time. Soldiers are at a low point. Don't know if it has something to do with blood sugar or just the biorhythms of the men, but we're at a low ebb about that time. If we're all awake, then he's in for a surprise."

Gerber sat in the fire control tower with the Starlight Scope to his eye. He nudged Fetterman. "Tony, we've got company."

Fetterman, who had been half asleep because Gerber was wide awake, asked, "How many?"

"Platoon. Maybe two. Moving slowly and coming out of the trees. They're bent low as if that will keep us from seeing them."

"What are we going to do?"

"I'm going to make a full sweep around the camp to make sure that no one else is sneaking up on us. Then, using my trusty rifle, I'm going to engage the enemy when he's about two hundred meters away."

Fetterman was now crouched behind the short wall that protected them. "I would have thought that they'd hit us with a mortar barrage before sending in the ground forces."

"This isn't the full-scale assault. That'll come tomorrow sometime."

At that moment, one of the M-60 crews opened fire. Gerber watched the red tracers flash across the open ground. One of them hit something solid and bounced up, spinning away. Gerber raised his rifle, tried to spot a target, and opened fire.

From the edge of the jungle there was a sudden sparkling as the enemy returned fire. They were shooting over the heads of the NVA who had nearly reached the outer ring of concertina. They ducked down, hugging the ground, now caught in a crossfire from their own soldiers and those in the base.

"Claymores should take out those guys in the open," said Fetterman.

"They're not a threat yet."

And then mortar rounds began to rain down. Gerber saw the flash from one of the tubes, but it was deep in the jungle and there was too much foliage in the way. He needed an indirect fire weapon. He needed his own mortars, but they hadn't gotten the pits dug yet and they hadn't been supplied with them.

"Tony, can you get some arty down on the mortars?"

"I didn't see the flash." But as he said it, there was another salvo and Fetterman spotted the flash. He picked up the radio handset and then looked at the frequency. He changed it and said, "Tay Ninh arty I have a fire mission, over."

"Say coordinates."

Fetterman provided them and waited. Then he heard, over the radio, "Shot, over."

He replied, "Shot out."

He watched the jungle where he thought the round should land. He heard the artillery shell pass overhead and a moment later saw the flash of the smoke round. There was a huge fountain of white-hot metal that vanished quickly.

"Add two hundred, right one fifty." Fetterman gave directions where he believed the mortar tubes had been.

"Shot, over."

"Shot, out."

Fetterman then said, "Add fifty. Right fifty. Fire for effect."

A moment later, he heard, "Shot, over."

"Shot, out."

The jungle near the suspected location of the enemy mortars erupted in a series of explosions. Fetterman used the Starlight Scope, but it did little to resolve the situation. He needed to see through the trees and the Starlight Scope did not have that capability.

There was another series of low flashes on the ground as the claymores were fired. The detonation hurled a wall of steel ball bearings at the enemy, cutting down everything in its path to a hundred meters. Firing from the bunkers increased, the ruby tracers bouncing over the ground or suddenly climbing until they burned out.

The sound of individual weapons being fired became a roar as everyone on the southside of the camp opened up. It was machine guns and M-16s against AK-47s and SKSs. There were detonations from the M-79 grenade launchers, and more artillery dropping on the jungle.

Over the radio, Fetterman said, "Adjust fire. Left one fifty, add one hundred."

"Shot, over."

"Shot, out."

There was a Willy Pete detonation as the smoke round dropped into the jungle. It was near to the base, and Fetterman advised, "You're dangerously close. Fire for effect."

As more artillery rounds fell, firing from the jungle began to taper off. It was clear that the enemy was retreating. It was just a probe, strong probe, but not an all-out assault. The enemy had learned that the base was better defended than they thought.

Over the radio, Fetterman heard, "Last rounds on the way. Tubes clear." That told him that the artillery has fired the last volley, unless he requested more.

Gerber, who now held the Starlight Scope, scanned the jungle. "I think that's it. I don't see anyone firing in the tree line."

Fetterman, binoculars to his eyes, concurred. He couldn't see much, other than the fires that had been started by the artillery. He turned his attention to the ground around the camp. There was no movement in the wire. The bodies of the attackers dotted the ground.

"Not much of a push," said Fetterman.

"They didn't send much of a force and it didn't get very close," said Gerber. "If you put the artillery in the right spot, then they lost some of their mortars."

"Guess we'll know more in the morning."

Gerber grinned. "You should have called for some illumination."

"Didn't really need it."

"No, I guess we didn't."

The following morning they checked for damage, which was light. One corner of a bunker had collapsed, but no one inside had been injured. There were no casualties at the camp. No one had been hit by shrapnel or by bullets. One man had sand kicked into his eyes by a bullet striking a sandbag near him, but the medic washed it out with water and told him to protect his eyes from the sun.

Gerber, Fetterman, Corley and Jordan met in the command bunker. They were sitting in lawn chairs around a makeshift table. There were lights from a light kit, that is, a long bar that held four lights and was attached to the roof. It was powered by a 10kw tactical generator that was in its own revetment, but hadn't sustained any damage during the night. The only problem was that it was noisy.

Gerber looked at the other men. "I think the big push is going to come tonight," he said. "Their little assault last night told them we are stronger than they thought. They won't want us to get any stronger than we are now before they launch the full-scale attack."

"What do you have in mind, sir?" Jordan asked.

"First, we need to set some mechanical ambushes. They haven't run into anything like that yet and it might slow them down. Just inside the trees, near where they grouped before. Sergeant Major Fetterman can be of assistance there."

He waited for Jordan to respond and when he nodded, Gerber said, "Second, we need to search the bodies, repair the damage to the concertina, and collect the weapons. One platoon should do it and they can be covered from the bunker line. We'll need to make sure that they know where their rounds will go if they have to shoot and they miss. We don't want any friendly fire casualties."

Gerber looked at Corley. "We'll want to strengthen the bunker line. Add another layer of sandbags to the top."

"According to the best estimates, two layers of sandbags should be sufficient to stop a sixty-millimeter mortar," said

Corley. "We need more for the eighty-twos. The beams and roofing structure is of sufficient strength to hold that third layer and we must remember that the mortar round, when it detonates, basically blows up rather than down. Given the structure of the bunkers, a single round won't be strong enough to punch through unless they hit the same place two or three times."

"We need to reinforce the berm and sandbag walls on top of it," said Fetterman. "That'll protect our guys and make it difficult for the enemy to get over it."

Corley nodded. "We could string concertina near the top. Isn't much of a barrier, but it might slow them down if they get that close."

"I'm thinking of bringing in the QRF," said Gerber. "Give us another company which Charlie might not be expecting. Have them land about sundown so that they're well rested. Gives our guys a little rest before things pop tonight."

"Chow?" asked Jordan.

"I know what you're thinking, Captain, but we're better off with C-rats tonight. If nothing happens, maybe we can get some hot food for tomorrow, but tonight we need to concentrate on the defense."

"Soldiers won't be happy," said Jordan.

"I suppose not, but when are they, really, unless they're somewhere other than here. I want everyone concentrating on defense tonight."

"Listening posts?" asked Fetterman.

"I don't know what they'll add to the defense. We know the enemy is out there and coming here."

"How about on the north side of the camp, Major. If we have listening posts out there, we can put the lion's share of the defenders on the south side. If there is movement in the north, we'll know about it."

"Good thought, Tony. Let's do that. Make sure the men know the score and that they're in the best locations to listen but not engage."

"Anything else?" Gerber asked.

When no one spoke, he said, "Then let's get at it."

CHAPTER 17

Gerber stood in the fire control tower, the Starlight Scope to his eyes, and grinned broadly. "It's too quiet out there. I don't like it," he said, in the finest tradition of nearly every western and war movie he had ever seen.

Fetterman shot him a glance. "You have got to be kidding me."

"Somebody had to say it."

"It's only a little after twenty-three hundred. Shouldn't be any activity for another two or three hours."

Gerber handed the Starlight Scope to Fetterman. "There is movement to the left. Just inside the tree line."

Fetterman nodded. "I see them. Looks like a platoon. Should we engage?"

"I thought we'd let them bunch up a little more. Then call artillery down on them. I've alerted the gun teams about the buildup. They're ready to launch on my request. They could be here in ten minutes or so."

"What about the fast movers?"

"On standby at Tan Son Nhut. They're only twenty minutes away. And we have one of the Puff gunships. All standing by for us."

Fetterman handed the Starlight back to Gerber. "I'll go down to the command bunker. I'll be of more use there."

"Well, I'd tell you good luck, but this isn't going to be a last stand. They have no clue what they're facing."

As Fetterman climbed down, Gerber heard the first sounds of the mortars firing. He looked over the edge, toward Fetterman, and said, "Incoming."

"Yes, sir. Heard it."

Gerber watched him drop to the ground and jog off toward the command bunker as the first of the mortar rounds hit. They were far short. Gerber scanned the trees, heard more firing and thought that he saw the flash. They had put the mortars in almost the same location they had used the night before even after the artillery had fallen close to them. It was that clearing that he and Fetterman had found during the helicopter recon.

Gerber got on the radio. "Tay Ninh arty, I have a fire mission."

He repeated the coordinates Fetterman had given them the night before. Once the marking round had fallen, Gerber said, "On target. Fire for effect."

As the artillery began to fall, another barrage of mortar rounds hit the camp. These came from a different location and were on target. They landed on the bunkers and in the center of the camp. Gerber heard the shrapnel striking the installation, sounding almost like a hailstorm. He crouched down behind the sandbags on the tower.

More firing erupted from the bunkers. But it was poorly aimed and the trees protected the enemy mortar crews. Gerber keyed the mic again and said, "Tay Ninh arty. You need to drop fifty and right five hundred."

There was a single Willy Pete round that marked the area targeted by Tay Ninh arty. Gerber said, "Right one hundred and fire for effect."

More heavy artillery exploded at the edge of the trees a little more than a mile from the camp. But it didn't stop the enemy crews from pumping rounds through their tubes. It looked at one point as if they were attempting to blast a path through the wire for their assault teams.

The air was filled with shouts and bugles and whistles that added to the din. The enemy rushed from the trees, running for the paths that their mortars had attempted to open in the concertina. Gerber reached for the landline to tell Fetterman in the command bunker to open fire, but saw that wasn't necessary. The machine guns were hammering away.

The whole area to the south of the base looked as if it had burst into flame. The muzzle flashes of the machine guns reaching out three, four, ten feet. Ruby-colored tracers flashed through the night, answered by the emerald tracers of the enemy soldiers. It looked almost festive.

There was a series of detonations and the assault broke. Fetterman had triggered the first line of claymores. As the the enemy ran for the safety of the trees, they ran into one of the mechanical ambushes. They hit the trip wires and the claymores, hidden under the bushes and next to the trees, which fired, but not in any sequence. That confused the NVA soldiers, who turned again, this time running along the trees rather than at the base. It was no longer an assault but a search for cover.

Tay Ninh arty had silenced the enemy mortar teams. For the moment, nothing fell on the base. A few fires ignited by the explosions quickly faded for the lack of fuel. There just wasn't much in the base to burn.

Over the radio, Gerber heard, "Last rounds on the way. Tubes clear, over."

Gerber said, "Understand tubes clear. Stand by, out."

On the landline, he asked Fetterman, "How goes it down there?"

"They didn't penetrate the first barrier. Claymores stopped them."

Gerber wanted to say that they'd be back because the first assault had been turned too easily, but it was just another movie cliché. Fetterman knew as well as he did what the enemy would do.

And then more mortars began to hit the base. But these weren't 60mm. These were large, 82mm mortars, coming from another area. The first rounds detonated in the center of the base, destroying the small bulldozer that had not yet been airlifted out, riddling two of the water buffaloes that held most of the base's drinking water, and destroying the tactical generator, which cut down on the noise but made communications that much more difficult.

Fetterman had never liked mortar attacks but thought of them as somewhat harmless. He just didn't respect them, especially the 60mm mortars. True, he could be killed just as dead by the shrapnel, but he had stood in other camps and watched as the mortar rounds dropped, walking toward him. If they got too close, he might kneel or take cover behind a sandbag wall, but he watched and listened and felt safe.

Now there was a new wrinkle to this attack. There was the sudden flat bang of a 122mm rocket. These couldn't be precisely aimed, other than in the general direction of the base. They were just as likely to fly over the camp, landing harmlessly, as they were to hit inside the perimeter, doing damage. The general practice was to aim at the center of the target area, hoping to hit something vital. They were more destructive and, depending on where it hit, could destroy a bunker, killing the occupants. These rockets were dangerous because of their random nature.

Fetterman got on the landline to Gerber. "We have rockets."

"I know. I'm on the horn to the gunships. They're on the way."

A half dozen more rockets hit, two of them flying overheard, the others landing inside the perimeter. The flat bangs distinguished them from the thump of the landing mortars.

Fetterman, still on the landline to Gerber, asked, "Did you see the launch points?"

"Negative."

"We need the guns," said Fetterman unnecessarily.

"I have alerted the gun teams," said Gerber, then added, "they're launching now."

Firing erupted in the trees, the rounds striking the sandbags protecting the bunkers and the berm. It was more suppressive fire than aimed. It was meant to keep the defenders from engaging the attackers, but it failed to keep the defender's heads down.

When the rockets and the mortars stopped impacting, there was a shout from outside the camp, joined by bugles and whistles. As one, the enemy surged forward from the trees.

As the enemy crossed the first strands of concertina, the machine guns began to hammer. Tracers flashed from both sides, but those of the enemy were ineffective.

Fetterman aimed his M-16 through the firing port of the bunker. He didn't use the iron sights on the weapon because there wasn't enough light for the sights to be effective. It was more point and shoot, but, unlike some of the soldiers, he was not firing on full auto. He took single shots, aiming low. He saw one man fall and then another.

"Need ammo," said one of the soldiers.

"Bandoliers behind you," said another.

"Fire discipline," said Fetterman. "Make the shots count."

Fetterman heard the brass bouncing off the walls and landing on the floor. The muzzle flashes made it difficult to see the enemy now and the hammering of the weapons made it impossible to hear.

The enemy penetrated the second line of concertina, but they were now more fully exposed. Fetterman, still firing on single shot, saw more of them drop. He thought about the claymores, but sensed the attack was faltering. The firing from the enemy had tapered off and it looked as if some were retreating back to the trees.

And then the enemy just vanished. One second they were in the wire and the next they were gone, back into the safety of the jungle. Fetterman stared out for a moment and then yelled, "Cease fire! Cease fire!"

The shooting tapered rapidly until it was only sporadic firing. Fetterman pressed close to the firing port but could see no movement in front of him.

With the enemy withdrawing to the woods, Fetterman said, "Everyone grab some water. Get ready for the next assault. They've opened paths through part of the wire and there are a lot more of them out there."

"Where are the gunships?"

"Coming. We've got enough firepower to hold them without the guns."

"It's hot in here," said one of the soldiers, but no one responded to him.

Kneeling behind the sandbag wall at the top of the fire control tower, Gerber felt exposed. It was the highest point on the base and the highest point in the surrounding territory. If the VC or NVA mortar men knew what they were doing, they'd use the fire control tower as their aiming point. They didn't have to see the base, just the tower standing some twenty feet in the air.

He turned to Corley and asked, "You going to stay here?"

"Why?"

"I'm going to check on things on the ground."

"You can see that from here."

"I have to get closer. Talk with the soldiers. See the damage for myself rather than hear a report about it."

"Who's going to direct the artillery?" asked Corley. "The gunships?"

"Since we have gunships in the area, you have to be careful of the gun target lines. The artillery is firing from the north with the impact just south of us. The gun target lines are generally from there. However, if one of the other fire support bases in the south is tasked, that changes everything. The pilots know to check that."

"Mack, I don't like this."

"One of us has to stay here. I'll come back, but I have to see what is happening in the bunkers. I have to get on the ground."

With that, Gerber climbed over the sandbags and then down the ladder. He jogged toward the command bunker and heard the pop of a mortar firing. He dodged to the right and couched near the sandbag wall of a bunker. The round landed on the other side of the perimeter.

As he stood up, a soldier approached him. "Sir, we've got a wounded man."

"How bad? Do we need a medevac?"

"Yes, sir. He's got a sucking chest wound. Medic has him patched up and he's breathing, but it's labored."

Gerber looked back over the top of the bunker, at the tree line. There was no sign of the enemy. "Show me."

They ran toward a bunker on the southeastern side of the perimeter. One side had collapsed, opening up the interior. There was a twisted M-60 off to one side but no other damage.

"We're inside," said the soldier.

Gerber entered from the rear, dropping down to the floor of the interior. The rocket had torn out part of the wall, but the sandbags had stopped most of the shrapnel. A man was sitting up against the opposite side of the bunker, a bloody bandage wrapped around his right upper arm and part of his shoulder. Blood stained his ripped jungle fatigue jacket.

"How you doing?"

The soldier grimaced. "Hurts like hell."

"Medic give you anything?"

"Didn't have anything to give me."

"We'll get you to the evac hospital soon. They'll take care of you."

The man nodded but didn't say anything more.

The other wounded man was lying on his side against the rear wall of the bunker. His jungle jacket had been removed and a sterile, plastic bandage pressed over the wound to his chest, sealing it. The man was conscious but not moving. He was watching Gerber.

"I'm going to call for a medevac. We'll get you out of here in twenty minutes or so."

He said nothing.

"We've got a bit of a lull here. I'll try to get the medevac in before Charlie makes another run at us."

"Can we get them out, our guy, I mean," asked the soldier.

"I think so."

Gerber climbed back out of the bunker and ran over to the fire control tower. He scrambled up the ladder, nearly fell over the sandbags and then reached for the PRC-25. Ignoring standard radio procedure, Gerber said, "We need a medevac."

The reply came from one of the gunship pilots. "I'll relay the message."

"Roger. The sooner, the better."

Major Fox entered the officers' club, stopping just inside the door. Most of the officers were watching a 16mm western that Fox had seen several months earlier, before he had been assigned to the company. There were three officers at the bar, two with beers and one with a shot glass in front of him that contained whiskey. All three were disqualified from the mission.

Fox raised his voice and said, "Turn off the movie for a moment."

The projectionist, another officer, turned to make sure it was the company commander, and then complied. The lights in the club brightened.

"Who among you has not been drinking?" Fox asked.

Only four of the officers raised a hand.

"Who among you is senior?"

"That's a complicated question, sir," replied Warrant Officer Steven Douglas. "I think I have the most time in-country as an aircraft commander. Norris is the senior officer not drinking."

"How much time do you have in-country, Norris?"

"Something like two hundred and fifty hours."

"Okay," said Fox. "I need to see you and Douglas in my office immediately. The rest of you can go back to the movie and drinking, though I remind you that you need to stop drinking by —" he looked at his watch — "ten for takeoff tomorrow morning."

Douglas, Norris and Fox left the club and walked to the operations bunker. Once inside, Fox waved to the chairs in front of the situation map. "Have a seat."

When they were seated, Fox said, "We have a priority mission that just came in. There are badly wounded at that forward base. We have a heavy fire team headed there now, but we need someone to evac the wounded. Looks like you two have drawn the short straw."

Fox moved to the map. There was an overlay on it, showing the location of the base, the surrounding terrain, and the approximate positions of the enemy forces as they were known or suspected forty-eight hours earlier. That was mainly guesswork based on the information supplied by those at the base as they had relayed it, and as it appeared to them now that they had called for gun support.

"They are a couple of badly wounded guys. The consensus is that they won't live until morning if they're not evacked now."

"What's the status on the ground right now?" asked Douglas.

"They're under attack. Mortars and some rockets. You'll have gun protection and you can land near the center of the camp. You'll need to watch out for their fire control tower and other obstacles on the ground. There are some fires burning but I don't think they'll be a problem."

"Until something blows up while we're sitting on the ground."

Fox stared at Douglas. "The situation, the tactical situation, isn't that bad at the moment."

Norris shook his head but didn't say anything.

"Isn't this one of those volunteer missions?" asked Douglas.

"You're one of the best pilots in the unit and Norris here is a good Peter Pilot. Are you suggesting that you're not going to take the mission?"

Douglas looked at the floor. "Please don't think of me as a volunteer." He held up a hand to stop Fox's response. "I just mean that I'm not a volunteer, but I think of this as a necessary mission. But why not put another aircraft commander in the cockpit with me?"

Fox spoke in a low voice. "Because I can't afford to lose two aircraft commanders. That's why you have a senior Peter Pilot."

Douglas closed his eyes and didn't say anything for a moment. When he opened them again he said, "This is a shit mission… But I've always said that we have to do everything we can for our fellow soldiers. We'll get them out."

Taking this as confirmation that he would go, Fox said, "Crew chief and door gunner should be at the aircraft now. First Sergeant selected them personally. They are the best in the company. You just have to get in and get out as quickly as possible. You shouldn't be on the ground longer than a minute."

"Oh, I plan on getting in and out as fast as I can." Douglas glanced at Norris and said, again, "This is a real shit mission."

Fox said, "Grab the SOI."

Douglas turned to Norris. "Grab your helmet and meet me at the aircraft."

Norris started to say, "Yes, sir," but realized he outranked Douglas and instead just said, "Yes." The lines of authority in an aviation unit were often obscured.

At the revetment, Douglas saw that the door guns were mounted and the blade untied. He said to the crew, "You know what's going on?"

"Medevac."

"Probably in an extremely hot LZ. Keep your eyes open and if there is anything that you can do to get the wounded onboard faster, do it. And make sure of your target before shooting. We don't want to hit someone on our side."

The crew chief, who looked to be fifteen but was nearly twenty-two, asked, "Have you done this before?"

"Medevac? Sure. Into a hot LZ at night during a ground attack? No. We'll be running blacked-out which gives us a bit of an advantage. Our biggest advantage is speed. Get in and out before the VC know we landed."

Douglas climbed into his seat, buckled himself in, and yelled, "Clear."

He started the engine, watched as the engine and rotor RPM climbed and then reached over and turned down the panel lights so that the instruments were barely visible. The red lights, though not very bright, even when on full, were bright enough to illuminate the pilots, especially close to the ground. Douglas could think of no reason the lights had to be bright.

Having cleared his take off with the tower, he lifted to a hover, started forward and pulled in pitch, climbing over the bunker line around the base camp. He reached fifteen hundred feet and turned to the south. He figured he was about ten minutes out. Over the radio, using the company fox mike, he said, "Gun leader, this is one two."

"Go."

"We're inbound," said Douglas.

"Roger. Come straight south and you won't foul the gun target lines. Artillery has been coming from the south side of the base." Then a few minutes later, he said, "I have you in sight."

"What's going on?"

"We've been making runs on the suspected mortar and rocket sites. Arty has been called off while we're in the area and we're going to be joined by another heavy team. You'll have plenty of help."

Although Douglas didn't want to say it, afraid that the enemy might be monitoring their radio traffic, there was no way to communicate except in the clear. Douglas said, "Once on the ground, I'll turn around, head back out to the north. I have the base in site, assuming that the fires are inside the perimeter."

"Roger that. No action on the north. We'll try to pin them down on the south."

"Going dark," said Douglas.

"Roger."

Over the intercom, he said, "Turn off the nav lights and the rotating target."

Norris flipped the switches that turned off the lights.

To the crew chief and gunner he said, "Okay back there, keep your eyes open. We're running dark and if you engage, the muzzle flash will give away our position, but take out any threat that you see."

Douglas entered a rapid descent.

"Put your hands on the controls but I'm flying. Just follow me. If anything happens, the universal evac hospital frequency is sixty-two decimal five. Tay Ninh is the closest."

"Got it," said Norris.

Douglas leveled off at fifty feet but held the air speed at ninety knots. Then up ahead was the base. He saw the fires and the fire control tower. Someone on the ground, inside the camp, aimed a strobe light at him. He hadn't been told about that, but figured that was where they wanted him to touch down. Over the intercom he said, "Got a strobe light on the ground. Don't shoot it."

As they reached the concertina area, Douglas pulled the nose up sharply and pulled in pitch. The attitude slowed the aircraft quickly in a gravity stop. As he crossed the bunker line, he heard shooting but wasn't sure where it was coming from. He leveled the skids and touched down so close to the man with the strobe that he dived to the right, out of the way, fearing that Douglas was going to hit him.

Two men carrying a stretcher ran from cover. They reached the aircraft and one of the men climbed in backwards, still holding the stretcher but now guiding it across the cargo compartment floor. The other man pushed, knocking the first down, but they didn't dump the stretcher. They slide it in.

Douglas, watched for a moment and then thought he heard a mortar firing. He doubted that because of the noise the turbine was making. He was sure that it was his imagination.

A man climbed up on the skid and yelled, "We got a walking wounded."

"Get him on board now! We're getting the fuck out of here."

A man, his arm in a bloody sling, climbed into the cargo compartment and sat down on the troop seat. The soldiers scattered. Douglas looked out the door and yelled, "Clear!"

The crew chief held up a thumb. Douglas dumped the nose, and they began a rapid acceleration and then a steep climb out. Just as they crossed the last of the concertina, there was a ripping sound. Douglas knew that it was a fifty-one-cal machine gun. He saw the tracers, looking as large as basketballs, but they were nowhere near him.

An instant later, another machine gun opened fire from an enemy gunner who knew his business. Douglas felt the rounds hitting the aircraft. "Turn on the nav lights," he ordered.

"You sure?" asked Norris.

"Turn the fuckers on now." Over the radio he said, "I'm taking fire from the right. Fifty-one."

"We see him."

And then one of the gunships rolled in using the miniguns, the stream of tracers an unbroken red stream. The muzzle flash leaped out ten feet in front of the gunship, but the enemy stopped firing. As they reached fifteen hundred feet and were now a mile or two from the camp, Douglas felt the tension drain from his body. He took a deep breath and said, "You've got it."

Norris, his hands still on the controls, said in a voice unnaturally high, "I've got it. Damn that was hairy."

It was almost as if the landing of the helicopter pissed off the enemy. Just as it cleared the wire, there was a bugle call, then another and another, and the enemy surged out of the woods, in a single wave. They fired their weapons as they ran. From the trees, behind them, the crew-served weapons opened fire. They were aiming at the fleeing helicopter, at the fire control tower and at the bunkers. The sandbags weren't designed to stop the .50-caliber rounds. Corley saw what was happening and retreated to the far side of the fire control tower. He jumped over the sandbags, onto the ladder and slid to the ground as the top of the tower shattered under the intense fire.

Gerber met him at the bottom of the ladder. "Let's head to the command bunker."

"Right behind you," said Corley.

The noise outside the wire grew into a continuous roar as the camp weapons opened fire. Gerber dove into the bunker and then looked up at Fetterman. "Dial in the gun team leader."

Fetterman pulled the PRC-25 closer, dialed in the frequency and let the tuning squeal die before he gave the handset to Gerber.

"Team leader. They are hitting the south side now. We're all under cover."

"Roger that. Rolling in."

Gerber got to the firing point in time to see the stream of ruby-colored dance across the landscape. Firing from the heavy weapons in the trees turned toward the gunships.

"Breaking left."

"Got you covered."

"Hit that fifty."

"I got him in sight."

A pair of rockets from the second ship flashed into the trees, but they didn't silence that machine guns. There were three or four of them. Gerber couldn't see where they were. Instead, he saw the enemy had breached the third concertina barrier. To Fetterman, he said, "Claymores."

The whole line lit up with the detonations of the claymore mines, but that didn't stop the attack. They were still coming, yelling and firing, and reached the second barrier. The machine guns in the bunker were firing continuously, the barrels beginning to glow with the heat of the gunpowder and the friction from the bullets.

The sounds of firing seemed to die away, but it was only Gerber's concentration. He was developing tunnel vision, seeing only that which was directly in front of him and hearing only that from those with him. He stood to one side of the firing port, the brass from the machine guns bouncing on the floor and the strobing of the muzzle flashes nearly unbroken and hypnotic.

Over the radio, he heard one of the gunship pilots say, "Roll through there and draw fire from that fifty. I'll take it out."

"I've got rockets. You draw the fire."

"You see him?"

"Yeah."

"Then kill him."

The rockets flared overhead, dove into the trees and the machine gun fell silent.

"Got him."

Outside the bunker, more enemy soldiers appeared. Gerber realized they weren't facing one regiment but two, maybe three. He didn't know how they had managed to assemble the force so quickly.

"They've breached the second barrier," Fetterman yelled. "Wish we had foo gas."

Gerber stared at the number of enemy in the wire. He saw them take up firing positions using the little cover available. They were firing on full auto, burning through their ammunition rapidly. He knew that they carried three or four spare magazines and would soon be out of ammunition.

Detonations from the M-79 grenade launchers added to the destruction in the wire.

Over the radio, someone said, "They're on the northside."

"Who has any ordnance?"

"I've got rockets."

"Can you engage?"

"Roger. Breaking to the right."

There was silence and then the rockets began hitting the north side. "Breaking right."

And then, "I'm heading back to rearm."

Gerber picked up the UHF radio and keyed the mike, "Rounder, Rounder, have the fast movers launched?"

"They're one zero out. Where do you want it?"

"South side of the camp, run east to west."

"Roger that. On the way."

"They're about to hit the berm," said Fetterman.

Gerber nodded and climbed out of the rear of the bunker. Seeing that one of the machine guns was about to be overrun, he leaned against the side of the bunker and aimed. One man struggled to the top of the berm and sandbags and was caught in the concertina there. Before Gerber could fire, the man dropped, hit by several rounds from others.

The soldiers were beginning to retreat, but Gerber knew that would be fatal. He ran to the berm and knelt there. He aimed over the sandbags. "Take them!" he shouted. "Take them!"

He switched to full auto and emptied his weapon. He ejected the magazine, slammed another home, and continued to pour fire into the attackers. Around him the men did the same and then, suddenly, there were no more enemy in front of them. One VC had gotten to the top of the berm and was still there, hanging in the wire, cut down by the increased fire.

"Who's senior here?" Gerber asked.

Fetterman kept the handset for the PRC-25 pressed to his ear. He listened to the chatter among the pilots of the various units as they coordinated the attacks on the enemy positions in the woods to the south. Through the firing port of the bunker, he saw fires burning where rockets from the helicopters had hit. There was sporadic fire directed at the helicopters, but as the enemy guns fired, the helicopters returned it, neutralizing the site.

One of the soldiers in the bunker said, "Better them than us."

Fetterman snorted. "They're saving your ass. Without them, I'm not sure we could hold this place."

"Wild West, this is Sidewinder two two."

"Go two two."

"Fast movers inbound, napalm and machine guns. Where do you want it?"

"South side of the base. At the tree line. They're holed up there for the moment."

"Roger."

To those in the bunker, Fetterman said, "Pay attention. This should be educational."

"What about the choppers?" a soldier asked.

"They're tuned in to Sidewinder control. They know the jets are coming in."

Outside, they watched as the helicopters broke off their attack, turned to the north and flew over the base, out of the way of the fighters.

Fetterman didn't know what frequency the fighters were using for their plane-to-plane communication. He wanted to listen in but knew that if he needed to communicate with the jets, he'd have to do it through Sidewinder.

He suddenly heard the roar of the jet engines. They sounded low and were heading toward him at high speed. Through the firing port he saw two canisters tumble from one of the jets and then a wave of fire as the napalm detonated, lighting up the area in the yellow-orange glow of the flaming jellied gasoline.

From the trees, farther to the west, a single line of green tracers reached up, but nowhere near the jets. The gun fell silent as if it had run out of ammo, or the gunner had decided it was the better part of valor to stop shooting at the jets.

The second jet followed the first, dropping his napalm farther to the west. A large part of the tree line erupted into orange flames and black smoke.

The second jet pulled up and away. There was a call to Sidewinder. "We have dropped the napalm. Anything else we can do?"

"Put any additional ordnance in the same location," Fetterman said.

"Roger that."

Fetterman watched the airshow for another five minutes but there didn't seem to be any enemy activity. He said, "I think we broke their back."

"It's over?" asked one of the men.

"I think so. There doesn't seem to be anyone out there interested in us."

The soldier sat down on the floor of the bunker and wiped his face. "That was close."

"Not really," Fetterman said. "They didn't penetrate the bunker line. Got to it, but didn't have the force or ability to cross it."

"It was one hell of a fight," said the man. "But we beat them." There was elation in his voice from the tiny victory and from the belief that the fight was over.

"Don't get too cocky," said Fetterman. "Charlie can be a tough foe. He sometimes has resources that we don't expect. Take a drink of water, but keep watch."

Behind them, on the other side of the camp, there was a single burst of fire. Fetterman said, "M-60. Ours."

Fetterman climbed out of the bunker and stood up, looking across the camp. There was now sporadic firing from both M-60 machine guns and M-16s, accompanied by an occasional shot from an M-79. The firing wasn't heavy.

He wanted to run over there, but knew he needed to stay on the south side of the camp. There was always the possibility VC and NVA would be back. He stayed where he was. Gerber would handle it, whatever it might be.

There wasn't much cover to the north of the base. The fingers of jungle there were nearly a klick from the camp, meaning there was open fields of fire that made a frontal assault difficult. As the soldiers had erected the base, they had burned away some of the grass and bulldozed the few bushes to open up the fields of fire. Although they had placed claymores on that side of the camp, there weren't as many of them as there had been on the south.

Gerber stood beside one of the bunkers, binoculars to his eyes as he scanned the tree line and the jungle. The firing from the bunkers was sporadic and he couldn't see what the men were shooting at. The movement might have been from animals, though he doubted it. It was more likely to be the wind moving the vegetation. An attack from there seemed to be suicidal, especially after what had happened on the other side of the base.

And then there was a single bugle call, a series of whistles, and it suddenly looked as if the jungle had come alive and was moving toward him. There was an instant, just a few seconds, when it seemed that no one was shooting at anyone. The enemy was swarming from two or three points in the jungle and spreading out into a long front. All at once, mortars began to drop on the base, landing at first in the wire and then walking toward the bunkers.

Gerber slipped to the side and dropped into the main bunker on the north side of the base. "Where's the radio?"

"Here, Major," said a senior NCO, holding out the handset.

He took the handset and pushed the button on the side. "What gun teams are available?"

"Got a heavy team to the east of your location."

"We're under assault on the northern side. Looks to be of battalion strength. Can you engage?"

"Roger that. Turning in your direction."

Geber then said, "Break, break. Sidewinder Control, this is Golf Bravo Six."

"Go, Six."

"What is available?"

"Sky Raiders inbound. ETA in four minutes."

"Got a heavy fire team in the area. North side of the base. Heavy attack."

"Roger."

Gerber looked through the firing port. The ground was alive with movement. Hundreds of enemy soldiers were running toward the bunker line. As he watched, the claymores were detonated. The steel ball bearings ripped through the first wave, but it didn't stop the attack. Men were screaming, firing, and running right at him.

The machine gun next to him opened fire. Gerber watched the tracers walk into the coming onslaught. He saw men fall, but more filled the gaps. This was the major push. Gerber knew that the attack on the south, though heavy, had been something of a diversion. This was where the VC believed they could win the fight. If they could overrun this side of the base, the defense would collapse.

And then the helicopter gunships were on them. The lead aircraft dove at the ground, firing rockets that walked through the human wave. Anti-aircraft fire erupted from the edge of the jungle, the green and white tracers reaching out for the helicopter.

It turned suddenly, breaking to the left, over the base and away from the Triple-A. The gunship behind it rolled in, but it wasn't engaging the VC infantry. Instead it attacked the machine guns firing at them in a clash of red and green tracers.

That aircraft broke to the left as the third helicopter was lined up. With the heavy machine guns silenced, at least for a moment, the miniguns of the third helicopter rained down on the enemy in the wire. As he broke to the left, the first helicopter attacked again, using rockets.

And then all three took off to the west, heading for Cambodia, but turning north before reaching the border and violating the neutrality of the country. They were out of the fight and headed back to refuel and rearm.

As they disappeared, the fighters arrived. "They're in the wire on the north side," said Gerber.

"Roger."

A moment later, the first aircraft appeared, swooped in low and dropped napalm. The canisters exploded in a fireball of bright orange flames. The second aircraft followed with more napalm and a third added to the conflagration. The whole area was lit up by a wall of fire leaping into the air.

"Golf Bravo Six."

"Six, go."

"Damage assessment."

Gerber looked out the firing port but could see no one moving in the wire. He could still hear firing, but none of it with the same intensity as earlier. There didn't seem to be any return fire. The enemy had all disappeared.

"Sidewinder, I see no movement in the wire. We have no incoming. That last pass stopped them."

The machine gunner had stopped firing. He turned to Gerber and said, "I don't see anyone."

"I think that broke their back," said Gerber, repeating the assessment that Fetterman had used on the other side of the base. "Sunrise in about an hour." He hesitated and then said, "I think we're in the clear."

CHAPTER 18

An hour after dawn, Gerber stood on top of the command bunker on the southside of the base and surveyed the carnage in the wire. Gaps had been blown out by the mortars and by the VC or NVA soldiers who has used bolt cutters to cut their way through. There were craters everywhere, most of them small, made by the enemy mortars and a few larger ones where the 122mm rockets had struck. And beyond them, closer to the trees, were the craters from the American artillery.

Bodies were strewn across the ground. From his position, Gerber counted seventy-five, but he knew that there were many more that he couldn't see from where he stood. They lay tangled among the rows of concertina, right up to the foot of the berm, where a half dozen had reached what he thought of as the high point of the attack. That they had survived long enough to get there was a tribute to their courage and more than a little luck.

The retreating VC had managed to take some of the weapons lost by the killed, but more were left where they had been dropped. Finding weapons to rearm would be a problem for them. The AKs would be the hardest to replace and many of the soldiers had been armed with the older SKS's.

Beyond all that was the damage done by the helicopter gunships and the Air Force fighters. A few fires still burned and clouds of smoke rose from the smoldering remains of the jungle. It was difficult to start a fire in the jungle, but napalm burned hot, drying the wood, and then igniting it. Gerber wasn't inclined to send out soldiers to fight the fires which would now burn away more of the cover for the enemy.

Fetterman, standing beside the bunker, looked up at Gerber, a hand held up to shade his eyes. "We going to patrol today?"

"Maybe in company strength and not too far from the perimeter. I doubt there is anyone left behind that would cause us any trouble today."

"Corley said that it might take all day to repair the damage and to restring the concertina. We don't have many claymores left and we lost one of the fifties and two M-60s."

"Crew?"

"They were lucky. The damage happened during the mortar and rocket attack. The crews were nearby but sheltered. Little shrapnel wounds. Nothing that the medics here can't take care of."

Gerber moved to the edge of the bunker, crouched, and dropped to the ground. He turned and looked back, into the base. There was damage to all the bunkers, but most of it was from small arms fire. The side of one bunker had collapsed, but they had already evacuated the soldiers who had been injured.

"We get a casualty count?"

"You're not going to believe it."

"Give it to me."

"The worst of the wounded were evacuated last night. We've got another twenty, twenty-five with minor wounds. We should get them to the evac hospital but only to get the wounds properly cleaned and dressed to prevent infection."

"I don't understand that sucking chest wound," said Gerber. "The flak jacket should have stopped the shrapnel. It would take a fifty-cal to penetrate it and that would have killed him."

"My understanding is that he took it off. Too hot in the bunker. The other wounds were to arms and legs, areas not covered by the flak jacket."

Gerber shook his head and changed the subject. "I think we — the artillery, the helicopters and the fighters — damaged or destroyed three regiments. They meant to kick us off this little mound."

Corley walked up. He had an M-16 slung over his shoulder and a forty-five strapped to his hip. He was wearing a steel pot with the chin strap unsnapped in the best John Wayne tradition. He looked from Gerber to Fetterman and back to Gerber. He said, "I've got a few work parties organized but I haven't pushed too hard. Men are tired after last night."

"But in good spirits and a little giddy, if I might use that term for them," said Fetterman. "They'll be good for several hours until the adrenaline wears off completely and they tire out."

"I'm thinking we should get as many of them out of here as we can, with proper replacements, of course," said Corley.

"We've got one company on standby.. I'll get on the horn and find out who else we can get in here. The twenty-fifth should have a company or two we can bring in."

"We could run a simple rotation, Major. One company out today, back tomorrow to relieve another of the companies. Everyone gets a day off at a base camp."

"I'm not sure that we can get the aviation assets to do that."

"Trucks?"

"That's just a set up for an ambush. I figure Charlie beat feet to Cambodia where he feels safe, but if we're running a daily convoy in and out, they'll hit it. Maybe just a mechanical ambush, but they will hit it. Besides, there isn't a reliable road into here."

"I want to get with the company commander before the patrol leaves," said Fetterman.

"And I want to talk to the guys from the listening posts last night," said Gerber. "They didn't give us any warning."

"Probably just in the wrong place to pick up on anything," said Fetterman.

"Let's get to work."

Captain Martin Smith was the junior company commander, having arrived in-country only three months earlier. He was a graduate of ROTC, and had attended the basic course at Fort Benning before being deployed to Vietnam. He had believed that four years in college and then the months between graduation, call to active duty, and additional training would see the war over before he could get into the fight. It just hadn't worked out for him.

He was wearing his flak jacket, had two canteens attached to his pistol belt, and held his M-16 in much the same way that a hunter would hold his rifle as he waited for the wild game to appear.

Fetterman was dressed the same in flak jacket, steel pot, and pistol belt holding two canteens, a first-aid kit, and his .45 caliber, 1911A1 Colt pistol. "Mind if I tag along, sir?"

Smith turned and asked, "Any special reason, Sergeant Major?"

"Little intelligence-gathering, little assessment of the results of the air attacks, and a little curiosity."

"I have no objections. However, I would ask that if you have any advice, that you share it with me."

"Not a problem, sir."

Smith lifted a hand and waved. "Let's do it. First platoon, you have the point for the moment."

The first platoon left through the gate near the command bunker, followed by the second, the command unit that included Sergeant Major Fetterman, and then the last two platoons. They walked past the bodies still hanging in the concertina, the remnants of the claymores, dozens of weapons, and other equipment. The brutal force of the claymores had ripped through the enemy, leaving a bloody, mangled mess.

Smith turned and said, "Pass the word to the last platoon that I want them to begin collecting the weapons and ammo. Take any equipment of military value. Run a relay back to the camp with it."

They reached the last of the concertina wire and walked out into a swampy area. The water wasn't deep, but the mud sucked at the boots as if trying to steal them. In front of them they found where the napalm canisters had detonated, spreading fire over a large area. Inside the blackened area were more bodies that no longer looked human. Heat had melted some of the metal components of their weapons and burned away the wooden stocks. There was nothing useful to be recovered.

They entered the trees. The damage was evident. Bullets had riddled the trunks and stripped the leaves from the branches. There were craters in places and the tops of the trees had been shredded by the heavy artillery. There were more bodies of those killed by the artillery and the helicopter gunships.

Finally, they came to a small clearing where there had been a mortar crew. The bodies were scattered around the weapons. There was no ammunition near them and all the tubes had sustained damage. The weapons were now useful as scrap metal and nothing more.

"This is what I wanted to see," Fetterman said.

"Looks like they have fled the area."

"Let the men pick up the weapons but tell them to be careful. I doubt they had time to booby trap anything, but it doesn't hurt to be cautious."

"You really think they might have booby trapped the weapons?"

"No, but you can never tell. Some of us live by the motto that there is always something more to be done. Of course, if you're running from air attacks and there are bullets flying all around, that one more thing might be to run a little faster."

Smith grinned and had the men spread out, watching for signs of an ambush, but it was clear that they didn't expect anything. That worried Fetterman because that was always the time that the enemy attacked. But then the defeat might have been so convincing that no one on the enemy side was thinking of ambush. They were just thinking of escaping the slaughter in the hope of living to fight another day.

After little more than an hour, Smith called a halt. There was a ten-minute break with an order to drink some water, and then a return to the base.

For the fifth day in a row, the flight lined up in a staggered trail and then shut down to wait. Douglas, still flying trail, climbed into the cargo compartment, sat on the red canvas troop seat, and stared out the windshield. A couple of the flight crews had gathered close to lead, but Douglas wasn't in the mood to be social. He was more interested in the quiet of the moment. He didn't even have the energy to pull out the paperback book. He just wanted to sit quietly.

Thirty minutes later, as he dozed, the infantry showed up and began to climb into the cargo compartment. Douglas got out and then stepped up into the pilot's seat on the left side. The co-pilot, changed in the night, was already sitting in the other seat.

"You ready to crank, sir?"

Douglas saw the lead pilot standing near the nose of his aircraft, waving his hand in a circle, telling the flight it was time to start. Douglas said, "You've got it, Mike. Get us ready."

Ten minutes later, Douglas saw that there were no soldiers standing near any of the helicopters and all had their rotors turning. He stepped on the floor button to activate the company fox mike and said, "Lead, you are up with nine, loaded."

"Roger. Lead's on the go."

Over the intercom, Douglas said to Mike, "I don't feel like flying at the moment. You just stick with it."

As they approached the camp, the extent of the fight became clear. They could see damage to the bunker line, and bodies surrounding the camp. Douglas hadn't been able to see any of that during the night medevac. He said out loud, but not over the intercom, "Jesus."

Someone threw a smoke grenade that billowed yellow and lead shot his approach, landing just short of the smoke. Douglas said, "You're down with nine."

The soldiers jumped from the aircraft and spread out, but there was no one shooting at them and no one for them to shoot at. Douglas made the call. "You're unloaded."

"Lead's on the go.

"You're out with nine."

"Rolling over."

Over the intercom, Mike asked, "We done for the day?"

Douglas chuckled. "I seriously doubt it. They'll find something else for us to do. The war goes on in other parts of the country."

"Well, I can always hope."

Gerber sat in the command bunker, his feet propped up on an empty ammo can. He held a warm Pepsi in one hand and was fanning himself with the other. Around him were the men who had been at the listening posts. There were a dozen of them. None had a soft drink but some had their canteens out. They all looked tired and sweaty.

"I don't want you to think of this as a critique, nor am I planning to chew out anyone. I was just wondering why there was no report of enemy movement on the north side of the camp before the attack."

"I didn't see anything," said one man. "I didn't hear anything until you all started shooting. It was the first indication that Charlie was anywhere around."

"You could hear the firing on the other side of the base, couldn't you?"

"Oh, yes, sir. We could see the gunships and then the airplanes working the area. We'd had a few mortars and rockets hit around us, but not very close and I figured Charlie had overshot their targets. We were laying low, just as you said, listening for sounds of someone in the trees around us."

One of the others said, "We didn't see anything until after the attack was launched on the north side. We saw them come out of the jungle but they were two, three hundred meters away from us."

"But you didn't make a report?"

"No, sir. They were already engaged. There was no point in us making a report. We didn't know anything, other than they were attempting to penetrate the wire."

Gerber rubbed his chin. "The purpose of the listening post is to alert us to enemy movement."

"Yes, sir. But there wasn't anything to report. The enemy was engaged and I could see no one else coming in."

"Okay," said Gerber slowly. "I suppose I'm somewhat confused. There was enemy moving around in the jungle."

"Yes, sir. But not near us. We didn't see anything until they began to shoot at the camp."

Another man said, "We could have engaged from the rear, but that would have told them where we were and there were only three of us. They'd have overrun us in minutes."

Now Gerber grinned. "It does seem that you had a good handle on the purpose of the listening posts."

"Yes, sir. And when they disengaged, when it seemed they were in full flight, we did engage using the M-79 and hand grenades. That didn't give us away. All they knew was that grenades were falling among them, causing more confusion."

"In the morning, what did you do?"

"Well, once it was clear that there were no VC around us, we broke cover and then tried to find any bodies near us. We found some about twenty-five or fifty feet away, some as far as a hundred yards. It was clear they had been killed by shrapnel, which told me our grenade attack was affective."

"Okay," said Gerber, dropping his feet to the floor. "I've got some warm Pepsi here, if any of you are interested. What I'd like to do... Who's the senior man here?"

"I am, Major."

"All right. Get some of the information from the others and draft an after-action report for me. Names of everyone who was out on the listening posts, what each position witnessed and what action was taken."

"I don't know, sir. The lieutenant usually does that sort of thing."

"He wasn't with you and I don't want this filtered through the eyes of someone who wasn't there. Doesn't have to be precise. Just get the facts and I'll have someone look it over and put it into a military format."

"Yes, sir."

Gerber stood up and as he did, the rest of the men came to their feet. Gerber waved them down and said, "As you were."

He left the bunker and found Fetterman. "I've got some information coming from the listening posts. Probably be rough, but it'll tell us what we need to know."

"Sounds good, sir. I've talked to Corley, who, by the way, is staying here tonight, and learned that there will be a chopper or two coming in later this afternoon. Some major or lieutenant colonel from the twenty-fifth will be here to take charge."

"Where was he yesterday?"

"Probably sitting on his ass in an air-conditioned club, eating steak and sucking down the booze. Anyway, he's on his way."

"You know, Sergeant Major, that might be our cue to get out of here. There's really nothing more for us to do. Corley can fill that new guy in and we can avoid having to tell him why two Special Forces soldiers were here in the first place."

"I've been wondering that myself," said Fetterman. "I thought we'd be watching this from afar."

"Me too."

It was late afternoon when the flight of three helicopters, escorted by two-gunships, appeared on the horizon and descended toward the camp. A soldier ran from the bunker line, pulled the pin on a smoke grenade, and tossed it outside the outer concertina where the ground was flat and dry.

From just inside the bunker line, both Gerber and Fetterman, holding their weapons and shouldering their rucks, waited. The gun team worked over the trees. There were no enemy in there, as far as they knew, and the firing was suppressive in nature. Keep the enemy's head down until the helicopters had landed and taken off again was the whole idea.

Corley strolled up as the helicopters touched down. "Leaving us?"

"Our work here is done," said Gerber.

"Where are you going?"

"Saigon. MACV. On to Fifth Group at Nha Trang. Back to doing what we're trained to do."

A man carrying an M-16 and holding his steel pot on his head with his left hand as if the rotor wash might blow it away stopped in front of Gerber and asked, "You in charge here?"

Gerber shook his head and pointed at Corley. "He's in charge."

"I need a full briefing on what has gone on here."

"Who might you be?" asked Gerber.

"Major Clifford Nickson. I'm to take command here."

Fetterman turned to Corley and held out his hand. "Been good working with you. Drop by Nha Trang if you get the chance."

"Couldn't have done it without you, Sergeant Major."

"If you gentlemen are leaving, I suggest you get on the chopper now."

Gerber ignored him and said, "Good working with you, Joshua. You're not a bad soldier for an engineer."

With that, both Gerber and Fetterman ducked and jogged to the last helicopter in the line. As it lifted off, Fetterman shouted over the noise of the turbine, "Well, that was fun. Now what?"

"We find our way to Saigon and a steak dinner."

"Probably won't happen til tomorrow."

"Soon enough, Sergeant Major. Soon enough."

CHAPTER 19

The hotel's rooftop garden hadn't changed much since the last time that Gerber had been there. The plants looked a little more stressed and the décor wasn't quite as fresh or as bright. The band didn't sound all that good and Gerber didn't recognize the song they were playing. And, it seemed that the bourbon had been watered.

Fetterman, wearing a civilian suit that hadn't been pressed in a month or two, didn't look particularly happy. "I think this place is marking the decline of western civilization."

"Not so," said Gerber. "We're in the mysterious East."

"I forgot," said Fetterman. "I had hoped for something a little more, I don't know, better. This just isn't the way I remember the place."

"We're not obligated to patronize this establishment," said Gerber.

"Where would you go?"

"Bien Hoa."

"That's a military establishment."

"But the booze wouldn't be watered."

"Noticed that, did you?"

Fetterman held up his glass and examined the contents. "The color just isn't right. These sorts of things suggest a desperation by the proprietor, meaning he's attempting to make as much money as possible before everything collapses round him."

"What has brought on this philosophical treatise?"

"Don't know," said Fetterman. "I'm just uncomfortable for some reason. I have a feeling of impending doom."

"Because we are on our way to Nha Trang?"

Fetterman shrugged. "There is something in the air. Like Paris, just before the Germans marched in."

"Funny you should mention that, given this used to be French Indochina."

"Yes," said Fetterman, "I had thought of that."

The band fell silent and Fetterman glanced at them. "Well, at least they stopped playing. I don't know what that song was supposed to be."

At that moment, a voice said, "I knew that I would find the two of you here eventually."

Gerber turned. "Robin. What brings you to Saigon?"

"Building my credentials as a war correspondent. Furthering my career. Chasing the story."

"Story is out. Story is dead," said Gerber. "We have nothing of interest for you now. MACV made the announcement a day or two ago."

"I know. I was there, listening to their nonsense."

Gerber grinned. "Won't you join us?"

"Only if you're buying," Morrow said with a smile.

"I don't make as much money as you war correspondents. Shouldn't you be plying me with booze to get the story?"

"Is there a story to get?"

"Not anymore, apparently," said Fetterman, standing. "If you two will excuse me, I'll head downstairs."

"Oh, sit down, Tony," said Morrow. "And I'll buy you a drink."

"Why, thank you, ma'am. Don't mind if I do."

Brigadier General Jones sat in his air-conditioned office holding the top-secret after-action report in his hand. He'd scanned it quickly and then began to read it carefully. He was surprised that it had been written by Corley rather than Gerber, but he couldn't fault the detail and information included in it. The report was everything he could want in such a document.

According to it, they had destroyed the better part of three VC and NVA regiments and had no men killed in the action. Twenty-seven had been wounded, only one seriously. They had stopped the infiltration into that area of South Vietnam and had captured or destroyed dozens of weapons including mortars and light machine guns. Jones was pleased with the report.

There was a tap at his door and Jones looked up at his aide. "Come on in, Harker. Did you read this?"

"No, sir. Thought you should have the privilege of reading it first."

"Quite the victory for our side, don't you think?"

"From the little I've heard," said Harker, "I think they did quite well."

"Concept worked. One day to erect the base and they were able to hold it against overwhelming odds. Took close coordination with artillery and air support. Even the Air Force did their thing well."

"Yes, sir."

"Oh, for crying out loud, sit down and relax."

"Yes, sir. Thank you."

Harker dropped into a chair opposite Jones.

"As I was saying. The concept worked but it is now out of date."

"I'm sorry, General, but I don't understand."

Jones sighed. "Aides are supposed to keep up on current events, understand the strategies and tactics employed by various combatants, and read the general's mind so that he can anticipate what the general will want. A secondary purpose is to teach a young but bright officer what is going on beyond the immediate horizon."

"Yes, sir. The concept worked and we successfully blocked the North Vietnamese from supplying men, arms, and equipment to the south."

"It was intended," said Jones, "to provide an illustration on how we can move our resources around and within one day set up a base that keeps the enemy logistics and personnel out of the South."

"Yes, sir. That's what I said."

"But the President has announced that US forces, along with South Vietnamese and the Khmer Republic, read Cambodia, have initiated an incursion into Cambodia to take out the communist bases there that have been operating with the tacit consent of the old Cambodia government. It means that we have the cooperation of the Cambodians in removing that obstacle to our efforts and those of the South Vietnamese eliminating the communist strongholds."

Harker thought about that and suddenly the light went on. He got it. "So, we don't need to set up these temporary bases because the terminus of the Ho Chi Minh Trail, which was west of Three Corps, has been eliminated."

Jones nodded his approval. "Precisely. Of course, the North can still infiltrate across the DMZ or from Laos, but that creates a long path from those points to Saigon. The battlefield strategy has been altered. You can read the history on this in the classified reports, but the upshot is that the President, annoyed by Tet, and the overthrow of the government of Cambodia that was sympathetic to the North, created a situation where we could now move into Cambodia without the international ramifications that would have accompanied such a move a year ago."

"So, what happens now, General?"

"That's the sad thing. Our concept is relegated to the pile of good ideas that are now obsolete. Gerber, Corley and Fetterman did a good job of constructing the base and defending it, but we no longer have the need to do it."

Harker sensed the discussion, the history lesson, was coming to an end. He stood up and said, "You have a late afternoon meeting with the local mayor and then a dinner with General Kellahin."

"He provide an agenda?"

"Just said drinks and dinner. That's all I know."

"Let's do this. Ride with me to the meeting with the mayor and then take the rest of the day off. Use the staff car to get back to your quarters, if necessary, and then have it sent back to me."

"Yes, sir."

"Thanks. That'll be all."

GLOSSARY

AC — Aircraft commander. The pilot in charge of the aircraft.

AIT — Advanced Individual Training. The school soldiers were sent to after basic training.

AK-47 — Assault rifle normally used by the North Vietnamese and the Viet Cong.

ANGRY-109 — AN-109, the radio used by the Special Forces for long-range communications.

AN/PRR9 and **AN/PRT4** — Intrasquad radio receiver and transmitter used for short-range communications. The range is something under a mile.

AO — Area of Operations.

AP — Air Police. The old designation for the guards on Air Force bases. Now referred to as security police.

AP ROUNDS — Armor-piercing ammunition.

APU — Auxiliary Power Unit. An outside source of power used to start aircraft engines.

ARC LIGHT — Term used for a B-52 bombing mission. Also known as heavy arty.

ARVN — Army of the Republic of Vietnam. A South Vietnamese soldier.

ASA — Army Security Agency.

ASH AND TRASH — Refers to helicopter support missions that didn't involve a direct combat role. They hauled supplies, equipment, mail and all sorts of ash and trash.

AST — Control officer between the men in isolation and the outside world. Responsible for taking care of all the problems.

AUTOVON — Army phone system that allows soldiers on one base to call another base, bypassing the civilian phone system.

BDA — Bomb Damage Assessment.

BODY COUNT — Number of enemy killed, wounded or captured during an operation. Used by Saigon and Washington as a means of measuring the progress of the war.

BOONDOGGLE — Any military operation that hasn't been completely thought out. An operation that is ridiculous.

BOONIE HATS — Soft cap worn by a grunt in the field when not wearing his steel pot.

BROWNING M-2 — Fifty-caliber machine gun manufactured by Browning.

BROWNING M-35 — The 9mm automatic pistol that became the favorite of the Special Forces.

C AND C — Command and Control aircraft that circled overhead to direct combined air and ground operations.

CARIBOU — Cargo transport plane.

CHECKRIDE — Flight in which one pilot checks the proficiency of another. It can be an informal review of the various techniques or a very formal test of a pilot's knowledge.

CHINOOK — Army aviation twin-engine helicopter. A CH-47.

CHOCK — Refers to the number of the aircraft in the flight. Chock Three is the third, Chock Six is the sixth.

CLAYMORE — Antipersonnel mine that fires 750 steel balls with a lethal range of 50 meters.

CLOSE AIR SUPPORT — Use of airplanes and helicopters to fire on enemy units near friendly troops.

COLT — Soviet-built small transport plane. The NATO code name for Soviet and Warsaw Pact transports all begin with the letter C.

CONEX — Steel container about 10 feet high, 10 feet long and 10 feet deep, used to haul equipment and supplies.

C-RATS — C-rations.

DAI UY — Vietnamese Army rank equivalent to U.S. Army Captain.

DEROS — Date Estimated Return from Overseas Service.

DIRNSA — Director, National Security Agency.

E AND E — Escape and Evasion.

FEET WET — Term used by pilots to describe flight over water.

FIELD GRADE — Refers to officers above the rank of Captain but under Brigadier General. In other words, Majors, Lieutenant-Colonels and Colonels.

FIRECRACKER — Special artillery shell that explodes into a number of small bomblets that detonate later. The artillery version of the cluster bomb, it was employed as a secret weapon tactically for the first time at Khe Sanh.

FIREFLY — Helicopter with a battery of bright lights mounted in or on it. The aircraft is designed to draw enemy fire at night so that gunships orbiting close by can attack the target.

FIRST SHIRT — Military term referring to the First Sergeant.

FIVE — Radio call sign for the Executive Officer of a unit.

FOB — Forward Operating Base.

FOX MIKE — FM radio.

FREEDOM BIRD — Name given to any aircraft that took troops out of Vietnam. Usually referred to the commercial jet flights that took men back to the World.

GARAND — M-1 rifle that was replaced by the M-14. Issued to the South Vietnamese early in the war.

GRAIL — NATO name for the shoulder-fired SA-7 surface-to-air missile.

GUARD THE RADIO — Stand by in the commo bunker and listen for messages.

GUIDELINE — NATO name for the SA-2 surface-to-air missile.

GUNSHIP — Armed helicopter or cargo plane that carries weapons instead of cargo.

HALO — High Altitude, Low Opening.

HE — High-explosive ammunition.

HOOTCH — Almost any shelter, from temporary to long-term.

HORN — Term that referred to a specific kind of radio operations that used satellites to rebroadcast the messages.

HOTEL THREE — Helicopter landing area at Saigon's Tan Son Nhut Airport.

HUEY — UH-1 helicopter.

ICS — Intercom system in an aircraft.

IN-COUNTRY — Term used to refer to American troops operating in South Vietnam. They were all in-country.

INTELLIGENCE — Any information about enemy operations that would be useful in planning a mission.

KIA — Killed in Action.

KLICK — Thousand meters; a kilometer.

LIMA LIMA — Land line. Refers to telephone communications between two points on the ground.

LLDB — Luc Luong Dac Biet. The South Vietnamese Special Forces.

LP — Listening Post. A position outside the perimeter manned by a couple of people to give advance warning of enemy activity.

LRRP — Long-Range Reconnaissance Patrol.

LSA — Lubricant used by soldiers on their weapons to ensure they will continue to operate properly.

LZ — Landing Zone.

M-3A1 — Also known as a grease gun. A .45-caliber submachine gun favored in World War II by GIs because its slow rate of fire meant that the barrel didn't rise and they didn't burn through their ammo as fast as they did with some other weapons.

M-14 — Standard rifle of the U.S. Army, eventually replaced by the M-16. It fired the standard 7.62mm NATO round.

M-16 — Became the standard infantry weapon of the Vietnam War. It fired 5.56mm ammunition.

M-79 — Short-barreled, shoulder-fired weapon that fired a 40mm grenade. These could be high explosives, white phosphorus or canister.

M-113 — Armored personnel carrier.

MACV — Military Assistance Command, Vietnam. Replaced MAAG in 1964.

MEDEVAC — Medical Evacuation. Also called Dust-Off. A helicopter used to take the wounded to medical facilities.

MI — Military Intelligence.

MIA — Missing in Action.

MONOPOLY MONEY — Term used by the servicemen in Vietnam to describe the MPC handed out in lieu of regular U.S. currency.

MOS — Military Occupation Specialty.

MPC — Military Payment Certificates. The Monopoly money used instead of real cash by the U.S. Army.

NCO — A noncommissioned officer. A noncom. A sergeant.

NCOIC — NCO in Charge. The senior NCO in a unit, detachment or patrol.

NDB — Nondirectional Beacon. A radio beacon that can be used for homing.

NEXT — The man who said it was his turn to be rotated home.

NINETEEN — Average age of the combat soldier in Vietnam, as opposed to twenty-six in World War Two.

NVA — North Vietnamese Army. Also used to designate a soldier from North Vietnam.

ONTOS — Marine weapon that consists of six 106mm recoilless rifles mounted on a tracked vehicle.

ORDER OF BATTLE — Listing of units available and to be used during a battle.

P (PIASTER) — Basic monetary unit in South Vietnam worth slightly less than a U.S. penny.

PETA-PRIME — Tar-like substance that melted in the heat of the day to become a sticky black nightmare that clung to boots, clothes and equipment. It was used to hold down the dust during the dry season.

PETER PILOT — Copilot in a helicopter.

PLF — Parachute Landing Fall. The roll used by parachutists on landing.

POL — Petroleum, Oil and Lubricants. The refueling point on many military bases.

POW — Prisoner of War.

PRC-10 — Portable radio.

PRC-25 — A lighter portable radio that replaced the PRC-10.

PULL PITCH — Term used by helicopter pilots to mean they are going to take off.

PUNJI STAKE — Sharpened bamboo hidden to penetrate the foot.

PUZZLE PALACE — The Pentagon. It was called the puzzle palace because no one knew what was going on there. Puzzle Palace East referred to MACV or USARV Headquarters in Saigon.

RLO — Real Live Officer. Term used by warrant officers to refer to officers who were commissioned.

RON — Remain Over Night. Term used by flight crews to indicate a flight that would last longer than a day.

RPD — Soviet-made 7.62mm light machine gun.

RTO — Radio Telephone Operator. The radioman of a unit.

RUFF-PUFFS — Term applied to the RF-PFs, the Regional Forces and Popular Forces. Militia drawn from the local population.

S-3 — Company-level operations officer.

SA-2 — Surface-to-air missile fired from a fixed site. A radar-guided missile nearly 35 feet long.

SA-7 — Surface-to-air missile that is shoulder-fired and has infrared homing.

SACSA — Special Assistant for Counterinsurgency and Special Activities.

SAFE AREA — Selected Area For Evasion. It doesn't mean that the area is safe from the enemy, only that the terrain, location or local population make the area a good place for escape and evasion.

SAM TWO — Refers to the SA-2 Guideline.

SAR — Search and Rescue.

SECDEF — Secretary of Defense.

SHORT-TIMER — Person who had been in Vietnam for nearly a year and who would be rotated back to the World soon. When the DEROS was the shortest in the unit, the person was said to be *Next*.

SINGLE-DIGIT MIDGET — Soldier with fewer than ten days left in-country.

SIX — Radio call sign for the unit commander.

SKS — Soviet-made carbine.

SMG — Submachine gun.

SOI — Signal Operating Instructions. The booklet that contained the call signs and radio frequencies of the units in Vietnam.

SOP — Standard Operating Procedure.

SPIKE TEAM — Special Forces team made up for a direct-action mission.

STEEL POT — Standard U.S. Army helmet. The steel pot was the outer, metal cover.

TAOR — Tactical Area of Operational Responsibility.

TEAM UNIFORM OR COMPANY UNIFORM — UHF radio frequency on which the team or the company communicates. Frequencies were changed periodically in an attempt to confuse the enemy.

THE WORLD — The United States.

THREE — Radio call sign of the Operations Officer.

THREE CORPS — Military area around Saigon. Vietnam was divided into four corps areas.

TO & E — Table of Organization and Equipment. A detailed listing of all the men and equipment assigned to a unit.

TOC — Tactical Operations Center.

TOT — Time Over Target. Refers to the time the aircraft are supposed to be over the drop zone with the parachutists, or the target if the planes are bombers.

TRIPLE A — Antiaircraft Artillery or AAA. Anything used to shoot at airplanes and helicopters.

TWO — Radio call sign of the Intelligence Officer.

TWO-OH-ONE (201) FILE — Military records file that listed all of a soldier's qualifications, training, experience and abilities. It was passed from unit to unit so that a new commander would have some idea about the capabilities of an incoming soldier.

UMZ — Ultramilitarized Zone. Name GIs gave to the DMZ (Demilitarized Zone).

UNIFORM — Refers to the UHF radio. Company Uniform would be the frequency assigned to that company.

USARV — United States Army, Vietnam.

VC — Viet Cong, called Victor Charlie (phonetic alphabet) or just Charlie.

VIET CONG — Contraction of Vietnam Cong San (Vietnamese Communist).

VIET CONG SAN — Vietnamese communists. A term in use since 1956.

WHITE MICE — South Vietnamese military police who all wore white helmets.

WIA — Wounded in Action.

WILLY PETE — WP, white phosphorus. Called smoke rounds. Also used as antipersonnel weapons.

WOBBLY ONE — Refers to a W-1, the lowest of Warrant Officer grade. Helicopter pilots who weren't commissioned started out as Wobbly Ones.

WSO — Weapons System Officer.

XM-21 — Name given to the Army's sniper rifle. An M-14 mounted with a special ART scope.

XO — Executive Officer of a unit.

X-RAY — Term that refers to an engineer assigned to a unit.

A NOTE TO THE READER

Dear Reader,

This book is loosely based on events in April 1969 in and around Patrol Base Frontier City, in which I was marginally involved. For the action, the 187th Assault Helicopter Company (known as the Crusaders), Company C, 4th Battalion, 9th Infantry, 25th Infantry Division; Battery B, 7th Battalion, 11th Artillery, 25th Infantry Division; Company B, 25th Aviation Battalion (known as the Little Bears); Troop D, 3D Squadron, 4th Cavalry and 116th Assault Helicopter Company (known as the Hornets) were awarded the Presidential Unit Citation on General Order No. 14, dated 10 May 1973.

The following is the Citation:

With full knowledge of the enemy's intentions, Patrol Base Frontier City was constructed adjacent to the Cambodian border ... directly in the path of the enemy's intended route of advance. During the early morning hours of 26 April 1969, the patrol base was attacked by an enemy force estimated to be two reinforced battalions of Viet Cong and North Vietnamese regulars. Although the enemy fought savagely to seize the base, the defenders repeatedly repelled the determined, combined artillery and infantry assaults on their position. Purposely permitting the enemy to approach within a thousand meters of their position before bringing them under fire with artillery, mortars, machine guns, small arms and air strikes, the brave defenders devastated the enemy attack. Enemy forces were able to breach the perimeter wire at only one point, but were trapped in a blistering crossfire and were unable to exploit their gain. The attack was completely stopped and the enemy forces were routed with heavy losses of men and equipment. Totally defeated, the enemy was forced to withdraw to sanctuaries in Cambodia, leaving behind a large number of casualties, numerous weapons, and a large amount of ammunition.

If you have enjoyed this novel enough to leave a review on **Amazon** and **Goodreads**, then we would be truly grateful.

Sapere Books

Sapere Books is an exciting new publisher of brilliant fiction and popular history.

To find out more about our latest releases and our monthly bargain books visit our website: **saperebooks.com**

www.ingramcontent.com/pod-product-compliance
Lightning Source LLC
Chambersburg PA
CBHW051459030726
47592CB00006B/2006